Previously From Mitch Davies

A Wind In Montana

Stolen Breeze

The Inn of Fallen Leaves

Undertow of Loyalty

A novel by Mitch Davies
Digital Edition | Copyright 2017
Mitch Davies
This book is licensed for your personal enjoyment only. This
book may not be re-sold or given away to other people. If you
would like to share this book with another person, please
purchase an additional copy for each recipient.
www.pensmithbooks.com

PRINT ISBN 978-0-9843907-9-3
EPUB ISBN 978-0-9989570-0-5
Library of Congress Control Number: 2012931774

Undertow

of

Loyalty

Mitch Davies

1

—

Neil Henberlin rushed through the glass entrance doors of his company's 20th floor corporate office, pushing them a little harder than necessary. The etched-glass door slapped his shoulder as it rebounded off the rubber door stop. The gong sound of the glass vibrations caused the receptionist's head to pop up, lips pursed, eyes squinting. She looked at him as if she'd seen a phantom wavering in mist.

"Someone's in my parking spot," he said, as he leaned over her desk. "Those parking spots are sacred, how could someone move into mine?"

The receptionist shook her head and said, "Ah... we weren't expecting you."

"Hmm. Why? I'm only late, not absent."

"But..."

"I know, it's Stampede Week. My hat and boots are in my office. I'll change later."

Henberlin noticed the receptionist's white Stetson cowboy hat, denim skirt with a white fringe, and the red bull-rider boots. He nodded in approval, then turned in a hurry for the stairway and took off almost running. Taking the steps two at a time, he topped the stairs and walked past the corner office occupied by the Vice President of Sales. He hoped to get past without noticed. The VP's secretary, wearing a straw cowboy hat, Western-cut blouse, jeans, and cowboy boots, happened to be exiting the office. She closed the door and turned to see Henberlin. Stopping dead in her tracks she said, "Neil?"

"Yeah, hi Geneva. I'm late for the sales training class. Don't worry, I'll be Western before noon."

"Okay. Umm…"

But, too late—Henberlin raced by. He continued at a quick pace until he turned the corner and carried on to his office. Rushing in, he placed his PC carrier on a chair and turned, intending to hurry away, except the top of his desk caught his eye. Stunned, he saw that someone had cleaned and tidied its surface. No papers, none of his personal items, only the computer cables and the phone. He stared at the phone noting that the message light was dark. Usually by this time of the morning on a Monday his voice mail would be crammed.

When he saw the cardboard box sitting on the floor beside the desk a level of panic began a throb in his heart. No time now to figure out who had messed with his stuff, or why, he'd promised Emmitt he'd tell stories to the sales training class. If the Vice President of Sales had pulled a trigger, he'd find out soon enough. And he hoped that hadn't happened, it was the absolute worst time for that to happen.

He kept on moving to get to the classroom, knowing he was already late. Once he entered the training lobby, he crossed the small area and knocked on the only door from which he heard voices.

The door opened and Emmitt LeClare's smiling face emerged. Emmitt, wearing a red and white diamond-checked shirt with double breast pockets, each with white pearl snaps, and a bolo tie, lost his smile when he realized who stood before him.

"Neil?"

"Yeah. Sorry I'm late. Is it too late?

"No, no not at all." Emmitt seemed at a loss for words. "It's just, I wasn't expecting you."

"I was out of town this weekend. You didn't think I'd stand you up, did you? So why wouldn't you expect me? Today's the exam, right? I told you I'd be here."

"Yes, it is. Ah, I'm going over some of their work from Friday. Give me a few minutes and I'll call you in. Is that okay?"

"Sure. I'll be here."

'What's with all the strange looks?' he thought. 'Can't be that I'm in a suit like some out-of-towner. Why is my presence a surprise to everyone? Did the VP pull something off over the weekend? Have I been fired? Almost impossible unless something weird happened.'

Sitting in the industrial design-inspired waiting room, straight chrome chairs and variegated walls, Henberlin stared comatose at the utilitarian tile glued to the floor. He mulled over disquieting thoughts. Having to park in one of the lower levels of the garage, the similar yet odd reception each of his colleagues had given him this morning, and the possible antics of the VP... maybe he'd have been better off if he'd stayed in Vancouver.

He tried to think of his coming session in the classroom. He enjoyed addressing the new sales trainees before they wrote their final sales aptitude exam. Aiding the sales training department gave him a chance to boost his ego. And his ego needed a little boost right now. Due to a recent lack of new sales contracts, management and his fellow salesmen were giving him a lot of doubtful looks these days. It had been a while since he'd experienced the drug-like euphoria of signing a lucrative deal with a big commission check attached.

For the sales rep holding almost every sales record the company tracked, a slow sales period created a low-hung level of embarrassment that wafted like an unpleasant odor.

A presence clicked a few feet in front of him, dispersing his thoughts and wrenching his stare away from the floor. Looking up, thinking his summons into the classroom had finally arrived, the bottom drop out of his stomach. He recognized the business analyst standing in front of him. Not a regular business analyst, but the Vice President of Sales' business analyst. An intense young pest believing his high-level attachment implied that sales reps had to accord him a higher level of responsiveness. The analyst had no cowboy hat, but he did have a red neckerchief tied around his neck, a long sleeved blue-checked shirt, designer jeans, and shiny aqua-colored boots to match his large round turquoise belt buckle.

"Henberlin," the analyst said as he stabbed a message form in front of Henberlin's face. "I heard you were in the office. I didn't think I was going to get to do this."

Henberlin took the note but didn't look at it. He knew it had the VP's name and title embossed in the top center.

"What is it?" he said.

"Read it."

"Just tell me what he wants."

The analyst tilted his head and waited a few long beats then said, "In his office when you finish here."

"What does he want?"

"I think you know."

"I don't."

The door to the classroom opened, the sales instructor's head appeared and scanned the room.

"Good. Neil, we're ready for you now," the instructor said.

Henberlin stood up, brushed the front of his trousers, smiled at the analyst, and walked to the classroom. He stopped at the door when a disquieting thought crept in again: 'Why is everyone looking at me strange just because I'm not in my Western gear?'

Then the analyst popped the thought bubble. "Owen's office, *right* after you finish up here," he said.

———

For thirty minutes, Henberlin told sales stories to the mostly-from-out-of-town trainees, some of whom had dressed Western in the spirit of the Calgary tradition taking place this week. Those who didn't dress Western had either been caught off-guard by the festivities or didn't bother.

He found his heart wasn't in his presentation this morning. He told the usual success stories, only today they were tainted in their delivery because he'd had zero recent success. Being backed up by huge sales numbers always added an extra layer of embellishment to his presentation. His situation with the VP wouldn't let him go. It swirled through his head and twisted his anxiety. He knew the meeting awaiting him when he left the classroom was going to be contentious.

When he didn't self-deflate his sales stories, they usually got laughs from the young future sales reps as he entertained and inspired them with his tales. Some of the new recruits were aware of the legendary events of his sales career. The intent of having Henberlin in the class was to have the recruits meet the man who executed these sales to completion—and to make them eager to get back to the field and sell. This day, however, he delivered his speech in deadpan. Usually, he could see envy in the eyes of the young men and women. If he was really on that day, he'd see in them a desire to someday break his records, to someday be telling their own sales stories to a group of young recruits. This time, he saw glazed-over eyes, the looks of people who wanted to get to the next thing on the training agenda so they could be on their way home.

"Well, it looks like you can't wait to get to the aptitude test. Before Emmitt here puts you through that torture, did any of you have any questions?" Henberlin asked the class.

There were no takers, so he thought his time was over. Next the test and, shortly after that, he'd find himself in the Vice President's office. Then the hand of one soon-to-be salesman slowly, reluctantly, raised above his head. 'Out of sympathy,' Henberlin thought.

"With your intimate knowledge of the oil and gas exploitation market, have you worked with the new vectoring processor that R.E.S. is going to announce soon?"

"Ah." Henberlin smiled. "Another of the best-kept secrets in the computer industry. Yes, I have had early access to the product. I can't give you much in the way of details, but I can tell you that we've really come up with an industry-leading concept. One that is going to put us miles ahead of the current competition.

"Imagine the benefits of a quad architecture high-speed vector processor with built-in artificial intelligence that's kicking out six giga LIPS in a stand-alone workstation. Sounds scary. This level of AI computation is going to find solutions before the problems exist. It makes it possible for a mid-level reservoir engineer to discover an exploitation technique that blows any current simulator's work to binary shrapnel.

"It's taking us a little longer, and costing us a lot more to bring this product to market, but it's going to pay off beyond all forecasts."

From the edge of the classroom came a voice. "If you can regain your sales touch."

Henberlin and the whole class turned to look at a sales rep candidate sitting in a chair near the window. He had been the best performer in the class. His posture, the cut of his suit—he hadn't dressed Western—the precise sweep of his precise blond hair, and the smart smile he wore presented a confident salesman.

"Excuse me?" Henberlin said.

"How come, on all the sales bulletins that get distributed on a weekly basis, I never see your name? You aren't listed in the top weekly sales and you're not listed in the top year-to-date sales. So what am I going to learn from *you* about sales?"

Henberlin stared at the man without blinking, moving, or smiling. Then he said, "I'm not sure that you'll learn anything... ah, your name?"

"Lon Radzik."

"Mr. Radzik, you give me an opportunity to make a point about sales streaks and sales consistency. Of course, a streak is a wonderful thing to experience and I'm always hoping one will be brought down upon me, especially now. Sometimes, though, investing the time to cultivate new and larger sales is a necessary risk that every salesman has to take, and the time invested may cause a dip in current sales. You have to ride out the dip to get the eventual payoff of a long streak.

"Management keeps a sales rep around for a few hero-to-goat cycles, but when a goat cycle sticks around a little too long, well... let's just say management doesn't let the goat linger too long. Learn from that what you can."

"I don't plan on having a slump," the trainee said with emphatic syllables. The class hooted and laughed at the display of brazen confidence.

Henberlin smiled and shook his head. "Okay, it's good you can all laugh considering you still have a test to write," he said, turning the class back over to the instructor.

———

Emmitt LeClare had been a hardworking salesman for R.E.S. for a number of years, but he'd never cracked the list of the elite. His territory required weekly travel, which he enjoyed for the first few years. Then he met a girl in one of the small towns within his sales territory and asked her to marry him. Shortly after she moved into his apartment in Calgary, she insisted he stop travelling. She didn't want to be alone in the city, and she didn't want him travelling to small towns with nothing to do at night. She knew what opportunities presented themselves under those circumstances.

Emmitt approached the company looking for a territory that would keep him at home. The industry-wide downturn in sales at the time had R.E.S. wanting to shrink the sales force and increase the territories for those who remained. Emmitt didn't make the list of salesmen that were going to retain their position, but then a position as a sales trainer popped up, so he took it.

Emmitt loved the last day of a training session. He especially loved to share the fear the exam created in the trainees. And he knew that seeing the soon-to-be-reps' nervous state was what made

Henberlin willing to stand in front of the group and share his sales experiences.

From the first day of the course, the trainees had been told that the final exam would heavily influence the training performance reports sent to each of their managers. Emmitt emphasized the difficulty presented by the exam—how much he hated the final day due to the impact their test results could have on their sales career.

"How things go for you back in your offices isn't up to me at this point, it's up to you." Emmitt's rich, broadcaster's voice owned his audience's attention. "I'm sorry to say it but today is the day. Remember, your manager spent a great deal of his branch budget to send you to this session. They want to know if you have an aptitude for what you were hired to do.

"Unfortunately, human beings have the ability to mimic others, in our context, to act like salesmen but not have the substance to be one. That is what this test is all about. For your sakes, I hope you all got a good night's sleep."

He knew most of them had partied through the weekend. None of the trainees had been aware they would experience Stampede Week when they enrolled in the course. Good fortune had smiled upon them and their timing. How could they not take advantage of participating in a ten-day party with the company paying their expenses? The previous Friday, the first night of the festivities, they'd spent the night and early hours of the morning in one of the large cabarets. Who wouldn't enjoy singing and dancing with strangers from all over the world? When they found out that the same party kept on going Saturday and Sunday nights, they did it all again without hesitating.

For their final exam, the class seemed deflated, tired, hung-over and fidgety after a second weekend of alcohol and heavy meals. Emmitt detected a level of fear, dense and lingering beyond any other created on the last day of previous sessions.

He cleared his throat and began in a slow, duty-bound voice, "This examination consists of fifty multiple choice questions. Each question is a sales situation in which you will have to make a decision as to the best action you should take. The psychology of selling is woven into each question, so I advise you not to try and outguess the question."

Each student tried to make eye contact with him as he placed a copy of the exam on their desk top. During the course, Emmitt had expressed the importance of eye contact. He had told them how it showed confidence in oneself and respect for a prospect. This time, he refused to look at them.

When he finished handing out the exam, he returned to the front of the room and asked, "Is everyone ready?"

The class mumbled in the affirmative. Nervous coughs sounded and throats were cleared. Then every chest expanded with the slow, deep intake of air one takes while waiting for the start of a race.

"You will have twelve minutes to answer fifty questions starting from—*now!*" Emmitt said with deliberate acceleration.

The sound of pages flipping was loud but brief as the sales students tried to take the best advantage of their twelve minutes. Then silence. Their eyes clicked as they read the words of the first question.

1)   You and your manager are in the middle of signing the largest order of your career. The night before, you attended a good friend's bachelor party. Despite your best efforts to take it easy, you got caught up in the festivities and got carried away shooting tequila. Then you topped off the evening with a midnight buffet of spicy Mexican food.

At the signing you are suffering from your party enjoyments. Despite your discomfort it looks like you will get the order. Suddenly, without warning, your stomach starts to cramp. Involuntarily, you break wind. What do you do?

A) Challenge your prospect to do better.
B) Ignore it and deal with it if it happens again.
C) Move to South America
D) Give your manager credit.

"You bastard!" the fastest reader yelled at Emmitt and then hurled a wad of crushed paper at him.

The rest of the class began to laugh the laughter of relief as they realized they had been suckered.

"You should have seen your faces." The instructor looked at Henberlin. "Neil, what did you think?"

"Every one of them flunked," Henberlin said, chuckling.

"None of you should have worried about failing a salesman's aptitude test, even if it had been a real one. The real test today was to see how much confidence you had in yourselves. That's your last lesson of the course. I've enjoyed working with you people. Good luck out there. Are there any last questions?"

One of the trainees raised a hand. After a nod from Emmitt he pointed at Henberlin and asked, "Isn't he the guy you were telling us about this morning?"

Henberlin looked at Emmitt with a raised eyebrow and asked, "What were you telling them?"

"Ah, you know, bio stuff. Just letting them know who was coming to talk to them," Emmitt said, trying to sound offhanded.

"But what about–" the trainee began, but Emmitt cut him off and repeated, "Just bio stuff is all."

Henberlin shrugged, then pushed away from the wall and made for the door.

"I'll come by later," Emmitt said. "See what you're up to."

2

—

Leaving the lobby of the training area, Henberlin's peripheral vision caught flashes of aqua closing in on his left.

"I thought I'd wait for you so you'd be sure to go see Owen," the business analyst said.

"Well, you wasted your time. I have some calls to make," Henberlin said without looking at the analyst or slowing to a normal pace.

"He said right away."

"I need to get him an update. I've been away for a few days so I don't know where things stand. You guys kind of jumped the gun a little, don't you think?"

"We thought you weren't coming back."

Henberlin stopped and turned to the analyst who just pulled even with him.

"What? Why wouldn't I come back?" Henberlin asked, but didn't wait for an answer. He continued to walk the short distance to his office.

"You can't avoid this," the analyst called after him.

"I'll try."

He slammed his office door.

He walked to his desk, stood off to one side, and stared at what seemed like a foreign object: A disrupted desk. A disruption performed by someone who thought they had the authority to infiltrate his private space. Disruption to his normal neatness. With

Henberlin, everything had its place. Plenty of reports and books and printouts strewn over the surface; busy but not chaotic. What a stranger had done to his desk, he considered an evacuation. The glass top glowed, the wood polished to a gleam. Leather cleaner had been applied to the back of his chair and to the armrests, which had been discolored from contact with his bare arms. Now they were buffed and new again. Inside the cardboard box beside the desk he'd expected to see his personal possessions. Instead, he found only old unused notepads, paperclips, a stapler he never used because who does these days, and other anonymous items found in the back corners of abandoned desk drawers.

He turned to the bookshelves to find them cleared and dusted. In the closet, bare wire hangers without his spare shirts, vacuumed carpet without his extra pairs of shoes. His Western gear nowhere in sight. He stood in his own office, but based on the evidence, he appeared to be gone.

'What the hell?' he thought, then caught himself: 'No anger, the weekend was too good.'

He picked up the phone and dialed the VP's secretary. "Geneva, where's my stuff?"

"Owen asked me to—"

"Owen?" he interrupted. Then an interrupting knock on the door. The door opened and seeing the face entering his office, Henberlin said goodbye to Geneva and hung up. Kyle Badgerclaw stepped in wearing a large black ten-gallon hat with eagle feathers along one side. His shirt faded denim, jeans showing regular wear, scuffed brown leather boots.

"Kyle, can you tell me what's going on? I know Owen has plans to fire me if I don't have something concrete on the Shield Oil contract, but he's left the chute early and cleared me out." Neil pointed at the new guest chairs in front of his desk. Then, turning and taking a long look at his own desk chair, he ran his finger along the armrest before venturing to sit down.

"You think Owen is going to fire you?" Kyle asked. "I know he's not an admirer, but really."

"What would you call everyone's surprised reaction to seeing me here this morning? They must have seen Geneva clear out my office and now they think it's happened."

"Yeah, but Geneva gave all your stuff to the detectives. I don't think anyone thought you'd been fired. They thought you'd been murdered."

Henberlin pulled back, raised his wide shoulders and pulled his neck back, then eased it forward again. He opened his mouth. His jaw move but no words escaped.

"That's right... you were in Vancouver when your death hit the news," Kyle said, realizing Henberlin's wide, unfocused eyes and phantom speech amounted to disbelief verging on shock. "When they reported you'd been murdered in the apartment here in Calgary, I assumed you hadn't gone on your weekend trip. But I'm happy now to learn that you did. You wouldn't have heard about it in Vancouver so you wouldn't have phoned anyone to let them know it wasn't true."

Henberlin's voice came back loud but only one word escaped: "What?"

"Saturday, on the news. They reported a double murder. A man and a woman in your special apartment. The man was shot in the face."

"Holy shit." Henberlin placed his hands over his mouth and stared down at the surface of his desk. Thoughts of his wife's reaction while listening to her morning news show began a wormy shakeup in his mind. He looked up when Kyle's voice came again.

"The detectives noticed the custom suits and traced them to the tailor. The tailor said he'd made them for you. Then they announced that your name appeared on the lease so they released a report stating that you were the victim."

Henberlin blew air through his hands then said, "Right, right, right. Well, obviously it's not me. So Owen had my desk cleared out because he thought I was dead?"

"Yes, but at the request of the police. You need to call them."

"Yes… I will." He sat for a minute, his fingers pinching his lips. "I wonder if Leyna has heard any of this. The longer she goes without knowing about it the better. I should call her." He reached for the phone but stopped when his hand touched the handset. "Wait a minute, you said 'double murder.' Who else was killed?"

"Well, that's the thing. It was Yanmei."

"Yanmei? No…" Henberlin's voice trailed to almost silence, his eye focus dissipating again. "It can't be."

Yanmei Albin worked as a group manager in the Production Engineering department at Shield Oil. She was the sales prospect he needed to call so he could update the VP.

Shortly after Henberlin joined the new processor introduction team, he received an unsolicited call from Yanmei expressing an interest in the processor. She would never tell him how she knew the yet-to-be-released processor existed, but the sales potential he envisioned for the new high-powered workstations within Shield Oil diminished his need to know. Yanmei knew how to dangle the prospective sales carrot and knew Henberlin craved carrots. He fought hard to make Shield an introductory project partner even though Yanmei's group would never become power users of the new system. But they were a small, controllable first step into the energy giant.

The system, best targeted at the reservoir engineers looking for high computational speed, still harbored numerous benefits the production engineers could utilize. The slower pace of the engineers suited the slower learning curve needed to establish how the machine would work in a user environment. The reservoir engineers would want to run all of their simulators at full speed the minute they could open the onboard FORTRAN editor. Henberlin would have loved to run parallel customer introduction projects. After all, as a salesman, he had a deep belief in the-more-the-merrier philosophy of market penetration.

But Yanmei wanted to preserve Henberlin's attentions in her department. She knew that if Henberlin had to split his efforts between her group and the reservoir engineers, who would adopt the new system in a more quantitative manner, he wouldn't be spending too much time on the 23rd floor talking to her group. So Yanmei presented the argument that the walk-don't-run approach at the start would pay off with bigger dividends in her company. Controlled success would lead to explosive sales—if they followed her lead.

"Sorry Neil, but there's no mistake about that one," Kyle said, snapping Henberlin back into the present. "You should have heard the R.E.S. hotline chatter as a result. Saturday night, my phone rang off the hook. Everyone in the sales and tech departments called to say they'd heard the news. They also said they called everyone else and they all had an I-told-you-so tone to their voice. This morning, groups hovered around desks, then splintered off to hover at other desks. Nobody stayed in their office. They jackal-packed in your hallway hoping to see some police action until they found out the detectives had been through your office yesterday."

"What were they saying?"

"Well, it kind of confirmed what everybody thought about you and Yanmei."

Henberlin let this sink in for a minute.

Everybody thought Henberlin and Yanmei Albin had more than a professional relationship. They spent a considerable amount of time together and he self-confessed that many times they met for the flimsiest of reasons and made sure they were not reachable when they met. Conversations with Yanmei held his interest. No doubt he would pursue this intelligent and beautiful woman under different conditions. But no matter how much he enjoyed Yanmei's company, he wouldn't let it affect his marriage.

Before Leyna, for him to have an intimate relationship with more than one woman would've been acceptable under all circumstances. He possessed the energy and desire to experience a high-paced, balls-to-the-wall existence. Travelling on credit, investing on margin, enjoying the love of a woman, all performed without a second thought. Day trading thrilled him to a level that required other thrill-seeking activities for when the markets shut down. Anything he could do that proved he was smarter than everyone else was irresistible to his ego. There didn't seem to be a dare he wouldn't meet head-on. But that all changed when a friend asked him to go to Argentina on a business opportunity.

The friend had some business he had to conduct, and if Henberlin wanted to learn a very lucrative method of making money, his friend would be glad to show him the ropes.

Henberlin's caution flags began waving. In high school, his basketball team played an exhibition game at the provincial jail. He had been looking forward to the experience. Driving to the event, he participated in the jokes about whether or not to call a fast break or wearing their "con" running shoes. Then they entered the prison. Once the team passed through the first set of doors into the secured area, a terrifying reality seemed to cut off his air. The doors had thin metal mesh built into the bluish glass. A thick steel door panel frame, painted white, supported two-inch-thick steel dowels that slid into the wall frame in all four directions. The place closed in on him when he heard the clunk of the dowels engaging behind him. Temporarily incarcerated, he knew he never wanted to go to jail.

Still, he made the trip with his friend and it turned out to be what Henberlin had expected. Drugs.

His friend took him to meet with two men the friend had met a number of times. No special method yet. After the buy, they went to a central farmers market on Puerto Madero to buy various sizes of cheese rounds. In a cheap hotel, not the one they were staying in, the friend showed Henberlin the method: Hollow out some of the cheese rounds, stuff them with drugs and ship them back to Canada. Henberlin shook his head in disbelief.

"Drugs in cheese, that's the method?"

"Works every time. Cheese makes it so the dogs can't smell the drugs."

"Not for me. See ya." He left for the airport.

Back in Canada two weeks later, when his friend went to pick up the cheese rounds, the Royal Canadian Mounted Police were waiting for him. Once he took possession of the cheese, they arrested him. Henberlin spent a few jumpy weeks sweating it out to see if his friend would mention he'd had a companion on the trip. He heard the clunk of the jail doors every time someone knocked on his door at home or at work. Thoughts about how he'd almost broken the law and ended up on the wrong side of the steel and glass prison doors often caused him to close his eyes and cringe. The loss of freedom and spending time with the kind of people he'd seen watching that basketball game more than cemented the idea of being a law-abiding citizen in his brain. The RCMP never contacted him.

During those weeks, he took a good look at his current life trajectory. Although he had a lot working in his favor, a few changes could make him more secure, comfortable, and, more important to him, respectable. No more trips to South America, no more stupid manly challenges. This didn't mean living the life of a monk; he didn't plan to settle down, he only needed to tone it down.

His college degree in math didn't present too many opportunities for high-paying jobs. But all the work he'd done with computers gave him a good level of understanding of computer systems and their used by technical users. He canvassed the major companies in the computer industry. After a number of interviews, he accepted a position with a mid-range computer company known for scientific processing. He began a career in computer sales.

Now, after a few lucrative years in the industry, he sat in his office as the wrongly-assumed victim of a murder. He reached for the phone again, and again stopped before picking up the handset. "So who got shot in the face?"

"Who knows now? You should let the cops know it wasn't you so they can find out."

Nodding in agreement, Henberlin grabbed the phone for the third time. He looked at Kyle and shrugged, holding up the phone as a signal for privacy.

After Kyle left and closed the door, Henberlin dialed his call— but not to his wife and not to the cops.

3

—

The Vice President of Sales slumped in his chair, causing his suede leather vest with silver buttons to ride up behind his head, almost to his ears. His black shirt with red piping around the yoke supported a silver sheriff's badge that dangled loose from a safety pin. He held his fingers steepled, his middle fingers touched the tip of his nose, his index fingers against his lips. The glossy black bookcase behind him displayed awards, trophies, engraved crystal bowls, pictures of fishing trips, framed golf bag tags... but no books. Henberlin knew Owen always went over the top with the company's money to make an impression: Leather chairs, mahogany desk, white leather sofas. Along the walls hung shiny plaques acknowledging Owen's achievement of some pinnacle in sales.

Although Henberlin hated entering the shrine that Owen Brady had decorated in his own honor, he loved to stand in front of one or two of the plaques, making the VP wait a while before the meeting started. He'd smile knowing he'd surpassed each of the sales records Brady once owned.

When Henberlin finished looking at the awards, he turned to Brady. "Any idea where my plaques disappeared to? I heard you ordered them removed from my filing cabinet."

Brady ignored the question.

"Sit down. How do you think the weekend's events will affect the project?" he asked, twisting his mouth to one side. "Now that your main contact is dead, where does Shield Oil stand on their commitment to start ordering systems?"

"I haven't spoken to anyone at Shield yet. They're probably still under the impression that I'm dead, too. Probably wondering what the state of the project is just as much as you are. You, at least, know I wasn't a victim."

Brady sat, hands posed as if praying. He sighed and said, "So you're telling me you're going to miss the deadline?"

"What deadline? When was there ever a deadline?" Henberlin asked, as his anger flared a little.

"The first system was supposed to be installed by mid-July. That's next week. You're not going to make it."

"Owen, that wasn't ever going to be the deadline even when it was announced as the intended deadline. So many issues have cropped up since then—as we all knew they would. That deadline was dead from the outset."

"That's not what's been presented to the brass by the project managers," Brady said with a soft smile. "Since we didn't think you were coming back we initiated placing someone else into your role in the project. I think it's a good idea to stay on that path. It may take some time for you to get back to normal."

With heat rising in his face Henberlin hoped he hadn't turned red in front of Owen. He had to stay calm. This couldn't end in a shouting match.

"That might be true if I'd had a traumatic experience, but I didn't. Yes, a good friend has been killed and it makes things going forward with the project a little uncertain. But, get real. Replacing me is a mistake. I'm the only person who can keep even a speck of momentum going within Shield. That's especially true with Yanmei Albin out of the picture."

"Really? What will you do now to keep the momentum going?" Brady held his hands up and looked skyward for a sign.

Henberlin let Brady's sarcasm pass but noted the slight, satisfied smile Brady kept on his face. Henberlin refrained from speaking for a few seconds. "I'll gladly lay out the specifics," he said finally. "Once I've got a clearer grasp on the state of things at Shield. As much as you want to get me out of the picture, you know replacing me would be a serious blunder."

"Neil, no one is irreplaceable. You can't run a company or a department within a company when the sudden loss of one person will cause company-wide damage. We thought you were gone and we started to plan for the project without you. Truth be told, the prospect isn't that scary. Since you haven't brought anything in for what's become an intolerable amount of time, it also appears to be the prudent thing to do."

Henberlin lowered his chin and shook his head. "*Some* people have seen how much work I've done on this project. I'm sure they wouldn't think it prudent for me to be removed."

"Really? Who's going to stand up for you when you haven't produced any sales for months?"

Henberlin would have loved to have set Brady straight. Instead, he ignored the question and said, "I've done too much work on this to have it taken away from me now. Installation of the first few systems is imminent. Even without Albin, the other analysts at Shield are as excited about this product as she was. Who knows, maybe she was stalling. Maybe they'll want to get things rolling as fast as we can deliver."

Brady's smile reached a little higher. "Well, why don't you find out if that's the case? Then, if it doesn't look like you'll be booking anything by the end of the week, we'll consider you to be on leave."

It was Henberlin's turn to smile now. "You can proceed thinking we're working with that understanding if you like." Henberlin stood and started for the door.

"The end of the week, Neil, or you're on leave."

Henberlin stopped and turned back to Brady. "I'll be talking with Raymond about this."

Brady pursed his lips, his eyebrows moved closer together, Henberlin anticipated a blowout. "If you think going over my head is going to help you, feel free," he said, flicking his hands to brush Henberlin out the door.

"It's not going over your head when I report directly to the President on this project, is it?" Henberlin waited for Brady to respond, but Brady picked up his phone and spun away.

Outside the office, Henberlin directed his voice to the phone Brady's secretary held beside her ear. "Your boss is a prick."

The secretary clapped her hand over the phone's mouthpiece.

Henberlin made his way straight to Kyle's office in the technical analyst's area of the floor. Kyle sat facing forward at his desk, typing into his notebook.

"Who've you managed to get a hold of?" Henberlin asked.

"I'm responding to an email from Marlin Walker. How'd it go?" Kyle said without looking up.

"Brady's given me to the end of the week to book something."

"Ha!" Kyle stopped his typing and looked up. When he looked at Henberlin, his smiled dropped. "Neil, I know what it must mean to you to lose Yanmei. More than the loss of someone you were doing business with. Don't you think you should take a little time to let everything sink in?"

"Sounds like a good idea, but out-of-the-question right now. We have to take stock of where we are with Shield. Things have to start happening pretty quick. If I stop and think too hard about losing a friend right now, I don't know when I'll be able to get back to business. Right now I need to get this project back on the rails."

Henberlin bent over, placing his elbows on his knees. He stared at the carpet for a minute, holding his head in his hands.

"The end of the week isn't too likely. Brady can't be serious."

"I don't give a shit if Brady is serious or not," Henberlin said, sitting up and climbing out of his reverie. "I only went to his office to make him think I cared about his concerns."

"Right. Have you talked to your wife, yet?"

"I'm going to call her when I leave here."

"Have you called the police?"

"They're on their way. I think they're going to take up a major part of what remains of the day. I need to know what the thoughts are over at Shield. It's good you're talking to Marlin. Did you find out if Yanmei's husband is at work?"

"No word on Stephen, sorry."

"Okay, we have to keep that stream into Shield open. What's Marlin's take on Yanmei not being in the picture?"

"He's blown away by it, just like the rest of them. I only gave them my condolences. I didn't want to be ghoulish and ask if they still intended to buy systems. I told them you were going to be tied up with the investigation for at least today, and that you would get in touch as soon as you could."

"Great, but did he give any indication that they were still committed to the systems? I don't care about making anyone's deadline but my own, and I need to get some business closed."

Henberlin, against his wife's council, had purchased a multi-unit apartment complex in Arizona a few months before the stock market and real estate recessions struck. The renters had to honor their payments for the duration of their leases. But, as each one expired, rents had to be lowered to keep tenants in the building. He survived that loss of income the first time around. But as renewal time approached again, the market crashed like cheap wine glasses dropping on the granite countertops he'd installed in each of the apartments.

Next, the buying appetite of Canadian investors added to the pain of the crash. Henberlin thought he was ahead of the curve when he bought years before other Canadians were willing to invest in foreign property. His friends and colleagues thought he was either crazy or showing off. His wife agreed with the others but wanted to give him the benefit of the doubt. He really needed her emotional support to stick to what he saw as a major equity-building strategy. After he'd implemented his plan, his doubters began to wish they, too, had invested in the Arizona real estate market.

Then, with the severe reduction in the value of Arizona real estate and the leveling of the Canadian and US dollars, more Canadians could justify the purchase of an investment property in the desert. With lower purchase prices and therefore lower mortgage payments, the new Canadian owners had all gotten a better deal than Henberlin. The new Canadian buyers attracted more tenants by charging less for rent and still covering their costs.

This all added up to a crash in the rental market in Phoenix. Renters with apartment leases signed before this additional crash began to negotiate new payments before their about-to-expire leases ended, and landlords were willing to drop the rates to keep their properties occupied. The threat of moving to another building when the current lease expired worked, and some building owners were falling into an upside-down rent situation—Henberlin being one of them. His building income no longer surpassed his mortgage demand. Even sending every cent of that income to his bankers didn't prevent him from falling behind on his loan.

But money? He didn't worry about money. He could always generate cash. What people thought of him as a businessman is what concerned him. What his wife thought of him as a smart businessman meant the most.

Kyle said, "You can read the email Marlin sent if you like, but he stayed clear of business."

"That's understandable. I just wanted to rub Brady's nose in a system commitment from Yanmei's group. The problem is that a commitment would smell so sweet—and Brady still gets secondhand credit for a sale. I think Raymond would like to rub Brady's nose in it, though. Brady doesn't have the ability or the class to hide his desire to take over as president."

Kyle's phone rang. He picked it up and said, "Hello, Geneva."

After a short pause he said, "Yes, he's here."

Another few seconds went by. Then Kyle hung up, turned to Henberlin and said, "They're here."

"Okay. Try and locate Stephen would you?"

Kyle nodded.

Henberlin turned away from his office. Instead of going to meet the detectives, he went into the stairway, pulled out his cell phone, and turned it back on. There were numerous phone messages. He knew his fear of how his wife would react to the news was why he'd delayed making this call. His stomach had sunk deep and his chest cringed. He took a deep breath then pushed the speed dial for his wife.

"Where have you been?" she answered. "I've been calling you all morning."

"I see that. As you can imagine it's been a little crazy around here."

"What happened? Why are they saying it was you? Why are they saying you owned the apartment and that your suits were in it?" Leyna's words accelerated through the phone.

"I don't have all the details yet, but the police are here to question me. I'll know more after I've talked to them."

"But isn't the girl a person you know? Isn't she a customer?" Again Leyna's voice clipped her words.

"Yes. As soon as I know more, I'll call you. Where are you? Are you all right?"

"No, I'm not all right. People now know you weren't killed but they're still treating me like I've lost you. I'm still at work. I thought of going home but then I'd only be sitting around wondering what was going on."

"Right. Have the police called you?"

"Yes, I had a message when I got in. I called them and put them off. I assumed it was a joke and told them so."

"Of course, why wouldn't you think that? I don't think talking to them would do any harm. Don't be surprised if they call you back. I should go, they're waiting. You're my first call when they're gone."

4

—

Detectives Gordon Sweetland and Victor Richie stood waiting outside Henberlin's office. During the introductions, Henberlin tried to get a read on their moods but found them both pillars of stony charm. They were dressed in suits, not the typical Stampede Week western wear. The cut and press of their suits marked them as different from the regular inhabitants of the office. Utility over vanity, loud and clear.

"Detectives, would you like something to drink? Coffee, tea, water?"

Detective Sweetland declined for both of them. Both men seemed about the same age, around fifty. Sweetland stood a fraction taller. His dark hair, tight to the scalp on the sides but long and full on top, sat like a cap on his oversized head. A scar appeared beside his right eye. Round like a hot fireplace poker had jabbed and melted the skin. It looked like his navel had shifted north. Richie had a stocky build, his hair a little thinner. If Henberlin had to guess which of the two men might have smiled earlier in his life, he would have mulled it over for a long time. The detectives looked at each other with confusion on their faces then looked around the office with the same look.

"Someone cleaned up in here," Sweetland stated.

"That's what they told me," Henberlin said. "So you were here on the weekend going through my stuff?"

"Your vice president gave us permission. We took some of your belongings and made a little bit of a mess, but you had a lot of personal items in here. Where did they go?"

"Hmm, I was just trying to find that out when you arrived."

The detectives continued their visual search of the office as they took seats in front of Henberlin's desk.

Detective Richie cleared his throat. "So, needless to say, we were surprised and confused when your wife called to inform us that you were alive, and most likely at your office."

"I can imagine. I talked to her a minute ago and she said she had a message waiting for her when she arrived at work, asking her to call the police."

"That was us. Obviously we have some questions for both of you."

"I'll help as much as I can. I'm really sorry to hear about the death of Yanmei Albin. We'd been working together a lot on a project."

"Yes, we know." Sweetland smiled. "Can you tell us where you were this past weekend, starting last Friday"?

"I went to Vancouver for the weekend with my wife. She had a marketing seminar and asked me, last minute, to join her," Henberlin answered.

"What time did you leave Calgary?" Sweetland said.

"I took an eight-thirty flight on Westjet. Arrived about the same time and took a cab to the Bayshore downtown."

"What did you do in Vancouver all weekend?" Richie asked.

"Late dinner on Friday. Spent the day hanging out at the hotel while my wife attended her conference. When it ended she met some colleagues for a short time afterward. After she showered and dressed and we went for another late dinner.

"Sunday we spent the morning at False Creek. I have to have my Benny's Bagels when I'm in Van. Then we walked around downtown, spent time at the hotel together, and again went for a late dinner. Got up early this morning and took the first flight in. Got to work about nine-thirty, running a little late."

"On Saturday you said you spent the day at the hotel. Can you tell us what you were doing until your wife met with you again?"

"Sure. I had breakfast in the room at about nine o'clock, then went to the spa around nine forty-five. My wife had booked me into a number of spa activities. Massage, mud detox, men's facial, and I think one other thing. I spent a long time in the steam room afterward. It took all day and, truth be told, I had the creeps about spending that much time on body cleansing. My wife returned to the room about six-thirty, and I'd arrived minutes before her after having a drink, a Caesar, in the bar."

Both detectives nodded, but Henberlin couldn't tell if they were nodding in belief or to acknowledge he'd finished his sentence.

"You said you went for a late dinner. How late?" Sweetland asked.

"Eight-thirty or thereabouts."

"What did you do from when your wife returned until then?"

"Well, like I said, my wife took a shower but there are certain things that couples do when they're alone and have free time. Especially when they're in a hotel room, at least especially for me." Henberlin smiled a bashful smile. "Dinner lasted maybe two hours. We stopped in the bar for a nightcap and then back to the room."

Henberlin didn't mind telling them about his activities during the weekend and would have provided more detail if it would help find Yanmei's murderer. He'd seen television and movie detectives question witnesses and persons of interest, and knew they could get personal. He knew his fellow employees considered the existence of a sexual relationship with Yanmei a foregone conclusion. He didn't want the detectives or his wife to think that way as well.

He decided he would try to keep his responses sounding strictly business, but first asked, "Do you have any idea who killed Yanmei and the other person in the apartment?"

"I'd rather not say," Detective Sweetland said. "Things are moving a little faster since you returned."

"Yes, I'm sure they have. Any idea who the other person was?"

"Like I said, your return threw us a bit of a curve."

"Yeah, I'm sure it did. I feel so bad for Yanmei. She was a good person to work with, very professional."

The two detectives looked at each other. Then Detective Richie said, "Okay. Tell us about the project you were working on with Mrs. Albin."

Henberlin began the history of his involvement with Yanmei Albin by describing the company's project to introduce the new computer work station into the oil and gas market. He had been chosen to be the first to approach prospective users of the system for testing and eventually sales. His history of success in the oil industry meant that he would be best at choosing where the system would be most applicable.

He and his best tech analyst, Kyle, agreed that the reservoir simulation application would be their first choice for the workstation. They drew up a list of the most advantageous oil companies to approach.

Since the technology utilized was new and sensitive on both trademarking and national security levels, the US Government stipulated that the chosen companies could have no foreign ownership, and that the new encryption algorithms were not to leave North America. Canadian companies were exempt if they were American owned. Shield Oil met this requirement.

Then, before they made their approach to Shield, Yanmei Albin, a Shield employee, contacted them.

Mrs. Albin headed a small department in production engineering responsible for simulating the performance of the sucker rods employed on the pump jacks of Shield's producing wells.

"So, our new system can handle the workload of sucker rod analysis with relative ease, if you believe the specifications," Henberlin said, moving things along. "We were gung-ho to chase the reservoir group for the first test, but this lesser application has its merits."

Again both detectives nodded, then sat silent for a moment. Detective Richie asked, "How did Mrs. Albin know to contact you?"

"You know, I asked her a few times where she'd gotten her information and my number and she never gave me an answer. It was always a silly quip of a response like, 'I have my sources.' Or 'you'll just have to wait and find out.' Stuff like that. We didn't want to put too much pressure on her to provide an answer."

"Why's that?"

"Her husband. Stephen Albin is the top reservoir simulation analyst at Shield. He's doing the work on Shield's South East Great Slave reservoir, Shield's largest asset. He's one of our main targets. We didn't want to come across too determined to find out how Mrs. Albin heard about our system because we wanted her to provide a strong lead-in to her husband's department. And she let us know she could do it, or not do it. After a while, we discovered how much we were dependent on her."

"How so?"

"I said we decided to go after the smaller application for testing, but we only got agreement from our tech group when we said we would still try to make contact with the reservoir simulation techs. When we did contact them, word came down from Stephen Albin that they would wait until the testing with the sucker rods was complete before they would look at testing with reservoirs. Yanmei had us."

"Yanmei?"

"Yes, we were on a first-name basis. When you work with someone for a long-enough time you get a little less formal. It's horrible calling her Mrs. Albin as if we weren't close friends.

"Yanmei didn't threaten us or bully us if the testing didn't go her way, but that fact lingered in the backs of our minds. She did let me meet her husband on one or two occasions. I wanted to make contact so I could show my company that we were making inroads to the other department. I explained to her how critical it was for me to have some contact with her husband so that my overlords didn't come down hard on me, accusing me of dragging my feet. What I was trying to tell her was that she was dragging her feet, and I had to show action on other levels within Shield."

"With regard to your relationship with Mrs. Albin, how close was it?" Sweetland held eye contact with Henberlin.

Henberlin wondered if the detectives were ready to start implying more than a professional relationship. "We were good working together and then we became friends," Henberlin responded.

"Friends...?"

There was a light tap at the door and the three men all turned their eyes.

"Yes?" Henberlin called out, relieved a little at not having to reply to the detectives implication.

The door opened and the secretary of the Sales department stood hunched at the door with a grimaced smile. "Sorry, but there's a call for either detective. It's parked on seven-oh-four."

"Thank you." The door closed and Henberlin picked up the phone to connect the call. "You do want to take this, right?"

"Yes, please," Sweetland said.

Henberlin connected, then sat back and watched Sweetland as he listened to information that sounded like electronic trembles from across the desk. Sweetland made hums of understanding and crunched his eyebrows down before first looking at Detective Richie. Then lifting his head and covering the mouthpiece of the handset, he said to Henberlin, "I hate to ask you to leave your own office, but would you mind?"

Henberlin snapped his body forward as he lifted from the chair, saying he didn't mind at all. He left the two detectives to their call.

Outside his office, the Sales secretary stood waiting after delivering the message to the detectives. She started when she heard the door open and saw Henberlin come out and shut the door behind him.

"Oh good, it's you. I had another message for you but didn't know if I should deliver it to you while you were with the police." The secretary held out the message slip. "It's a request for an appointment from the man at Contract Geo about the inversion software."

"Okay, thanks."

"He wants to see you today. I told him you were tied up and likely would be for some time. He said he understood, but that it was important to deliver the message as soon as possible."

"That's fine." As Henberlin said this the door to his office opened and the two detectives stepped out into the hallway.

"Sorry, Mr. Henberlin, we're going to have to leave now, but we do need to talk with you again soon. Will you be at your home this evening?" Detective Richie said.

"I should be. That would be fine."

"Thanks for your time," Sweetland said with a quick nod. Then the two men left.

5

—

Rent-An-Office facilities had cropped up everywhere in Calgary's downtown core. Freelance engineers, landmen, and computer analysts used them to present a downtown presence to their clients. The stigma of doing things on your own evolved to become a badge of entrepreneurial courage. In the past, it meant you weren't good enough to get a job at an oil company or you'd received a golden parachute from an oil company and got hired back as a contractor—double dippers who received a pension check and a contractor's fee for doing the same work they'd performed as an employee. The new crop of tenants in the rented office space were oil- and gas-savvy mercenaries willing to provide their skills on retainer, by choice—young, aggressive, intelligent players in the patch.

The shared office facility Contract Geo occupied had once been the offices of a large business computer company which, some years earlier, vacated the two floors atop a moderately-sized tower on the edge of Chinatown. Since the fifties, Chinatown had been dominated by the Chinese community. Now all of Asia shared real estate in the popular area at the downhill end of the Center Street Bridge. Thai restaurants, Vietnamese sandwich shops, Korean fast-food kiosks, Japanese teppan counters, and Indian lunch buffets treated the working people of the area to the great tastes of the East.

Henberlin parked by the river and walked along the sunken section of Center Street, where the street level was three feet higher than the sidewalk. He passed in front of a row of attached two-story buildings. Some brick, some wood construction—all old and brittle, seeming to rely on each other to stay erect. They housed vegetable markets that gave of the scent of overripe tropical fruit, electronics outlets with a wide variety of rice cookers in display windows glowing with neon signs advertising DVDs. An ancient herbal remedy store with its doors opened smelled of anise. The same old man always sat in the window manning the scale and cash box, a neat stack of small brown paper bags beside the scale.

Shade from the buildings darkened the sidewalk. Henberlin could make out the figure of a person in the distance. As he moved closer, he saw an old man wearing baggy clothes too big for his thin frame and a baize cloth hat, its rim slanted down, almost covering the man's ears. He was short and stood facing Henberlin, as if waiting for him.

"Neo…" he said, "Neo, have tea with me."

"I'm sorry, what?" Henberlin, said shocked that the old man was addressing him.

"Neo Henbrin, right? Have tea with me."

"Ah, I'm sorry, I think there's some mistake here."

"No, you are Neo Henbrin, right?

"Yes."

"Have tea with me so we can talk."

Henberlin waited a beat then said, "I can't, I have a meeting I'm headed to."

"Not today. Tomorrow. Same time, meet me here in front of this green door."

Henberlin looked to his left. At the edge of the sidewalk were three thick, misshapen steps that led up to a wooden door. Its tired paint a faded shade of green. The windows showed years of dusty buildup that blocked the view inside. There were no numbers or letters to identify the location.

"I don't understand. Why?"

"We should talk. Tomorrow, right here. First we talk about your father."

Henberlin looked harder at the old Chinese gentleman.

"My father?" He stared, his brow knitted over his eyes. "Which one?

"Number one father, of course. I know about him. We should also talk about your wife."

"What?"

"You see, we have things to talk about."

"Who are you? Why would you know anything about my wife or my father?" Things beyond his knowing were closing in on him.

"I'm Yanmei's father, Jian Liu. We'll talk tomorrow. It's important."

Henberlin swallowed hard as his brain ticked through a large database of his and Yanmei's conversations. He searched for facts regarding her father, worried that she'd been afraid of her old man and that he should be too. Also, he wondered why Yanmei would have told her father about him.

Hesitating, he said, "Okay, I'll try and make it, but what do my wife and father have to do with this?"

"Tomorrow, it's important."

Henberlin nodded, then stepped to pass Jian Liu. As he did, Jian Liu's small hands grabbed Henberlin's bicep with strong fingers. The fingers couldn't wrap much of the arm, so their hard points dug into the muscle. Slight pain penetrated the flesh. Jian Liu looked straight and deep into Henberlin's eyes. The smaller man's gaze saw through to his real intention—to get away as fast as possible. They stood in that pose for seconds that seemed extended beyond time. Jian Liu tensed his fingers for emphasis, then let go of Henberlin's arm. Still holding his gaze, he said, "Important, it's important."

With a slight bow of his head, Henberlin agreed to meet the next day.

After the short walk to the corner, in the confusion of the old man's interruption, it took Henberlin a full minute to remember what had actually brought him to this downtown intersection.

'Yanmei's father, my father, Leyna, how are they mixed up in whatever's going on?'

These and mists clouded his thoughts as he rubbed his bicep.

Inside the reception area of the Rent-An-Office, the shared receptionist asked him to wait a few minutes for the meeting room. He'd been to the office twice before and still wondered what had made him agree to help the man he was about to meet. The previous two times he'd been ushered right into a room with an eight-seat conference table surrounded by fabric chairs and state-of-the-art audiovisual equipment, none of which their meetings ever required.

He now noticed the reception area contained the same type of fabric chairs, a few glass tables with oil and gas magazines angled in neat columns on their surfaces, and a modern lamp in each of the room's corners.

Strange chimes rang out. It wasn't until they rang a second time that he realized it was the ringtone he designated for long distance calls. He answered and heard a mechanical voice say, "Please wait for an important call from Melanie Jackson."

Henberlin knew he had to take the call, but couldn't link the name with the context he should know it from. A few clicks from the phone, then a beep.

"Hi. Neil? Are you there? This is Melanie Jackson in Phoenix."

The context fit together.

"Yes, I'm here. How are you, Melanie?"

"I'm doing well, thank you. But I have an issue. One of the vacant second-floor units in your building has had a water heater failure and it's flooded the carpet and soaked the drywall. Plus it's flooded out the vacant apartment below. I've had my maintenance man go over and shut the water off to the entire complex. But I'm afraid that, with the way things currently stand with regard to your management fees being in arrears, I can't go beyond that point."

Henberlin mouthed the word 'Shit' between clenched teeth before responding, "That's terrible. What have you told the other tenants about their loss of water?"

"Nothing. I can't operate on your behalf."

"Okay, that's unfortunate, but we can't have things remain at a stand still. We have to get the next step started. How is it that a water heater goes bad anyway?" Henberlin wanted to get his Arizona property manager talking about a subject other than money.

"It happens all the time in Arizona. The hard water causes mineral buildups that cause the heating elements to stay on all the time, and they corrode the tanks. Eventually the tank pops."

"Wow, I've never heard of that." Henberlin paused and hoped what he was about to say would come out with a high level of sincerity. "I'm going to need your help, Melanie. I imagine I need someone to take the responsibility to get the tank replaced and get the water on again. Then I'll need someone to manage getting the two apartments back into shape, but that comes a little later. First, I want you to trust me about the management fees that I owe you. I will pay you in full and I'll do that very soon. But right now, if I don't get the water back on and the tenants leave the building and then sue me, I'm going to have to shut it all down and bankrupt my Arizona holdings. Then you get nothing, because of course the banks get their share first, and there's nothing left after their share. What I need from you is to get your maintenance man to get the replacement water tank and a plumber to install it. I'm going into a meeting here soon. When I'm done I'll wire you two thousand dollars to get this rolling. Then we'll talk about getting you more. Can you work with me through this?"

As he finished his request, the man he'd come to meet walked in the main entrance of the suite. "Neil, sorry I'm late. Come on in," he said with a sweeping gesture.

Henberlin nodded and held up his hand, index finger in the air and palm out, showing the man his cell phone. When he brought the phone back to his ear, Melanie was in the middle of her answer:

"...right after your meeting and make it five thousand or my bosses aren't going to take you seriously."

"Five's going to be tough unless you'll take part of it on my AMEX card."

"I'll take it all on your AMEX card."

"Great. Please have your maintenance man get started right away. Are you ready to write down this card number?"

Henberlin provided his card number, then stood and shook hands with Horace Delaney, a freelance reservoir analyst who marketed a software package used by reservoir simulators. The men turned and walked past the receptionist on their way to the conference room.

Once inside the room filled with audiovisual equipment, Henberlin turned to Delaney and said, "What the hell's happening? Yanmei? Is she really dead?"

Delaney held up his hand. "Wait, give me a minute." His tone was superior to subordinate, and he held Henberlin in a stare until Henberlin acknowledged how they were going to proceed. Then Delaney turned and began turning on the audiovisual equipment. The room filled with the sound of cooling fans with a soft static background. He then pulled out his cell phone and played with the screen for a minute. When he looked up, he acknowledged Henberlin and gave him a nod.

"I don't have an answer, Neil. We're trying to find out what happened. When we thought you were the other body with Yanmei in the apartment we were scrambling. Now that we know you're alive, we at least have a direction to go in."

"What direction can I give you? I was out of town and hadn't had contact with her in a week. And I'm not really involved, I'm just a credibility contact so you can have her feed someone whatever it is you want to feed them. I'm barely a go-between for Christ's sake. You said this was going to be simple. I meet with her periodically so that anybody that's watching her sees that she's actually meeting with someone who knows about the new system. You never said people could get killed. Shit. Do you think they're going to come after me now?"

"Maybe."

"What? Are you kidding me? Really? Maybe? What the hell does killing me accomplish? You set me up to look like I was passing information. I wasn't actually doing that."

"They don't know how involved you are, how much you know."

"Jesus. And now Yanmei's father has cornered me on the street and wants to talk to me."

"Her father? What did he say?"

Henberlin found himself staring out the window looking at nothing in particular about the wall of another building. He needed to look away from what he heard coming from Delaney. Then he shook off his panic. Something in Delaney's tone angered him. Something alerting him to Delaney being a move ahead.

He thought back to his first meeting with Delaney, the casual introduction and chat at a bar while watching a soccer match. After a beer or two, the conversation turned work-related and Henberlin's opportunity radar pinged when Delaney mentioned his reservoir simulation software. 'Amazing how Delaney's product fit perfectly with the specifications of the new workstation that R.E.S. intended to introduce to the market,' he'd thought. Then a reference to Shield Oil and their interest in Delaney's software. Yanmei had already talked to him about using the system for finite element analysis on sucker rods. But Henberlin's real target was the reservoir simulation group, a group that could really utilize the new systems. Reservoir simulation involved simulating the stresses of a geological structure underground. Analysts introduce various stresses mathematically to mimic the structure's previous production data. Based on the accuracy of simulating the past production of an oil field, the company could predict future production levels based on newly-applied stresses like fracking. And here sat a man with a possible introduction to that very group at Shield Oil. The salesman made his play by asking Delaney to have lunch with him the next day. They could talk a little more about his software and its potential for working in a scalable parallel processor environment. The naïve prospect said he hadn't thought about parallelism, but maybe the software had possibilities in that environment. At their second meeting, Delaney enlightened Henberlin to a situation he thought he'd never be involved in. He told him that he, Delaney, had initiated the contact between him and Yanmei. That his simulator didn't exist and that the real reason for their meeting in the bar was to set up a mechanism for passing misinformation about R.E.S.'s new computer system to people who were illegally trying to duplicate the technology.

Once the Yanmei card hit the table, Henberlin realized Delaney had actually set a hook for him and the point of a harpoon came hurling his way. The setup worked and Henberlin found himself helping the Canadian Intelligence Service with an operation to counter corporate theft.

"I told you what the old man said. He wants to meet me and talk with me. I imagine since my name was linked with his daughter's on the news, he figures I might know something about her death. What I don't get is how he knew me on the street."

"Yeah, well your picture is still on every television channel, and has been for the past few days. I imagine most people would recognize you. When does he want to talk to you?"

"Tomorrow."

"Where?"

"Not sure. He wants to meet at the same spot, same time tomorrow."

"You're going to be there right? You agreed to meet him?"

"I said I'd try."

"What did he say when you said you'd try?"

"He said he hoped I'd be there."

Delaney sat still and watched Henberlin who, not knowing how to sit and be watched, endured Delaney's non-reactive face and cold eyes searching him for movements and twitches. He smiled, shook his head in tight little shakes, and held his hands out, inviting comment.

"I was watching," Delaney said.

"What do you mean you were watching?"

"He said a lot more to you than he hoped you'd try and make it. He grabbed your arm and spoke tight-lipped, staring you straight in the face like it was a threat. What did he say?"

"Jesus. Now you're following me." Henberlin crossed his arms, grabbing his biceps. He reached and rubbed his forearm due to the hairs on his arms tingling. He took a breath. "He told me it was important. He said so twice. It was important that I meet him."

"Did he say what he wanted to talk about?"

"Yanmei."

"What else?"

Henberlin lowered his hands, clasping them in his lap. The thought that had permeated his mind since the second time he'd met this man took over his thoughts again: 'Can I trust this guy?'

The thought that had scrambled his logic since the meeting with Yanmei's father burst ahead again: 'What do my wife and father have to do with any of this?'

"Neil?"

Henberlin looked up, his thoughts interrupted. "Yeah, first he said he wanted to talk about my father. Then he said he wanted to talk about Yanmei." When he limited his response to his father and Yanmei, he established that the answer to trusting Delaney with his wife was 'no.'

"Your father knows Jian Liu?"

"My real father, not my step-father."

"The loan shark?"

"Former loan shark. I don't know what he does now."

"Makes sense he would know Jian Liu. We hadn't seen anything in his file about it, but you never get it all."

"It sounds like you have everything. Why would you know anything about my real father?"

"We checked you out. Part of what we do."

"I only offered to help by being at some phony meetings. You said all I had to do was make appearances, look like I was involved, and lease an apartment. Simple stuff you said, and for that you check me out?"

"We checked you out because it seems the simple stuff always gets a bit more complicated, like it did last Saturday. We need to find out what Jian Liu wants to talk to you about. Mr. Liu has been active with some people we like to keep watch on. Yanmei was our contact with Liu and now it's going to have to be you. She provided her father with information that we wanted her to give him. She told him she had received the information from you. Because of your involvement with the new computer system from your company, you were the perfect person to provide the information. Now I'm going to have to tell you what Yanmei passed to her father."

Henberlin stared at the floor, not seeing it. He shook his head as Delaney spoke.

"So you mean that the person trying to illegally acquire information about our new system is Yanmei's father? You used Yanmei to incriminate her own father?"

"Yes, and by extension, the government of China. But Yanmei had her own reasons for going along with the plan. You don't need to know them.

"We'd been setting him up with tidbits. Yanmei dangled the information bait that she extracted from you via the appearance of having an affair with you. We were about to give him the information he wanted to get his hands on, when the rug got pulled."

"What information is he after?"

"We need to get you all caught up to speed. It's going to take a while."

"I have to get home, so it's going to have to wait until morning. The two detectives are expecting to meet with me again this evening, and I haven't talked to my wife since this ball-of... hit the fan."

"Any problems with the detectives?"

"No, they were just checking out anyone connected."

Henberlin told Delaney about the questions the detectives asked, then set up to meet early in the morning.

As Henberlin left the office, Delaney said, "Neil, sorry to be putting you deeper into this thing, but we need to see what's motivating Jian Liu. He's cold enough to take out his own daughter. Maybe we should have moved the info a little faster."

Henberlin held his hands in front of his chest, fingers splayed. His head tilted to one side, thinking. He opened his mouth but, for a moment he couldn't speak. He finally said, "You think he murdered his own daughter?"

"We think he killed one of his sons about a year ago. The police have called it an accident, but there's more to it than that. His sons both rejected his political views. To him they were a disappointment. Yanmei reflected his views until she had her eyes opened. If he found out she was passing information for us, he would never have forgiven her."

6

—

Leyna Henberlin coiled her long limbs tighter into the blanket she'd wrapped around herself the minute she returned home from her office. Her husband refilled her wine glass, then had to tap her shoulder to get her to realize he had returned with her wine. She'd managed to hold it together at work—supplying answers to a colorful range of questions, hoping her answers sounded reasonable. She detected a tip-toeing nature in the conversations of her fellow employees, but her clients, with bold right, ask whatever they wanted. The question they all wanted answered: "Did you know your husband kept an apartment downtown?"

She lied as she answered with what she thought was believable: "Yes, he often works late nights and early mornings. An apartment downtown made sense; I didn't want him sleeping in his office."

When she asked her husband why his name appeared on the apartment lease, the explanation Neil provided had a hard-to-believe quality. Hard-to-believe because the implied truth, spouted by the news channels, had gained ground with each seedy spin their idle minds could fabricate.

———

The actual truth of the lease's origin came from Horace Delaney. This was a truth Henberlin had to withhold from his wife.

To sell the value of the information that Yanmei had passed to her father, Delaney wanted to simulate an affair between Yanmei and Henberlin. To that end, Henberlin had taken the apartment where he and Yanmei met on a number of afternoons for the sake of appearing to be romantically involved. At first, they brought work with them to the meetings. Yanmei's sucker rod department did have a significant use for the new processors that R.E.S. was bringing to market, so many of the meetings involved the presentation and evaluation of the system's benefits. Through these discussions, they developed an understanding of each other, where they were coming from career-wise, life plans they had, things that indicated they both valued their lives. This understanding created a strong mutual respect for each other. Of course, thinking that Yanmei was a CSIS agent reduced the reliability of her personal information in Henberlin's view. What he knew as fact, though, was she really was an engineer with extensive knowledge about sucker rods. She'd been in the department with Shield Oil for the past eight years.

Over time their meetings evolved into subjects unrelated to their work. Movies, food, books, art, childhood dreams, current dreams, spouses, but never politics. And never the work for Delaney that had brought them together.

Yanmei had talked one day about her childhood when she served as her father's sidekick. This involved watching mahjong and poker games in dingy subterranean rooms while listening to stories of life in China—the old days and the new. Her father always filling in the meaning of the stories as they made their way home after the games.

They made a deal: If she told Henberlin something about her life, he would tell her something about his life along a similar line. He told her how his father would take him to the race track to bet on a few horses, and then turn him loose for a few hours while he handicapped races and met with a few people. Henberlin was just starting to know the track and who to watch between the races to know what was really going on when his mother kicked his father out of the house. Years later, he learned about his parent's divorce when his mother told him he was going to have a step-father.

"Wow, I'll bet that was a bit of a shocker," Yanmei said.

"Yeah, kind of. I didn't think very often about my real father after he was gone, and I never went back to the track because I didn't want to find him there if I did. My step-father changed our lives in a severely positive way. All of a sudden, we were part of the upper class. My mother suggested it would benefit us all if we forgot about the former head of the family. So we did."

All this truth and the real reasons for his meetings with Yanmei, the real reasons for having his name on the apartment lease, he had to keep to himself. Delaney issued specific instructions to ensure that he not tell his wife or his boss.

Henberlin's explanation of the apartment to his wife included a detail that he'd come up with to add a degree of innocence and a share-the-blame quality to the ruse. He'd offered shares in the apartment to the other salesmen at R.E.S. and they loved the opportunity. There were times when the sales staff wanted to get together, either formally or informally, in a private, quiet environment without having any visibility to management. Periodic meetings for help with difficult sales opportunities, afternoon drinking sessions, after work hockey games and pizza. The apartment let them bask in their status as high-earning salesmen without having the stress of management or the corporate environment. This shared use eased Henberlin's mind, making the apartment seem less like a love nest, should his wife find out about it. Since it was his idea to share the apartment space, it seemed natural for him to have his name on the lease, he'd explained.

There were also times when private customer meetings in a neutral environment—not a restaurant or a bar—worked wonders for a sale. The customers loved the idea that the apartment didn't have management approval. If their host's company wasn't aware of the apartment, then why should their own company' management know about it? It could be a no-holds-barred environment.

Customers and prospective customers, in the true nature of exploiting perks from people trying to sell them something, soon began dropping hints that it might be nice if they could use the apartment on their own. Salesmen, in the true nature of giving the customers what they wanted to get a signature on a contract, grinned and made the concession.

Henberlin had lukewarm enthusiasm for the private-use-by-customers idea. The other salesmen notched up his guilt level, letting him know their commission checks depended on the prospect's use of the apartment. He literally held the keys to their success. In this way, he became a sort of property manager, keeping a schedule and making sure the place remained clean and in order.

He only had himself to blame for his new duties. After all, he could have kept the apartment to himself and used it in the manner Delaney intended. Delaney wasn't keen on the shared use either, until he realized that the apartment's use for secret trysts by a group of salesmen made the supposed affair between Henberlin and Yanmei look even more real.

As the manager and lease holder, Henberlin did use the apartment for actual business purposes more than any of the other salesmen. He always wanted to have an edge to his sales efforts, something that made him different from the other salesmen trying to sell competitive products to his prospect. The apartment supplied that on one level, but he wanted to make more use of it for direct sales efforts with his potential and existing customers. Often he scheduled breakfast meetings with clients at the apartment. Breakfast meetings were an underutilized sales technique that he discovered his clients considered unique. No one got asked to a private breakfast meeting in this power-lunching city. Starting the day a little earlier than usual and discovering something about technology that could advance simulator performance kick-started the day and enabled a more personal work interaction.

After these breakfast meetings Henberlin usually worked the rest of the morning in the apartment. Other days, in the afternoon, he would drift over to the apartment to write proposals or review test results that Kyle had supplied. He had laptop access to the R.E.S. virtual private network via the apartment's Wi-Fi. This method allowed the review of data stored on a company data server using the extensive security of the VPN. This guaranteed no unauthorized access to the new systems where the processing actually took place. To get onto one of those systems to monitor performance and look at process-specific data in real time, he needed to access a back door that required verification of original location IP addresses. Since Henberlin wanted to keep the apartment hidden from the company, he hadn't attempted to register its IP address with the system administration authority.

On days when he knew he would work into the night, he moved to the apartment after making sure all the data he would need would be located on the regular company server. Then he worked the last few hours remotely before going home to Leyna. He always made his way home. It didn't matter how late, Leyna always wanted him home. He knew she laid awake in bed until he arrived, even though she pretended to be asleep. He loved that about her and it touched him that she waited for him to arrive home before she could rest. He also knew that she fell into a deep sleep shortly after he laid down beside her.

But lately, she'd showed signs of heightened anxiety regarding his late work nights. In the past, she rarely called him to find out when he would be coming home. Now she called daily and often, and called him a second time to confirm the time he said he'd come home.

To alleviate this new level of anxiety, he agreed to go on the last-minute trip to Vancouver. He could have used the weekend to catch up on a technical analysis of the software conversion estimate he'd received from a potential simulation partner. However, one of his wife's coworkers had a ticket he wasn't using. Since she already had a room, there would be no additional cost to him joining her. She said it would be nice knowing they were together, even though she would be at the conference all day. He could spend the day at the spa, her treat, and they would be together in the evenings, then all day Sunday. Her relief when he said 'yes' was palpable.

It had turned out to be a great weekend. Leyna seemed edgy after the conference on Saturday. After she downed the drink she said she'd been thinking about all day, followed by a session of urgent lovemaking, she settled down and eased into a relaxed, contemplative state. She'd become a little detached after their shower, evidence she'd taken one of her anti-anxiety pills.

The next day, Sunday, she remained calm and perhaps a little too laid-back throughout their activities in Vancouver. The same casual attitude remained that last evening in Vancouver and right up until their return Monday morning. When they talked for that brief moment during the day, finding themselves in the middle of a double murder, he detected a change in Leyna. She sounded excited and frustrated by the events they came back to in Calgary. But what exactly had caused the change? The questions hurled at them by the media, coworkers, clients, and police? Or by his not contacting her as soon as possible to try to set her mind at ease? His actions had burst their lives open to public view, leaving her alone to defend those actions with no prior knowledge or time to prepare. He couldn't blame her for her frustration. She was discovering things about her husband that, out of context, could easily be interpreted the wrong way and it seemed everyone—media, friends, associates, and the general public—had settled on believing the worst. He had to make sure she didn't settle on the same conclusion, for the sake of their marriage.

Now, in their home, the two of them had a chance to catch up, for him to sooth her concerns with an explanation. He could tell she'd had more than a glass of wine before he got home. What he couldn't tell was if she had taken her pills. Her smoothed-out demeanor made it hard for him to read her reaction to his explanation of the apartment. A stare, a nod, a raised eyebrow, but no comment, no sign of belief.

"Are you okay?" Henberlin asked while leaning in to make eye contact.

Leyna shook her head as if to wake herself. Then she lifted her head, opened her eyes wide, smiled, and nodded.

"Leyna? Do you believe me? Mrs. Albin had been to the apartment on a number of occasions, but every one of them was for business only."

Henberlin almost missed the side-to-side movement of her head as she stared at nothing. "I want to. But that's not what they're saying. That's not what it looks like. That's not what I'm starting to believe."

"Leyna, don't believe them. Believe me, the man who loves you and takes care of you and wouldn't do anything to hurt you."

"It's so easy for you to just say that. You're so sincere." She paused, a vacant smile on her face. "But I think you could lie to me and I would never know it, unless I already knew the truth."

"Unless you were in the apartment with us, you wouldn't know the truth. That's why you have to believe me. I accept no guilt over the time I spent in the apartment with Mrs. Albin. I didn't do anything to be ashamed of. There was no affair. She was a viable prospect with lead-ins to other areas of her company. Like any other prospect, I used the apartment for what it was intended to be used for, nothing more."

"Nothing more," she said. "Nothing more."

"Would you like another glass?"

Leyna extended her hand with the glass. "Who was the other person murdered in the apartment?"

"I don't know."

As they held each other's stare, the doorbell rang.

"Oh, they're here," Henberlin said.

"Who?"

"The detectives. They said they wanted to talk to me again tonight. They were interrupted earlier in my office, remember?"

Leyna shrugged. "Do they have to do this now?"

Henberlin let the detectives in. Once seated, the questions began.

"When did you last see or talk to Stephen Albin?" Detective Sweetland asked.

"Hmm, probably early last week. I'd called to invite him to meet for breakfast at the apartment." Henberlin looked at Leyna when he mentioned the apartment.

"You were going to meet him at the apartment? Your love nest?" Detective Richie asked.

"Wait a minute now. The apartment isn't a love nest. It's—"

"It's where you met your mistress," Richie interrupted. "And now you were going to meet her husband there. What happened when you met him?"

"You're taking this the wrong way. Nobody's seriously asked me what we used the apartment for, so you're all getting the wrong impression." Henberlin knew his frustration was visible.

"What happened when you met him?"

Henberlin stared at the detective, shaking his head. "Nothing. We never met. He didn't even entertain meeting me. That call was the first time I'd talked to him aside from the brief introductions Yanmei had allowed. For all my previous attempts to make contact, he'd had an assistant contact me to reject my requests for a meeting. I don't know how I got through to him last week. He's pretty well insulated."

"So he refused to talk to you?"

"I was starting to think that."

"Maybe if you weren't having an affair with his wife, he would have taken your calls."

"I wasn't having an affair with his wife." Henberlin paused, took a breath. "We'd heard he was a bit reclusive. All work, not good in public. Very direct individual who cut meetings short when he'd heard enough. Told you when he thought you were wrong. We thought he refused to talk to us because he didn't talk to anyone."

"Your people and his people said he didn't like you. Said they wouldn't mention your name to him because it caused him to go off. They said he knew about you and his wife."

"Wrong. There was nothing between his wife and me."

Henberlin thought Detective Sweetland had stopped breathing—he held his stare so long. A time long enough to make Henberlin wonder if they were holding something back, weighing whether or not to bring it up in front of his wife. Finally, Detective Richie stood and towered over Henberlin, who naturally leaned away and raised his hands off the chair arms.

"I've had enough of this bullshit," Richie said. "Neil Henberlin, please stand. You're under arrest for the murders of Yanmei Albin and her husband, Stephen Albin."

"What? Stephen was the other person in the apartment? Wait, you're arresting me?" Henberlin swung his head between looking at Detective Richie and his wife.

"You have the right to remain silent..." But before the detective could continue reading Henberlin his rights, a groaning cry rumbled—then accelerated as the pitch of the cry reached scream level. Grunts gasping for air punctuated the screams causing the three men to snap their necks in the direction of the collapsing figure of Leyna. She stretched and extended her arms, each hand gripping her bunched-up blanket. She caught her breath, then pulled all her limbs into her stomach and sobbed a loud, "Noooo, not now."

The detectives watched as Henberlin went to her side to try and comfort her. "Leyna, Leyna, just breathe. Easy, just breathe." He turned to the detectives but said nothing.

Richie said, "We'll stay until an ambulance arrives." Then he finished reading Henberlin his rights.

7

—

The cell had no bars. In their place, strips of steel painted a flat Dijon yellow formed the enclosure. Henberlin heard the door clank shut behind him as he entered a small meeting room. There, a man he thought was his assigned lawyer sat waiting. The lawyer stood to introduce himself as Henberlin entered the room.

"Mr. Henberlin, I'm Hec Taylor. Call me Hec," the lawyer said.

"Public defenders wear fifteen hundred-dollar suits these days?"

"If they do that's no surprise in this town. You have to pay to get good people."

"Who's paying for you?"

"Don't worry, it's taken care of." Hec smiled. His expensive suit and immaculate hair let down by crooked, coffee stained teeth. "Now, let me tell you where things stand."

"But I don't know who you are or if I want you to be my lawyer. How do you know where things stand?"

"Mr. Henberlin, you're in jail facing murder charges. I'm going to have you out of here in a little over an hour, the charges are going to be dropped and the cops will be certain, beyond any doubt, of your innocence." Hec Taylor leaned back in his chair. "Do you want to hear the deal?"

"Deal? Who are you?" Henberlin wondered if he was imagining this man. He'd slept little during the weekend and last night, in the jail cell, he'd jerked and jumped with every noise that clattered through the other cells. This morning, he knew he had to call a lawyer to try to get control of the situation. He never made that call. Worry about his wife consumed his thoughts. "Wait, do you know what's happened to my wife?"

"She had a rough time of it when she got to the hospital, but they gave her something that settled her down. She'll likely be released this afternoon. And you could be there to take her home."

"Okay, okay. Tell me what you're up to."

"We're up to helping you, Mr. Henberlin. I'll get you out, soon. You go home and get your wife relaxed and settled in. Then, when she's having a restful time, you go to your nightstand and pull the drawer out. Taped underneath the drawer is a sim card. Take a look at the video on the card and then call Jian Liu."

"Jian Liu?"

"Yes, you had a meeting scheduled with him this morning. Under the circumstances, he understands that may be an inconvenience. Will you call him?"

Henberlin tried to recall his conversation on the street with Yanmei's father. Jian Liu seemed more interested in talking about members of Henberlin's family than talking about his daughter. He'd work those thoughts later.

First, how could Jian Liu and this lawyer clear him of the murders when the Calgary detectives were certain he had done it? But why deliberate over details when he could be free from this mess altogether.

"Yeah, I'll call him. I told him I'd meet him. He said it was important."

"Good. This may take an hour. When it's done, you'll need to get a different lawyer."

"Okay."

"One more thing." Hec Taylor smiled, this time with his mouth closed. His smile comforted Henberlin. His clean features, grey eyes, perfect eyebrows, and that trust-generating smile. He held the look for a beat or two, then said, "We had no trouble getting into your house to provide you with the sim card. We don't anticipate any trouble that would make us have to do it again." Then the smile again.

Henberlin sat and stared at the face, then stared at Hec Taylor's back as he left the meeting room, then stared at the closed door until the guard placed a hand on his shoulder to let him know he had to return to his cell.

––––––

Before Hec Taylor had taken three steps down the hall after leaving the interview room he'd dialed Detective Sweetland's phone number. In Sweetland's office, he presented his information.

"First, Henberlin had indeed been in Vancouver for the entire weekend," Hec said.

Both detectives started to speak but Richie yielded to Sweetland. "Henberlin's name doesn't appear on the manifest of any flight from Calgary to Vancouver on the Friday nor on any of the Monday morning return flights," Sweetland said. "How can you say he *indeed* was in Vancouver?"

"Mrs. Henberlin's coworker's name did appear on the manifests of the flights Henberlin stated he'd taken. Somehow, with a fake ID or by someone he knew at the airport, he'd travelled as the coworker. We confirmed with the airline that the passenger had checked in. If you check with airport security I'm sure you'll see Henberlin on the security cameras at times matching the flights.

"Second, the hotel room was booked in Mrs. Henberlin's name. Though none of the hotel staff remember seeing Mr. Henberlin arrive, I discovered a Ms. Ester Ng. Ms. Ng is a freelance spa technician who picks up sessions on busy weekends to take specially-booked clients through a day of activities at the spa. If you check with the hotel and ask to contact Ms. Ng, she'll confirm that Mr. Henberlin had spent the day in the hotel spa and therefore made the trip to Vancouver. He was there when the murder took place."

Hec paused to allow the detectives to ask questions. They remained silent. Taylor observing as their thought wheels spun fast. Finally one of them asked, "Anything else?"

"Yes." Hec handed Detective Sweetland a small sim card. "I suggest you take a look at this video."

Sweetland took the sim card and looked it over, flipping it in his hand.

"Any PC or smart phone will work. I should watch it with you," Hec said.

"Okay, come with me."

The file loaded. Hec Taylor said, "A stationary e-camera is going to show a restricted view of a small entryway in Henberlin's secret apartment."

"What the hell?" Detective Richie said, looking at Hec Taylor, who pointed at the monitor.

Light-colored paint, an entry wall that prevented a view of the door, a thermostat on the wall. A woman is in view immediately as the camera's motion detector picks up the woman rushing backward toward the door.

"That's Yanmei Albin," Taylor said.

"Where did you get this?" Again it was Richie speaking.

"Watch. I'll explain after."

The woman screams then lifts her hands as a shield and repeatedly yells the word "No!" Then the sound of a small caliber gunshot. Yanmei Albin, stops moving backward and falls limp to the floor like a dropped towel. Another person walks into camera range, pointing a small handgun at the body on the floor.

"That is another woman, not Mr. Henberlin." Hec Taylor said.

The woman is wearing loose, dark jeans, a dark waist-length jacket, a dark safari hat, and gloves. She steps up beside Yanmei Albin, stares at her from above for a second or two, then fires another shot. Without further hesitation, she disappears behind the small entrance wall. The door is heard opening, then closing. After a few seconds of inactivity, the camera turns off.

Hec Taylor broke the silence by saying, "Do you agree with me that the shooter was a woman?"

Sweetland looked at the stone-faced lawyer for a second and nodded in agreement.

"Then you'll let my client go?"

"I have a few questions first," Sweetland said, rubbing his chin while his eyes wandered around the room. "Where did you get this?"

"Her husband's computer."

"How did you get it?"

"Her father went to her home after the police notified him of her murder and asked if he could let them into her home. He arrived before the police did and looked around the house. At the time, no one knew her husband had also been killed. The screen of Mr. Albin's PC was open to the file viewer and Yanmei's father clicked on it. For whatever reason, he took the sim card and didn't mention it to the police. Instead he called me. I copied it to this sim card, and I'm here giving it to you."

"He should have given it to us immediately. We didn't find anything on the PC."

"Sorry, he must not have been thinking. He did just find out his daughter had been murdered. I copied the file to the card and got it to you."

"He corrupted a crime scene and you tampered with evidence. We'll want the original sim card Mr. Liu took from the PC," Sweetland said and exhaled from his nose.

"There was no crime at that location, so it wasn't a crime scene. Mr. Liu wanted to be near his daughter and was there at your request."

Sweetland appeared to think for a moment before asking, "How would the camera have gotten there in the first place? How would Stephen Albin get into the apartment to place it?"

"This is pure conjecture now, you understand?" Hec Taylor waited for Sweetland to agree, then continued. "Stephen Albin was a potential customer for this new fast computer, or whatever the hell it is, and that apartment was used for certain informal activities. The salesmen that shared the place would allow their customers to use it. I'm guessing Albin knew about his wife and Henberlin, asked to use the apartment for his own purposes, and planted the camera."

"What happened to the camera then?"

"Okay, let's say Albin is watching as it happens or even sees it sometime later. He's shocked and goes to see if it's real. He finds his wife and figures while he's there he better remove the camera."

"Don't forget, he was killed there too."

"Before or after his wife was killed?" Hec Taylor asked.

"If we had more video we might be able to tell," Detective Richie said. "I assume that if the motion detectors worked once, they worked every time someone came or went into that room. Mrs. Albin is moving backward when the camera turns on. Where is the video from when she arrived and moved past the camera to go to the back rooms?"

"I agree with you, but I don't know the answer. I copied everything from the video onto the card I gave you," Hec Taylor responded.

"All the more reason why we need to have the original sim card." Sweetland thought for a moment. "I've been wondering: Why is Jian Liu's lawyer representing the man we think is his daughter's killer?"

"I'm Mr. Henberlin's lawyer until he's released. He says he will be getting his own lawyer and plans to use him. Jian Liu asked me to intervene since it appears Mr. Henberlin didn't commit the murders."

Two hours later, Henberlin walked out the front doors of the Calgary Police Department's downtown office. The waiting media were ravenous for details. They crowded in on him as he quick-stepped to either side of the blocking herd to attempt a getaway, but they soon stopped him. Once they had him scrummed, the questions shot out so fast and loud he couldn't make them out. He stood with his hands cupped behind his ear, shouting, "I can't understand what you're saying." Over and over he repeated this line and the media people became frustrated. But, in fact, he could make out the questions, he just didn't want to answer them. The most popular ones were "Did you kill your mistress?" and "Was your wife aware that you were having an affair?"

He refused to give them the satisfaction of an answer.

Then, rising above the general din of questions, he and the media pack heard the clear voice of the reporter from the *Herald* ask, "Why did Yanmei Albin's father's lawyer come to your defense, and what did he tell the cops that got you released so quickly?"

Henberlin froze at the question while the members of the media looked at each other and at the questioning reporter from the *Herald*. One exclaimed, "What? Say that again."

But the reporter didn't repeat himself. Instead he stared at Henberlin, waiting for an answer.

Henberlin, in the silent time required for thoughts to catch up with new facts, realized he didn't know the answer to that question. He shook his head in answer and the media bunched before him began to launch a number of variations of the question. Before he figured out what he could say in response, two uniformed police officers pushed their way into the group and escorted Henberlin to a squad car to drive him home.

8

—

Instead of taking Henberlin home, at his request, the police officers dropped him off at the hospital. He found the ward where his wife had been admitted. After determining when she would be released, he called his tech analyst, Kyle, and asked him to pick him and his wife up at the hospital.

Leyna lay her head back against the seat and stared out the rear driver's side window. Henberlin leaned on his elbow, which he'd situated above Leyna's shoulder so he could lean in on her and look at her face.

"Is she okay? Maybe she should have stayed at the hospital another day," Kyle said.

"You may be right," said Henberlin.

As he did, Leyna closed her eyes and shook her head without saying a word.

"This may be a bit cold, but Yanmei's assistant and Stephen Albin's second-in-command both contacted us and said they wanted to get the ball rolling on installing systems. It seems both Albins were the road blocks in their departments."

Henberlin pulled his gaze away from his wife and stared at the back of Kyle's head as his thought process kicked in. "They were the road blocks?"

"Yes. Stephen because he didn't like you, but you know how erratic and hostile he could be. And Yanmei because she could retain negotiating power if she delayed a while longer. Yanmei's assistant fed Stephen's assistant everything he had about our system's specifications and testing results. He wanted Stephen to take a meeting with you and take the steps necessary to start installing systems in their department."

Henberlin had wondered about how Stephen perceived him and his association with Yanmei. The presumed affair that he willingly went along with to help CSIS must have come across as believable if Stephen disliked him enough to hold back a system that would benefit his organization. Even the detectives had indicated everyone knew that Stephen Albin disliked him. It hurt a little. He never wanted anyone to dislike him, and aside from the Vice President of Sales, considered himself to be enemy-free.

"Okay, so what do we have to do?" Henberlin asked.

"I've set up a meeting. I'm going to update the reservoir group on the status of their data structure and the guy in the sucker rod group is going to update me on his analysis of the sample rod."

"When?"

"Tomorrow."

"Shit, I can't leave Leyna."

"They asked if you could be there. They want to talk contract."

"I'll be all right," Leyna said, her unblinking stare unfocused out the car window.

———

The interest level of the reporters waiting for them at the house seemed blunted by Henberlin's lack of knowledge regarding the reason for his sudden freedom. They realized the details regarding the investigation were going to have to come from the police. That didn't prevent them from asking questions pertaining to the apartment love nest and assumed mistress. Their tone with respect to the murders had throttled back due to a lack of expectation in receiving substantial answers to any of their questions.

It took Henberlin about an hour to get his wife settled and at rest sleeping in the guest bedroom. He told her it would be quieter for her in the room situated at the back of the house. She didn't care where she rested as long as she could lay down. Next, he plugged his dead cell phone into his charger. Within minutes it rang. He looked at the caller ID, swore, but didn't answer. Things in Arizona were going to have to wait. When he plugged in the phone that Delaney had provided him, also dead, it too rang once it had a little juice.

Henberlin took the call but used his wife's condition to beg off meeting Delaney until sometime during the evening. For the next day's meeting, Kyle would start with the tech people from Shield Oil, and Henberlin would make it into the office before they wrapped up. Right now he only wanted one thing, to find the item left in his house by Jian Liu.

Moving into his bedroom, he closed the door. He didn't want his rustling around to draw his wife's attention. The lawyer said that Jian Liu's men had taped the sim card to the underside of the drawer of his nightstand. Not a simple drawer that slid on rails, but one with an auto-close function that required tricky latches to hold rails in the slide track connected to the slow-pull mechanism with the air-piston.

The extraction of the drawer tested his dexterity. He cursed at his own klutziness as he tried too hard to get the drawer out of its guides. Once he removed the drawer, he flipped it over to find a two-inch strip of silver duct tape in one of the back corners. Underneath and in the center of the tape, a thin raised-square shape stood out. Henberlin peeled the tape back and removed the sim card from where it stuck to the white adhesive. He flipped the sim card and looked at both sides as if it might reveal something. Then he reached for his phone, still plugged into his charger.

Then he stopped and picked up the phone Delaney had provided to see if it could accommodate the sim card. It could. He slotted the card, then searched the apps for a file directory and found the only file on the sim card. When he tapped it, a video began to play on the small HD screen.

He immediately recognized Yanmei walking into the living-room area of his downtown apartment. The time and date stamp showed the previous Saturday when he was in Vancouver.

In the video, Yanmei stops shortly after entering the area from the apartment's entry and kitchen area. It's when Yanmei stops that Henberlin first noticed the dark figure sitting in the chair straight across from the camera. The person stands and points a gun at Yanmei. While standing, a substantial area of the person's face is visible.

Henberlin registered the face.

Yanmei begins to back out the door from which she had entered the room with her hands out in front of her. She says "No" multiple times as she disappears from view. The other person continues to walk toward her. Then, standing in the door, fires one shot. The person pauses then also disappears through the door, then an instant before the camera turns off, another shot is fired. The screen blinks black. Then the video that Hec Taylor showed the police plays.

Henberlin realizes there were two motion cameras in his apartment. In the second video, the person in dark clothes stands over the fallen Yanmei, then fires another shot. Maybe the one Henberlin heard when the first video ended, but it could have been a third shot. The person leaves and Henberlin could hear the apartment door open and close.

"Shit, shit, shit," he said.

The screen returned to the file management app, so he made a copy of the video file in the phone's internal storage. Then he pulled the sim card, went to his home office and plugged it into his computer. He did not make a copy but watched the video over and over again on the larger screen. He stopped the video when the person in dark clothes stood up from the chair. Each time the person stood, he knew he was looking at Leyna.

9

—

'What now?'

Leyna remained in the deep sleep she'd been in overnight. Henberlin didn't know whether or not he wanted to talk to her about the video yet. He'd already arranged for a friend of Leyna's to come and sit with her while he left to go to the meeting with the Shield Oil techs. His acceptance of the relief that overcame him when he left the house surprised him. That and the awkward conversation with the friend made it sink in that things in his marriage were never going to be normal again. Getting back to the normal activities of his work environment—where he knew how to execute the activities expected of him—couldn't come fast enough.

He concentrated on work as he drove to his office. Before heading down the hill to the downtown area, he made one stop at a large department store. In the electronics department, he purchased a pre-paid cell phone. He activated it when he got back to his car and threw it into the glove compartment.

His coworkers paused, stunned when they saw him walking down the hall to his office. He grabbed the proposal file listing the system specifications of the computer systems he planned to propose to Shield, then made his way to the meeting.

He found the group session already in progress, taking place in one of the specially-equipped media rooms. Inside, projected on a drop screen in a split presentation were, on one side, columns of raw data and on the other, a three-dimensional color representation of the same data. They all stopped as Henberlin entered, but he asked them to keep going. At an appropriate break in their discussion, they brought Henberlin up-to-speed on a new concern that had popped up in the data.

"It's something flaky that we didn't expect to see. There's more data than originally anticipated for this particular reservoir," the Shield analyst said with a puzzled tone.

"Kyle?" Henberlin said, looking for an explanation or hypothesis.

"It's the data that Stephen provided me, straight up. Before you got here, we looked at the original file size specs on the delivered media, and the file we're looking at here has the same specs."

"Could it be a precision difference because our system can compute in more detail?"

"Probably not," Kyle responded, "but our system will be able to identify the anomalies a lot quicker. We were discussing a filter we could develop that would help us clear the mystery."

"It's also possible that Stephen loaded more into the data sets because he thought it would be a good test of your system's power. It would be so like him not to share his intentions with anyone," the Shield analyst offered. "At any rate, it's on the right machine to comb through the data and give us an idea what we're up against."

"Another chance for us to show off," Henberlin replied. "Do you guys need more time? I can come back."

"Why don't we go over the proposed configuration, and then have you give us a timeline for delivery of the first block of systems?" the analyst suggested.

"Great, I've got those right here."

When the meeting ended and the Shield people left, Kyle tried to approach the data problem again. Henberlin told him it had to wait. He said Kyle should look into it further and tomorrow they would decide what to do. Tomorrow would be a normal day, he hoped.

Alone in his office, Henberlin closed the door. He pulled the new pre-paid phone from his desk drawer and dialed the phone number Hec Taylor had given him.

"This Jian Liu."

"What's this all about?" Henberlin asked with impatience.

"Ah, Neo Henbrin. It looks like your wife kill my daughter."

"Have you shown this to the police?"

"Some."

"What do you want?" The frustration of his wife's situation and finding out about it from Jian Liu caused him to clip his words.

"Nothing can bring my daughter back. Your wife is free for now, but maybe someday I will make her pay."

Henberlin flashed to his feet. Holding his phone in front of his face, he shot back, "What do you mean, make her pay?"

Jian Liu ignored the desperate query. "Yanmei was working on a matter with me and I wish to continue the efforts in her honor. Yanmei supplied me with information about your computer system. It is very good information and I want the rest of it."

"I can't help you with that and I don't care about any of it. She shouldn't have supplied you with anything. I only want you to leave my wife alone."

"Of course. But Yanmei did give me good information, and I want more."

"I can't help you."

"Can you help your wife? She can't kill my daughter and not pay something. You can help her pay."

Henberlin remained silent as he evaluated the answer.

Jian Liu let the silence run on for a full minute then added, "She's awake now, talking to her friend. When we left you the video, we installed the cameras from your apartment in your house. We don't care what you and your wife do or say in your home, so go ahead and remove them."

He angered at the sound of the dial tone but, halfway through redialing the number, Henberlin stopped himself. He needed to think this through before contacting Jian Liu again. Instead, he called Delaney and told him about his meeting in jail with Hec Taylor and about his conversation with Jian Liu, leaving out any mention of the video and his wife's involvement in the murder. When he hung up, he went straight to Delaney's office.

The wait in Delany's lobby didn't last long. When Delaney took Henberlin to the back, he didn't take him into a meeting room but straight to his smaller office. When he stepped inside, Henberlin saw Kyle sitting in a chair in front of the desk next to the wall. Henberlin looked at Delaney and said, "What's this?"

Kyle looked dumbfounded, like a student who'd snuck outside school grounds for a smoke—only to find a teacher who'd done the same thing.

Delaney cleared his throat. "Well, no offense, Neil, but some of the information we passed on to Yanmei is a little beyond your technical capabilities. You've both been involved in this without knowing about the other."

Not knowing what to think, Henberlin could only look at Kyle dumbfounded. After a few seconds he shrugged. Heat surged in his head as the kernel of anger grew. "Why would you need me at all when you've got Kyle's information at your beck and call? The only thing I can add that he can't is pricing. I don't think that's the kind of information Jian Liu is after. You could have left me out of this and none of it would be happening to me right now."

"For appearances. Jian Liu would ask Yanmei to corroborate information from within R.E.S. You were a second source—at least, we made you look that way. Also, we presented you as the main source for information on the encryption capability of the new operating system. That's their main target. Your developers hit a home run with that technology. The more the American military look at it, the more they want to take it away from commercial entities. The Chinese got wind of the coming ban and they want to get everything they can on it before the operating system becomes classified.

"Yanmei had been supplying them with bits and pieces of crippled real code, but before they could get deep enough into it, Yanmei would tell them of the bug. Then she'd delay them while she worked on getting updated versions—versions the Americans crippled in a different manner."

"So the American military is pulling our strings and they're about to take away the product that we're all counting on?" Henberlin said, waving his arm and pointing his finger between himself and Kyle.

"I didn't say it was the military, but the military's concerns are being respected. Anyway, who it is doesn't matter to you. They still need your help. You can walk away right now if you want, there's nothing forcing you to continue to supply information. Unless, that is, you wish to continue doing something for your country and its allies. Yanmei wanted to make sure the Chinese didn't get their hands on this new technology. The computers and the reservoir simulation software were reason enough for her to foil their plan to steal technology. But for the encryption, she had a special earnestness in preventing them from getting their hands on it. Preventing them from hacking into government and business databases, something they seem to accomplish with ease, gives us a more secure country and economy. We hope you'll want to continue with us to complete ours and Yanmei's objective."

During Henberlin's private discussions with Yanmei, they'd never discussed her mission. He had no idea of the level of determination she held toward foiling the Chinese plan to steal the new technology. He did know what seemed to make her tick with regard to her own future. She anticipated a limited time in her current occupation. This required her to develop an exit strategy from the oil patch, an exit that involved leaving and never looking back. He believed she spoke metaphorically. With his current knowledge that they were being recorded whenever they were in the apartment, he wondered if she had been providing inert conversation that wouldn't alert any third party eyes and ears watching their activities.

Working against her father and the Chinese meant she had to be cautious. The CSIS people thought she'd been discovered by the Chinese and eliminated. Henberlin knew his wife killed Yanmei, but he couldn't share that truth.

He looked at Kyle and asked, "Why are you doing this?"

Kyle cleared his throat. "Not completely sure, to be honest. I didn't think it would hurt to supply the technical points needed to deliver sabotaged information to the Chinese. That changed when Yanmei got murdered. I wonder if they're coming after me next."

"What did Delaney tell you about that?"

"That it was possible," Delaney answered for him. "We don't know what they know about the false data, or if they know at all. We do think they know about Kyle. If they know about the false data, they probably know where it came from."

"If they didn't know you were involved before, they sure know now. They've been following me for quite a while. They must be following you too, Kyle, and even you, Delaney. If they see us all together, they'll think it was us." Henberlin's words came faster and louder.

"Calm down, Neil. We don't know that. My cover as a reservoir simulation software developer goes pretty deep," Delaney said matter-of-factly. "They may see our meetings as regular sales activity. You came to work to meet with the people from Shield Oil, why wouldn't you also meet with me? No reason to believe we've been made."

"If they don't think it was us, wouldn't that be why they killed Stephen Albin?" Kyle asked. "Wouldn't they think he falsified the data?"

"That could be one explanation," Delaney said.

"Do you have others?" Henberlin asked, as his eyes searched the office's nooks and crannies for motion-sensitive video cameras.

"Everyone said Stephen had erratic tendencies. Maybe he knew Yanmei was passing bad data and told her father. Her father takes them both out in the apartment to make it look like a jealousy killing with Henberlin as the cause. Maybe Albin knew nothing, but they still used him to present the same motive. People are looking into it." Delaney then changed subjects. "You said Jian Liu wanted you to continue to provide data."

"Yes."

Turning to Kyle, Delaney asked, "And the analyst from Shield Oil noticed the false data you included in the data file?"

Kyle nodded, then looked at Henberlin, who raised his chin in understanding.

"So one analyst discovered it," Delaney said. "Do you think the Chinese will?"

"I don't see how they wouldn't. I'll have to rework the data sets and try to get them by Shield again."

"Right. Meanwhile, Neil, you have to meet with Jian Liu and tell him there's been a delay with the data. We have to stall. That is, unless you're going to walk away."

Henberlin's eyes shifted between the other two men who waited for his response. "Not sure. What about the sales? Can we proceed with the contracts and installation of the systems?" Henberlin's financial emergencies weren't going to let up and sticking it to the VP of Sales still had its appeal.

"By all means. You have to make it look like business as usual. Shield Oil is moving forward. If the Chinese see R.E.S. starting to drag their feet, they'll think something's wrong. They expect a salesman to think sales first, so you have to keep pushing for the contract."

Henberlin nodded in slow-motion. "In that case, I need a contract for a system from you too. That'll make our meetings more plausible. You could be the first and I'll use that to get Shield Oil to make their commitments as well. I'll tell them your order is in front of them in the production line unless they order more than five. You don't care when you get a system, so your order serves a bigger purpose. Is that salesman enough?"

Delaney smiled. "Okay, but I want you to call Jian Liu again. Get him to tell you what Yanmei told him. If he leaves anything out and asks you to supply information he already has, then we know he's got some doubts about that information, or he's testing you. Whatever he asks you to supply, tell him you don't have firsthand knowledge and you'll have to find out who does."

Henberlin nodded and said, "I'll set it up."

"Neil?" Kyle said in a soft, querying voice. "How was Leyna when you left her?"

"Ah, fine. Sleeping. Talking with her friend. She's been through a bit of a shocking time these last two days."

"No doubt."

"In fact, I have to get back to her," he said, rising to leave.

"Let me know when you're set up with Jian Liu," Delaney stated as Henberlin walked out.

10

—

"Jian?"

Fifteen year old Jian Liu closed his eyes, then drew breath through his nose, filling his lungs to capacity. His father had been trying to corner him into packing family heirlooms all week. Jian ignored him without trying to hide his lack of interest in helping loot the riches of the country. How the family had accumulated its wealth embarrassed Jian more with each success gained by the People's Liberation Army. He believed in their cause and followed their progress through China, wishing for them to destroy Chiang Kai-Shek and the Nationalists for the good of the people.

He shared this desire with only his closest school chums, those who also believed that Mao Tse-tung's vision for China would lead their country to be the equal of any nation.

As his belief in the Liberation grew, so grew his resentment of his father. Jian now believed his father wasn't courageous enough to remain in China and support his fellow Nationalists. Even though Jian believed the Nationalists' time was up, if their members were true believers in their country they should remain in China to support the new leaders and to see the wrong direction their former ways had led them. Instead, his father intended to abandon his past, abandon his people, and abandon the system that allowed his ancestors to exploit the country's agricultural resources. His father, unlike most of the wealthy intellectuals, would flee, taking as much of his family's fortune as its members could carry. Jian's father often stated that the others were being fooled by communist lies. But the others held a sincere belief that their views and their way of life would be respected. His father thought that every communist promised at every negotiation meeting would be disregarded the instant the communists took power.

After burning all evidence of any family connections with the imperialists, Jian and his family would make their way to the sports ground in the center of the city. Its conversion into an airport, providing escape flights to Taipei.

Jian would help with zeal to destroy the evidence of those connections so the people he wished to stand with would never know about his family ties. But he had other things on his mind right now.

Jian continued to pack the bag with the few things he would need when he joined with the Liberators. He had no intention of leaving the people he believed in.

"Jian?" His father's voice was closer. "When are you going to do as I ask?"

"I'm not going to do as you ask," he said under his breath as he closed the bag and stuck his head out the door.

'Good,' he thought. His father, too busy preserving his greed, hadn't come down the stairs.

Jian turned and made his way to the servants' stairway, then climbed the stairs to the main floor and slipped out the servants' entrance.

Beiping, though under siege, showed no signs of civil war except for the availability of certain items. Surrounded but not stuck inside, the citizens could make their way through the demarcation line with caution and a little persistence. If you intended to leave and meet with members of the Liberation, there were no obstacles for exiting the city. Jian had been leaving almost every night to spend time with the Liberators. Using the same location again this night, he crossed with ease. He no longer required an escort as he walked the neighborhood on the outskirts of the city. It was busier than most nights. He noticed more foot traffic and more noise emanating from the courtyards of the bigger houses taken over by soldiers of the freeing army. Now past dusk, the streets closed in on darkness. Fire glow backlit the entrances of the large residences, the scent of burning wood carried by invisible smoke.

The crack of heat breaking branches and the orange sparks rising above rooflines indicated something different happening this night. His comrades sang and the smell of meat cooking over the fires mixed with the smoke of the open flames.

When Jian arrived at the camp where his friend in the Liberation Army held post, his new friend beamed with excitement and slapped his arm around Jian as he approached.

"These are great times, Jian. Comrade Mao is powerful. His message is getting through," said Dong Fai.

"Didn't you say that it would? What's happening? Why are things so boisterous tonight?"

"The Nationalists are coming around. The pig kisser they call a general has returned to the negotiating table where he will continue his enlightenment."

"That's good."

"The battles on the west side have them scared. They don't have the soldiers to resist. When they accepted that, they once again realized talking would save them."

Dong handed Jian the bottle he cradled to his chest. Jian had never been asked to drink with the soldiers. "It's medicinal wine— it's all we have. Have some."

This was the first time Jian had seen liquor in the camp. Its presence further indicated celebration. The bottle offering jesture making him part of the army he had come to join. He took a swig. A burn descended his throat as vapors rose in his sinuses, he firmed his will so he didn't cough.

"My family is going to flee tonight," Jian said. "I've come to be a Liberator."

"Ah. Good. I told Commander Zhang you would be with us soon. Come, I'll take you to him."

Dong took back the bottle and led Jian past the fire where the men cooked over steaming pots. Along with the usual smell of boiled greens, the smell of the greasy meat produced an empty pain in Jian's stomach.

Commander Zhang slurped the last of his bowl of stew, then took a long pull of a bottle of yellow wine. He held his hand over his mouth as his cheeks inflated and he released a belch. He smiled, satisfied. "Dong," he said when he spotted Dong and Jian, "have some stew."

"Yes, thank you Commander Zhang. This is Jian Liu. The young man who has been telling me about what is going on inside the city."

"Liu? Your father is a grower? Welcome, have some stew."

"He's joining us tonight," Dong said.

"China needs you. Thank you for coming, but with you in our camp we won't be getting information about movements in the city."

Jian shook his head. "My father is leaving Beiping. He was forcing me to go, so I've left to join the People's Army."

"Good... good. Have some stew." Zhang pointed at the pot hanging near the edge of the fire, steam escaping from the wooden lid. He stood and watched Jian search for a bowl. After receiving a bowl from one of the other soldiers, he stepped to the pot. But before he reached it Zhang called him back.

"Liu. Your information is very valuable. Where is your father taking you?"

"Taipei."

"When?"

"Later tonight."

"I've never been in an airplane, have you?"

Jian shook his head.

Zhang sipped his yellow wine then stood in a contemplative quiet for a moment. "I think you should go with your father."

Jian's eyes widened. He lowered his head and stared at Zhang's feet. "But I want to fight for my country, Commander Zhang. I'm old enough and strong enough to be a good soldier."

Mitch Davies

Zhang placed his hand on young Jian's shoulder. "I know, you are already a good soldier. You are stronger than a rifle, stronger than a bomb."

Jian lifted his head and looked the commander in the eye. The words sturdy with purpose cementing his commitment to their cause, but he didn't completely grasp their meaning. His recent arrival meant he had yet to prove his real worth to anyone.

"I'm sure I will prove to be so," Jian said.

"Yes. Liu, I want you to continue to do what you have been doing, only now I want you to do it from Taipei. The things you've been telling Dong don't end with Dong. Your information is highly regarded. Go to Taipei. Keep watching. Let us know who your father talks to, and if possible, what they talk about. Let us know who else you see in Taipei."

"How?"

"I don't know, but someone will contact you."

"But I want to be a soldier for China." Jian saw his new heroic life slipping away.

"You will be more than a soldier," Zhang said, "more than a rifle, and more than a bomb."

Going with his father meant more years of living with the imperialists. But if that was how he would serve the Liberation, then that is what he would do.

Jian's arrival home added to the chaos that his father orchestrated in the house. The angry old man yelled at everyone in turn, assigning them objects to squeeze into bags they'd already over-packed. He reprimanded Jian for disappearing with a slap to the face, then sent him to his room to get his suitcase.

The slap stung, and hours earlier he would have resented his father's attack. Now he had a new purpose: He would fight for the People's Army while hidden among their enemies. He could stand his father's assaults knowing he would defeat them all in the end.

"Bring it here empty. You don't deserve to take any of your own belongings," his father snapped.

Jian filled his suitcase with an ancient golden bowl, some ivory carvings, a jade mahjong set, scrolls his father pulled from an ancient box Jian didn't know the family possessed, and a number of small porcelain vases he knew wouldn't make the journey in one piece. He returned to his room to get packing material to cushion the artifacts. His father began slapping him, yelling that he wasn't allowed possessions until he saw how Jian had layered them in his suitcase to protect the treasures.

At departure time, there were no servants to help carry the many cases and boxes the family had packed. Their driver had disappeared along with the car, so they would all have to take taxis. The few taxis they were able to negotiate with couldn't accommodate all of their belongings so the first episode of paring down their belongings took place before they could even begin their journey. As the taxis rolled away, Jian turned to watch from the back window as the boxes and suitcases they'd left behind shrunk in the distance. Their former servants appeared from behind fences, bushes, and trees where they'd been waiting for the family to leave. At once they began fighting over the remains. Some went straight for the cases on the street but a large crowd—more people than they had servants—sprinted to the front door of the house where they pillaged everything that was left.

Four hours after landing in Taipei, the Liu family sat with their remaining luggage on the curb in front of the airport. Hours had passed since they had slept and a lack of food made them wonder if they could achieve sleep even if given the opportunity. Jian's father, his head cradled in his hands. From time to time he shook his head and moaned.

"It looks like they aren't coming. What should we do?" Jian asked, finally building up the courage to find out his father's intentions.

"They said they would be here when I called before the flight. But you're right, it looks like they aren't coming," Jian's father said as he stood up.

What he didn't say, and what Jian didn't know until much later, was that when his father had called from Beiping to let his contacts know he was coming, the people who answered the phone in Taipei had never heard of the people he asked for—people he'd paid to make arrangements for them in Taipei, people whom he realized had betrayed them. Jian had noticed a deflation in his father's attitude as they boarded the flight in Beiping, then noticed his father's silence during the flight and after their arrival in Taipei. He knew something had changed. His father's preparations would not turn out as he promised.

"We'll make our own plans," Jian said to his father.

"Yes, but what?" His father's eyes had no focus.

"We need a house, an apartment, or a hotel room so we can rest and then begin to find work."

Jian's father looked at his son's face. Jian saw his father's perception of a threat, that it seemed his son had grown up. Then his father raised his shoulder, determined that he would still provide for them in this unknown China.

11

—

After a bit of nice chat about plans for the rest of the day, Henberlin shot inquisitive looks at Leyna's friend Marion. He craved a silent update regarding Leyna's disposition—silent because he didn't want to talk about his wife as if she were a problem child.

Marion's noncommittal gestures tainted Henberlin's already dreadful expectation of the conversation he and Leyna had to have.

The instant the door closed on Marion's departure, Henberlin turned to his wife and asked, "Where were you and Marion talking after you woke up?"

"In our bedroom. She came in after she heard me running the water for a bath. Why?"

"You'll see," he said as he made his way to the bedroom.

It didn't take long to find the first small camera sitting on top of the armoire. He yanked it down from its position beside the woven straw basket that Leyna had fallen in love with on a romantic weekend in South Carolina. When Leyna asked what he had found, he provided a short answer, "Just wait."

The second camera took a little longer to locate: In the family room off the kitchen on a book shelf in a gap between two books a fraction back from the bindings. It wasn't meant to be concealed for long, it was meant to prove what Jian Liu had said about the ease of getting in and out of their home.

"What are those things?" Leyna asked, her voice close to breaking.

"Cameras."

"Cameras? Why? Were you spying on me?" Leyna placed her hand over her mouth, squeezing her cheeks, tilting her head away from her husband. Then her hand dropped as if her strength leaked from her arm muscles. He saw her eyes go into a squint and bore in on him. "What do you have to spy on me for?"

"No, no... nothing. I wasn't spying on you, someone was spying on me. But while doing so they caught something you and I have to talk about."

Leyna blinked and shook her head as she lowered into one of the light grey suede love seats. She reached for the table where she often had a glass of wine waiting but saw no glass of wine.

"Do you think you should have a drink after the sedatives you've taken?" he asked.

"That or another sedative." She closed her eyes, her chin making slight twitches to the left. "This is becoming too much. What are you talking about? What did they catch on camera and who are 'they'?"

Henberlin walked to the liquor cabinet and poured himself a glass of whiskey. He returned to the love seat and sat beside his wife.

"Leyna, I know you killed Yanmei Albin."

Color drained from Leyna's face. Then her skin flushed red again. "I did no such thing."

Henberlin nodded, confirming to Leyna that he knew the truth. Unable to look at her for a moment, he returned to the liquor cabinet to refresh the drink he hadn't touched. He hadn't expected her to deny her action. He had expected her to confide in him, ask for his help. He stared down at his drink for a moment and said, "That's what they caught on video. Those cameras were installed at the apartment. They were watching live when you shot Yanmei. They moved the cameras here to let us know they could get to us. While they were here, they left a copy of the video."

Henberlin described the scene that he'd watched on the sim card but didn't tell her where the card was hidden. The color left her face again and she laid back, letting her head drop, her hair hanging down behind the love seat. She stayed in that position a long-enough time that Henberlin checked to see if she had fallen asleep.

"Leyna?"

"I couldn't let it go on. I don't deserve that kind of treatment."

Leyna Henberlin grew up an unnoticed yet over-accomplished young woman. The last of five daughters, by the time she reached her teenage years her parents had had enough of child rearing. They'd been through it enough times and eagerly moved into empty-nest lives even though they still had one chick living at home.

For a while, she competed with their desire to move on with their lives. Finally she realized it was a losing battle and moved on with her independent life as well. Independent until her father decided to run for mayor in this rich city full of oil and gas millionaires.

The multi-term incumbent looked to have another sure win until Leyna's father, Renn Gauthier, presented an image the independent voters of Calgary fell in love with. The party system had no real place in civic politics in the West, so a modern man with ties to western values and a beautiful family appealed to a large portion of the population.

At the time, Leyna held a managerial position in the creative department of a midsized advertising agency. The agency allowed her a leave of absence to work on her father's campaign as long as she made sure the agency's name had strong visibility in all campaign materials. They also wanted her to make sure it showed up in her personal profile, as she would be very visible throughout the campaign.

As the advertising director for her father's organization, she employed many of the online and telephone fact-gathering techniques she had used in her work. She identified which images worked best. Their campaign adapted strategy with more expediency than the incumbent's and Renn Gauthier made significant gains in the early days of the election.

The image of a family of females stuck in the minds of voters, particularly women. Here stood a man who lived his whole life making the women in his life happy. How could he not be a good man? A distinctive contribution to that image was daddy's dedicated daughter working hard to get her father elected. This image cemented the idea that Renn Gauthier was sensitive to all manner of concerns. Leyna's outright attractiveness also aided in creating a memorable image.

The Gauthiers almost pulled it off.

After a recount her father conceded the election, but the media wouldn't let him, or his daughter, disappear. For the next few months, either Renn or Leyna were asked to second guess every development at City Hall. Renn pulled no punches and enjoyed stripping flesh off his former opponent's policies. Leyna, with blunt honesty, made it clear she had moved on with her career and didn't care about the mayor's doings. Within a year of the election, Renn was the only Gauthier appearing in public. That is, when it came to politics. Social gossip was another media playground, and Leyna attracted more than her share of attention.

Her advertising agency had grown thanks to her visible participation in her father's run for mayor. Receiving a promotion, greater responsibility, and a raise, she relished her return to work. Her business life developed into another point of interest for the media and she often appeared in industry-related publications. Who knew better how a pretty face drew interested eyeballs from the reading public than she?

Through it all she continued to live with her parents in the home she grew up in, as if to thwart her parents' empty-nest desires. The media loved the home-girl image as well, speculating in the social pages every time she ventured out to a new restaurant or club with a new man. Would this be the man who could get her to move out of the house she loved so much, away from her mother and father? The media would dig into the companion's background to determine via public opinion if he had the stuff required to settle down with Leyna

Gauthier. This scrutiny caused more than one man to back away from the circus, and resulted in at least one instance of Leyna rejecting a suitor due to past behavior.

None of it mattered to her. Given time, she knew the media would lay off, and they did. When Neil Henberlin entered her life, a casual meeting in a downtown bar, the media paid no attention. When they announced their marriage, though, it was like old times.

A picture of Renn smiling beside his daughter adorned the front page of the paper and was greeted with enthusiasm. People thought they were running for mayor again and they became a little disappointed when they discovered that wasn't the case. The wedding of the beautiful, dedicated daughter was on par in acceptability but happy occasions didn't stir muck the way politics did. Digging into the fiancé would have to do. Maybe there was muck to be found after all. It had worked on previous boyfriends, so why not with the fiancé?

No such luck.

Henberlin had no muck, and only came across as boring. A salesman. Successful, yes, but still, a salesman, and a high-end computer salesman at that. The regular media wouldn't know what to ask the guy to try to draw him out. If they did, they wouldn't understand his answers. They'd have to leave the interviews to the tech reporters.

This all added up to Leyna becoming a public focus again in her social life, business life, and her marriage. All because she was newsworthy. And soon she would add something new to the newsworthiness: Murder. A murder she had in fact committed, a murder her husband knew of. Who else knew?

"You weren't being treated that way, Leyna. No one was trying to harm you or take anything away from you."

"Did her husband plant the cameras? Was he trying to get proof of your affair?" Leyna asked. She walked to the mini-fridge built into the liquor cabinet and poured a glass of wine.

"There was no affair. It's time for the truth."

They held eye contact as she returned to sit beside him. She continued looking into his eyes after she sat.

"Okay, you start," she said.

Henberlin blinked then said, "There was no affair."

"C'mon, you said we're telling the truth."

"Leyna, there was no real affair. It was fake."

Henberlin began telling Leyna about Delaney and their first meeting. How he got played and then got patriotic over the idea of helping his country foil the Chinese attempt to steal technology. He also bought in more deeply to how great the company's new computer system appeared to be once it had become an international object of desire. He wanted to represent that greatness, so he made his commitment to Delaney. Then things started to snowball and, before he thought things through, he'd agreed to go along with the pretend affair.

Through it all, he thought he was only going through the motions. He had no idea if anyone thought the affair was believable—for certain, he knew it wasn't. He and Mrs. Albin did spend time together, and it was uncomfortable at first but then a form of comradeship developed. They were both stuck in this ruse and could relate to the difficulties it presented. They sympathized with each other, but there was nothing else.

Faced with this new information, Leyna drained her glass of wine. Her lips tightened to a series of vertical ridges. He knew she counted internally, her trick to control what came out of her mouth when she was angry.

"You expect me to believe you're a spy? Time spent with this prospect of yours, time in a love nest you rented in your name, all an act? You had no desire for this woman? A beautiful Asian girl didn't entice you to... do things you wanted to do?"

Her stare burned into him. Henberlin looked away. "I'm not a spy, I'm helping a spy. I'm still helping him, and not because of Yanmei's death or because I'm being patriotic... not any more. I have to help because you killed her. Her father is the person who wants the information about the system, her father is the one who placed the cameras in the apartment, her father is the one who gave me the video of you committing murder. He gave the police the last portion of the video to get me out of jail so I could continue to provide him with information. He says he'll give them the rest if I don't continue.

"He wants to punish you, Leyna. He wants us to always be expecting the police to come and take you to jail. Supplying him with the information he wants and living in fear is the only way I can save your freedom and somehow I'm going to save it. But tell me why. Why did you do this?"

"I didn't deserve what you did to me."

"What you thought I did to you."

Leyna snapped her mouth shut, stopping her inward breath, which she held a long second before saying, "People were talking. Your people, my people... saying nasty things. Do you know what it's like to have people insinuating that you're not good enough for your husband? That he has to have another woman in his life?" She paused and looked down at her hands. "I watched you leave your office and go to your apartment. I watched her arrive a short time later. I waited to see how long you were in the apartment and it seemed such a long time. The longer it went on, the less I could stand being there, waiting on you. When I left it had only been fifteen minutes. It looked like an affair, Neil. What else could I think? Why didn't you tell me you had this... extra project?"

"Why didn't you ask me about what you thought I was doing?"

They fell silent. The answers to both questions as difficult as they were obvious.

12

——

The timeout to refill their drinks had opposite effects on the Henberlins. Neil found energy. He believed that his wife now believed him about the nonexistence of an affair. Once they reestablished trust they could work out a plan. Leyna seemed to have collapsed, staring down at the floor, not responding to his question about getting her another glass of wine. Finally, she shook her head as if clearing away bad thoughts, then indicated she would have a refill.

"How is it you were in Calgary last Saturday?" he began in an attempt to figure out her current state of mind.

Leyna turned and looked at him with a direct stare. "Are you sure you want to hear this?"

He held her look, trying to decide the right thing to do. As if she knew his thoughts, before he answered her question she said, "If you don't turn me in right now, you go to jail if I go to jail. The more you know, the more you become a part of my crime."

Again he remained silent—due to her calculating awareness or because he didn't know what he should do. Finally he said, "Not necessarily. Tell me what you did. It won't make it right, and I don't know if I can help you… or even if I should."

"I think you should," she said, holding his eyes with hers again. "This is what happened. I'd booked my reservation to the marketing conference months ago. As the conference grew nearer, the thought of leaving you home alone with your mistress for an entire weekend

86

raised my stress level to the point where I couldn't let that happen. So I came up with a way to take you to Vancouver with me.

"The Aaron Codair story?"

"Well yeah, I chose him because he has the same dark hair and head shape as you. Well, I booked a flight in his name so I could tell you he dropped out at the last minute to make it seem like a great opportunity to get away together."

"So you set all this up as part of a plan?"

Leyna smirked and gave her shoulders a slight shrug.

"Next I contacted the spa at the hotel and arranged a schedule to keep you busy while I attended my meetings. Then we met for lunch and I sprung the trip on you."

———

At noon on the Friday of the conference, she'd met Henberlin for lunch.

"Guess what? I have some good news about some good luck for you," she said with a devious smile.

"Good luck for me? What's up?"

"Aaron from work told the boss he can't make it to the conference this weekend. The agency is going to have to eat his plane ticket. Instead of wasting it I suggested that I take you along. They're fine with that. They get their money back on the extra hotel room and Aaron's per diem, so it's a wash with the cost of the plane ticket. You get to come to Vancouver with me for the weekend. Isn't that great?"

"Well, yeah. I mean, if I can go. What about the ticket, though, isn't his name on it?"

"Yes, but look what I've got." Leyna handed her husband a copy of his own license only it had Aaron's name printed on it.

Neil looked at the plastic card. Not perfect but close enough, he thought. "How the hell? Isn't this identity theft?"

"Only if you use it in an inappropriate manner."

"*This* isn't inappropriate?" he asked crooking his eyebrows.

"Come on. It's a mere weekend trip. Aaron's not going to mind. We have all these graphics producing machines at the agency that make this kind of switch easy and provide good results. Look at how close this is to a real driver's license." Leyna seemed proud of the work her coworkers were capable of performing.

"I don't know. Why don't we change the ticket?"

"The reissue cost is more than the original ticket. What makes this all seem so perfect is scoring a trip together at no cost to us. Come on, try it, it'll work. Besides, I leave on an earlier flight. I have to pick up my credentials and attend a cocktail party, so I'll be waiting for you in the hotel. And I mean, I'll be waiting and I'll have been waiting for over an hour. You know how a hotel room with a big bed and clean sheets effects what I'm willing to do for you. Imagine my state of mind when you finally arrive. I'll make your trip worth it, I promise."

His imagination didn't have to work too hard to conjure up the images of previous bouts of hotel sex with his wife. He thought he was alone in his heightened pleasure from making love in a bed different from the one they shared each night. But once, on a sales reward trip he'd earned to San Diego, after a particularly athletic session, Leyna untangled herself from sheets, blankets, and her husband to replenish her oxygen and restore her energy. After a few deep breaths she raised up onto her elbow and in the almost dark could see her husband's heaving shiny chest. She smiled as she rubbed her free hand over his lower abdomen and told him how much she looked forward to their naked encounters in hotel rooms. He bolted to a sitting position and suggested they turn the lights on and take their time to explore. The memory warmed him to the idea of a weekend in Vancouver.

"What time's the flight?" he said.

Henberlin, a little nervous, shuffled along in the security line at eight-thirty that Friday evening. The security agent looked at the boarding pass and license. The names matched so a blur of scribbles transferred to the boarding pass and the agent called for the next person in line while handing Henberlin back his documents. Nothing to it, except using someone else's identification to sneak through airport security and board a plane filled him with the guilt of a terrorist. But the guilt disappeared when he picked up the grey plastic tray to fill it with the contents of his pockets. He didn't find his cell phone in any of those pockets. The sense of loss pounded in on him. 'Alone, I'm alone,' he thought. 'How is this going to work? What if I need to call Leyna? How are we going to stay in touch?'

But thinking about his wife changed his outlook in an instant. Leyna waiting for him in the hotel adjusted his state of mind to the oozy, sexy state she'd promised she'd be in when he arrived. The flight seemed longer than the normal short hop to Vancouver.

Finally, in the hotel's hallway, he knocked on the room's door and watched the peephole lens. It darkened and the door opened. Leyna had noticed on two previous occasions when she wore her blue dress with the shimmering fabric, her husband's eyes spent a lot of time roving over her curves. He couldn't resist taking her in his arms, not able to overcome the desire to touch the body the dress encased. She'd bought the dress for the very way that her curves were accentuated by the tight fit and smooth texture. The plunge of the neckline dropped low enough to show the start of round ampleness and the weight of her breasts. He noticed her perfect makeup, dark around the eyes, lips more red than she usually colored them, her hair down, casual and loose. He had expected naked, but liked the idea of Leyna clothed in this dress. His eyes on a quest to see through the fabric to the flesh he knew lay below, his want for her stronger that if she'd been naked. Their trust in each other meant they shared their bodies without question but as they made overtures leading up to lovemaking he was always hesitant, wondering if she would share those pleasures with him again. In his peripheral vision a taunting image, a hotel bed with clean crisp sheets he knew they would toss together. Taking the time to again appreciate the attractions of the interesting woman he had married, anticipating the joy of removing the teasing dress to reveal and enjoy the yielding body. A body showcased by a garment perfect for its intended purpose. The joy and yearning created while looking at her body foreshadowed the expected experience, the pleasure of loving Leyna.

Drinks, sly smiles, and innuendos led to lovemaking like they hadn't enjoyed for a long while. Both hungry to accept the pleasures offered, both willing to supply everything wished for by the other.

Off to dinner and more drinks, then a return to the hotel room and sleep.

In the morning, Leyna turned off her alarm and rolled over onto her back, delaying her usual immediate rise from bed. He didn't disappoint her waiting tactic and reached over, cupping a hand on her breast. An invitation to intimacy. They made morning love, then she left for her shower. He entered a comfy post-sex slumber, broken a short time later by her kiss goodbye.

Saturday morning, the only day of information sessions for the conference, Leyna filled a cup at the coffee station and stood off to the side watching the attendees arrive. Then, seeing someone she knew, she joined the line right behind him.

"Bob? They allow the people at Mackie-Boudreau to be exposed to outside influences?"

"Ha! Leyna… Only if they've been very good. I don't know how I got here."

"You're always good. What are you expecting from this event?"

"Good coffee, great Danish, and very little else. I have some side meetings that should be the most productive part of being here. How about you?"

"Same. The lineup of presenters doesn't impress me too much. I imagine I'll split time and catch bits and pieces in the same time slots. Shall we go in?"

Being early, they found seats in the second row on the middle aisle. Ten to fifteen thin tables with stiff, almost floor-length tablecloths made rows in the conference room. Each table dotted with pitchers of ice water. Green slices of cucumber and yellow lemon wedges floated among the cubes. Small pads of cream colored paper and shiny brown plastic pens with the hotel's logo sat in front of each tucked-in chair.

The noise level increased as the rows began to fill. Leyna, chatting with her acquaintance, ignored her coffee until one of her hand gestures contacted the saucer, tipping the cup and sending a dark splash spreading over the white cloth. She jumped to her feet and looked for anything to stop the flow of coffee when an attendant appeared with a rag to soak up the stain. The attendant absorbed as much of the liquid as she could manage, then placed a clean white cloth napkin over the stain and apologized for the little she could do at the moment.

"No, no, thank you so much. I should be apologizing," Leyna said. Then she turned to her companion. "I'm sorry, Bob. I hope I didn't splash any on you. I guess I'll go get another cup. I plan to leave halfway through, anyway, so I'll lurk in the back for a while then take off. Maybe I'll see you again later."

"I hope so. I'll keep an eye out for you," he said.

Leyna left to get another cup of coffee. She returned and sat in the back row for the first fifteen minutes of the presentation. She paid no attention to the speaker and finally stood and left the room.

Before leaving she went to the coat desk.

"This beats trying to check a jacket before the conference starts," she said to the check steward.

"We sure were crowded this morning. Here you go."

Leyna took her tag and walked to the farthest room in the hallway near the exit. She climbed the stairs to street level, coming out on the side of the hotel. It took but a minute for her to hail a taxi. Climbing into the back seat she said, "The airport please." Then she leaned back into the seat and turned her head to the window.

"Surprising how light the traffic is. It's never like this," the driver commented.

They made excellent time.

At the airport, she purchased a ticket on one of the small airlines servicing the small cities in British Columbia and Alberta. She used her sister's married name. At Security, she presented her sister's driver's license, which she'd previously extracted from her sister's purse. The flight made one stop in Kelowna, then flew into Calgary.

She grabbed a cab, telling the driver to take her to City Hall. From there, she walked to a department store and purchased a black hoodie, black sweat pants, thin synthetic tan gloves, and canvas running shoes. She paid cash, then went to the food court on the second floor. In the washroom, her hands were shaking so much she had trouble tying her shoelaces. Adjacent to the food court stood a row of light green lockers for shoppers to store purchases while they continued to shop. Leyna pulled a key from her pocket and opened one of the lockers. She placed her good clothes inside, pulled a small plastic bag out, then relocked the locker and pocketed the key.

A short walk later, she used a key she had previously copied to enter her husband's secret apartment. She took a quick look around, then sat down in a chair in the bedroom before pulling out her husband's cell phone. It took her two guesses to come up with his four-digit security code. He hadn't used the four digits of their home address but his fallback, their anniversary month and year, gained her access to the phone. She scrolled to Yanmei's contact record, clicked on the message icon and typed:

➜ Vancouver cancelled. At the apartment waiting for you.

She touched the send button.

Within a minute, the cell phone vibrated. She entered the security code again and saw the message with Yanmei's name below the speech balloon:

➜ Be there soon. What's up?

Leyna didn't text back.

She reached into her pocket and removed the small handgun she had retrieved from the locker. It was the scariest thing in her life right now. Scarier than the way she went about acquiring the gun. Dressing down and approaching desperate-looking people in dangerous parts of East Calgary. She had no choice but to acquire a gun in such a way; she couldn't approach anyone she knew. Though the approaches were dangerous, they were also productive. She watched a young, unshaven man with a mess of curly hair extort something from a homeless person. He'd slapped the sitting man in order to take the man's cigarettes. As he lit a smoke he looked at Leyna, lifted his chin to ask what she wanted. She stated her request. After giving the young man fifty dollars, she got the name of a small grocery store and who to ask for. She went to the store and asked for the person whose name she'd been given—a man's name. To her surprise, a woman came to meet her and led her to a back corner of the small grocery store and asked what she was after. Hearing the explanation and questioning Leyna about the person who had sent her, she hesitated at first then told Leyna where and when to meet for the delivery and how much money to bring.

At the delivery, she met a different person. During a noon hour in a downtown park, she received a key to a locker and directions to the locker's location. She handed over her payment, trusting a criminal with blind faith that she would get what she paid for. Inside the locker, wrapped in a plastic bag, she found the gun along with a box of ammunition. 'Time to rethink what I'm doing,' she thought. 'This is a real gun and I intend to use it on a real person.' She closed and relocked the locker.

Sitting in the apartment, she held the gun in her hand for the first time. She tasted her morning coffee and the heartburn it brought on. Her stomach ached not from hunger, not from illness. She mouth-breathed short, shallow breaths. She thought she would faint because she couldn't get enough oxygen into her lungs.

The door clicked and she heard a whoosh of air as it opened and closed. She waited, amazed she held the gun up and kept it still. She didn't wonder if she would do what she had to do. The time was now. Make no mistake, the thing would happen. She knew she would do it. A body came two steps through the bedroom door, then sensed another person and stopped. Leyna pulled the trigger twice and the body fell to the ground. Still seated, she thought, 'That was a man.'

She stood over the body, saw the key lying beside his hand and shook her head. She said in a low voice, "No idea."

She stepped past him, walked out, and sat in another chair outside the bedroom door in the living room. Again she waited. Minutes later the door lock clicked, then opened and closed again. Leyna heard Yanmei enter. It sounded like she placed something on the kitchen counter then opened the refrigerator for a second or two before closing it again.

Leyna stayed still in her chair until Yanmei walked through the opening from the kitchen into the living room. Leyna stood and walked toward Yanmei, who raised her hands in front of her and began walking backward out of the living room into the kitchen. As Leyna moved toward the doorway, Yanmei started to yell but Leyna didn't register the words. Not interested in communication, she thought only about firing the gun. She pulled the trigger and the shot knocked Yanmei down. Leyna continued into the kitchen, stood over Yanmei, and shot her one more time.

She paused. Relief trickled top down in slow motion and filled her body. Relief that the affair was over, relief that she did what she had to do, and relief that she wouldn't have to do anything like this ever again.

She moved to the door and left the apartment to return to the food court of the department store. Back in her own clothes, she placed the other garments back in the store bag she received when she purchased them. One check in the mirror, then out to the street to take the C-train to the Kensington district.

She threw the gun and the bag of clothing into a dumpster behind a coffee shop where she guessed the dumpster would be picked up often. From there, she took a taxi to the airport and purchased a ticket on a different regional airline. This time through Kamloops to Vancouver.

The last sessions of the conference were still in progress as Leyna arrived at the hotel. She stepped into one of the sessions and sat emotionless at one of the back tables, breathing steady breaths, trying to determine the topic of the session before it ended.

"I met with some people I knew after the session and we went to the bar to have a drink before I met you back in the room. You know what happened then," she finished with a smile.

"Leyna, the way you're telling me this, it's like you're proud of yourself."

"Well, you have to admit, there's nothing that could possibly point to me. If for some reason they did check me out, there are so many things that point to my being at the conference for the entire day. But still…" Leyna waved her hands beside her ears. "If I'm to believe your story, that there was no affair, then I killed people for no good reason. How can I take pride in that?"

"*If* you believe? You still have doubts?"

"Accepting your truth means I made a terrible mistake."

"You think killing two people over a real affair isn't a mistake?"

"I couldn't stand what you were doing to me. I had to take it away from you."

"You should have asked me. I could have eased your mind and we wouldn't be in this situation."

"Are you going to turn me in?"

"It's the right thing to do, but I don't know. You're my wife and I love you. I don't want anything bad to happen to you, but the Albins deserves justice."

"Neil, I can't go to jail. I can't be locked up." Her frantic voice raked on Henberlin's concerns for his wife. He heard tones he hadn't heard since she became depressed after their second anniversary. Life had settled down for her. Her father had never entertained running for office again, so no more political exposure and no longer a frequent topic in the social pages. At the same time Henberlin's sales activity had been ramping up and he'd been getting considerable recognition from his company for what he had accomplished. Noticing Leyna yielding to his schedule and opinion without sticking up for her own concerns, she displayed signs of falling back into a depression. She started on mild a dose of medication. The drugs had the desired effect and Leyna stopped their use without showing signs of returning symptoms. That is until about two months prior to the murders when Henberlin noticed a bottle of the same prescription sitting beside the sink. It had a recent fill date. When he asked her about it, she only offered that she'd been flirting with the bad thoughts again, and wanted to take care of them in case things got to be too much for her.

He'd kept a closer watch on her since then, but hadn't seen anything that sent up warning signals until he saw her break down when the detectives arrested him. Since then, he tried to pay closer attention to her moods.

She moved to him, laid her head on his chest, slipped her arms around him, and squeezed tight.

"You can't let me go to jail. I did it to correct your mistake." She sobbed.

Minutes ago, she gloated at her success at committing murder. 'Now,' he thought, 'is she breaking down again or acting?'

13

"You're late," Jian Liu said as Yanmei reached the bottom step to the tiny basement apartment. For as long as she could remember, her father had taken her to the apartment under the produce market on First Street East.

Yanmei didn't respond. She walked past the doorway of the small living room where her father sat and went into the kitchen. She placed her hand on the teapot sitting on the bare wooden cupboard where the laminate had peeled away years before. A scratched aluminum border with brown rusty nails protruding surrounded the counter. A few chips of the long-gone laminate, like shark's teeth, appeared in places under the aluminum edging where the remainder of its length was packed with black grime. The pot warmed her hand so it was warm enough. She poured herself a cup of tea. In the living room, she joined her father at one of the card tables set up in the room, ready for future players to lay out mahjong tiles. A gruff old man sporting a sparse grey stubble beard sat across from her father. He stared at Yanmei, unable to take his eyes off her.

"Were you with your lover?" Jian asked his daughter, feigning no interest, yet getting straight to business. The stranger moved his stare to Jian Liu.

"In front of this man who I do not know?" Her tone implied recrimination.

"He's not a stranger. This Neo Henbrin's father. Did you get the computer instructions?"

Yanmei turned to take a closer look at the man. She stared, wondering about etiquette for such an introduction. She made a short bow of her head then turned to her father and raised her eyebrows. Jian Liu sighed. He turned to the old man. "Okay. You go now. I'll get back to you later."

"Is there anything you need me to do?" the man asked.

Jian Liu waved the back of his hand in answer. After the man left he lifted his face to Yanmei. "When is this going to happen? You keep telling me it will be soon."

She took a sip of her tea, staring over the rim of the cup, gauging her father. "I can't press."

Yanmei Liu grew up in the basement apartments and secret tunnels below downtown Calgary's Chinatown. Always tagging along with her father, who had a mini business empire consisting of strip-mall Chinese fast food restaurants and a newsstand known for its vast selection of Cuban cigars. He owned the businesses but spent no time managing them, and Yanmei never heard him speak about the businesses to any of his associates. They weren't the primary interest of his life. Otherwise they would extract some of his attention. She gleaned the primary interest of his life, after years of following him in this subterranean world.

She attended a great number of underground events. All of them involved mahjong games or poker, all took place in small dingy rooms that she doubted she could find on her own. In her early school years, her father allowed her to miss school for days on end so she could tag along with him while he played games and talked to other men from the downtown Chinese community. He wanted her to hear the stories they told about life in China and the virtues the Chinese system had to offer. After each session, he asked her about some of the stories she'd just heard. He added some interpretation that the other men chose not to share or couldn't supply due to lack of knowledge.

Jian Liu seemed to know more details regarding the events recounted than the men who actually experienced them. Yanmei listened and concentrated on the other men's words as she heard the original version of the stories. She wanted to remember the exact words used by the men when her father reviewed those stories later. He put meaning into the stories, providing the essence and insight of China's 20th century character.

Part of why she loved to go with her father and hear the stories was the fact that it was her and not one of her older brothers. She turned out to be her dad's sidekick. The boys were pressured into doing well at school and fought the pressure with rebellion. They weren't going to do anything their father wanted them to do, except take on the responsibility of getting an education. As Canadian-born Chinese, they wanted the freedom of a democratic country. Calgary offered that opportunity while letting them maintain their Chinese identity. They could give part of what their father wanted: Hard work, strong studies, directed education. But they wanted all those things to be in the field of their choice, not his.

Seeing his sons avoiding all involvement with the direction he planned for them, Jian Liu started to ask Yanmei to join him and he couldn't have been happier with the level of acceptance and the concentrated effort she displayed. On the days when he conceded she should return to school, they both wished she could be at the games. The men in the tunnels always asked where the young girl had gone.

During their days together, Jian promoted the benefits of the new direction in China. Communism with benefits. Big benefits. Big capitalist benefits.

And he promoted to Yanmei the idea that China needed people in other countries to learn about other societies. They could pass that knowledge on in order to help China advance in her new direction. Yanmei soon wanted to help.

In the summers when she was allowed to be out of school, she travelled to China to live with relatives she never knew existed. She'd always believed their family roots originated in the soil of Taiwan. The lifestyle she experienced gave her pause to think about what her father's country needed from the rest of the world. She had been indoctrinated with its virtues, the resiliency of centuries, the scientific aptitude, the ability to copy any technology, the volume of people, and the economic potential.

Now China searched for opportunity. Opportunities derived from raw materials and new technology. Opportunities for which China could provide processing, manufacturing, and re-creation in excess.

Her relatives lived in the constant wrap of Beijing smog without complaint. During her time in the city each summer, Yanmei had difficulty breathing the filthy air and never stopped complaining to her relatives. They called it the price the people had to pay to make China great. This attitude caused Yanmei to consider the extent to which the people of China are willing to sacrifice to make their country better. 'They rise early, they perform manual labor for long hours, they raise their children after work when they're tired. All this for very little money. They can't afford much in the way of rice and food, and nothing goes toward luxuries. And they perform all these sacrifices while sucking inescapable pollution into their lungs.'

She thought living in Calgary was tough. Her time in Beijing made her laugh at what she thought was difficult back home. At the end of each summer, she couldn't wait to get back to her easier life, but guilt over the ease of life in Calgary had her thinking she had let down her family in Beijing. They would have to make up for the work she wouldn't be there to perform.

Before entering high school, she'd asked her father how she could continue to help them while she lived in Calgary. His response was that she had to do well in school, that she couldn't spend as much time with him going to mahjong games. The most helpful thing she could do was excel, to be the smartest child in school. Learn so that someday, the knowledge she gained would help China become equal and better than today's modern nations.

Her brothers had been good students and their work habits were also ingrained in Yanmei. They, however, had fought with their father about what type of education they should pursue. Yanmei chose to do what her father had asked. Knowing that the city of Calgary was awash with oil and gas companies, he wanted her to develop a career that would get her into the bowels of one of the large exploration companies. So that's what she did.

She majored in petroleum engineering and found herself on the production side of the business, still upstream from the refinery. Her world in the industry contained a population of engineers and landmen. She could watch the activities of the exploration, exploitation, and land departments in a natural manner. And she paid close attention to them all. Her father always wanted to know about what she did at work and how her work related to these other departments.

This information-gathering task became a lot easier when she married Stephen Albin, at the time an up-and-coming reservoir engineer at Shield Oil. The marriage provided immediate access to that area, but she didn't start the marriage by going mining for information in her husband's department. She told her father about some of the work-related discussions she and her husband had but left out some details.

Then the desire for detail escalated. She wanted to please her father, and continued to do so, but now her father always had someone with him when he asked his questions. Quite often, the other person asked his own questions.

Yanmei soon realized her father was collecting information for the people of China. It's universal knowledge that China has a high demand for raw materials, and had already invested in a few very large projects in the energy sector. Their investment in the oil sands of Northern Alberta came after no other oil company could afford to participate. Having made the investment in such a valuable asset, China now wanted to protect that investment. They realized the depth of the knowledge hole they needed to climb out of, and began to accelerate their steps to fill the void. Entering the world of modernity demanded China take these steps. The methods of filling the void were training Chinese nationals and acquiring insights into the industry without the necessity of experiencing those insights firsthand.

Jian Liu presented this argument to Yanmei as an adult the same way he did throughout her childhood. He always pointed out his own dedication to what China stood for, and how China would rightfully take its place as the leading nation in the world. He convinced her that she performed the same function he performed, gathering information to make China great. Yanmei went along with his requests because she'd loved being her father's helper when she was a little girl. Always happy to do what pleased him.

To this point, thinking no harm had been done, Yanmei passed on her knowledge with the belief that her information could be acquired elsewhere through discussions with any petroleum consultant the Chinese could hire. When her father started hinting at areas of the industry that were a little more detailed and sensitive — areas he couldn't have known about on his own — Yanmei concluded some other person directed the line of inquiry. His questions dealt with information regarding specific geographic areas, and whether Shield Oil held assets in those areas or planned to acquire them. Critical information related to competitive situations.

Realizing he was escalating — both his desperation to acquire the data and the type of data he wanted — Yanmei's reluctance to provide such information grew. She needed to come to grips with being used to help strengthen her father's China. Was it her China? 'Yes and no,' she thought, 'but let's see how far he'll go.'

It took many attempts to direct her to gather information, and an equal number of dodges on her part to get him to explain his persistence. His explanation included his usual statements of how China needed the help of Chinese people living abroad to become strong. His new argument included the importance of family members helping family members. If family didn't help family, then why have a family? Hadn't he shown the level of that importance when he disowned his sons? They wanted their own lives, had forgotten their roots and therefore were of no use to China. He'd sent her each summer to Beijing so she could establish roots that grew alongside his roots and the roots of their family still living in Beijing. So she could see the needs of China and he knew she'd seen them. He reminded her how she'd asked him how she could help her family even while living in North America.

She chose not to question any of his logic, not to ruffle their relationship. She still hadn't gotten her mind clear on her role in her father's endeavors. She also began to wonder if she'd been programmed by her father throughout her life to become an information vacuum for China. The dis-ownership of her brothers in his explanation was something she accepted as a threat.

She began to avoid her father so she wouldn't have to make up excuses for not having the information he'd requested. She also didn't want to be asked to explore any new areas of interest within her company.

As she tried to get her head together, she met Horace Delaney. Delaney had contacted her because he'd heard of her involvement in the process of evaluating the new computer system coming to market from R.E.S. He wanted to know anything she could tell him about it. Yanmei, tired of being probed for information, provided a number of reasons why she wouldn't supply such information. Delaney switched gears and began to describe his own involvement in reservoir engineering. This opened discussions about her husband's activities at Shield Oil, and a great wall began to rise. She told Delaney that talk about her husband was further out-of-bounds than talk about R.E.S.

Delaney wasn't giving up. For his third attempt, he begged her to meet him for lunch. He wanted to explain his persistence in wanting to talk with her. She only gave in because he suggested a very expensive Italian restaurant considered the hardest lunch reservation in town.

Delaney stood to meet her as the maître d' escorted her to a private little table tucked into a small alcove to one side of a large brick fireplace.

"Mrs. Albin, it's nice to meet you," he greeted her.

"And you." She turned her head, looking around the restaurant. "This is a bit much for as little as I'm going to be able to talk to you about."

"Not to worry. Entertainment expense."

They each ordered a house salad and a small bowl of fresh made pasta. Delaney chose hand-cut pappardelle in a provolone sauce with nutmeg and crisp dices of pancetta. Yanmei ordered spaghetti with the restaurant's famous marinara, well-known for over indulging with garlic.

The lunch conversation stayed light as Delaney kept it rolling with questions about Yanmei's work history. Neither ordered dessert, yet confessed to thinking about having gelato or chocolate love cake with their coffee. By the time they got to their coffee, the restaurant had almost cleared out.

Delaney smiled at Yanmei and said, "Mrs. Albin, let me tell you what I really want to talk to you about."

Yanmei held her smile and noticed the serious timbre present in Delaney's voice. Her smile slipped. "Okay."

"We're aware that you have been passing sensitive information to your father."

"Oh?" Her jaw dropped as she thought of how this change of topic arose. "I wouldn't say 'sensitive.' It's more... general information that he asks me about my work."

"Mrs. Albin, I want you to think about how long you'll be willing to stick with that sort of response. I don't imply a serious breach like yours out of the blue." Delaney watched Yanmei's face, fixing her eyes until she gave a small nod and lowered her eyes to peer at the table top.

"I wondered if someone knew what my father was doing, and what I was doing." She lifted her eyes from the table and looked Delaney in the face. "Are you with the Government?"

Delaney ignored her question, saying, "We need your help with something. The next time I see you, I'll let you in on what that is. Your willingness to assist is important." Delaney paused again, giving her time to wonder what would come next.

"Now I should let you go. I don't want your office to think you're out having a good time." Delaney stood holding his hand out in the direction of the entrance, and waited for Yanmei to gather her things and leave. Neither said another word.

———

Jian Liu's impatience regarding the programming code for the operating system's encryption function had reached its peak. His contact inside the People's Petroleum of China Corporation had stepped up his demand for the code because the US Government intended to block its distribution to commercial systems. His contact inside the petroleum corporation didn't actually work on behalf of the petroleum concern.

The cell phone Jian Liu kept in a locked compartment in the small top-worn desk began a muffled ring. He kept a small room in the basement of an organization for the betterment of the Calgary Chinese community. Through the years, he had used the organization to provide scholarships to students of Chinese decent to attend the University of Calgary. For his work, he needed a small office. Because he worked on a volunteer basis, and because people in the Chinese community feared Jian Liu, he enjoyed limitless privacy in this room.

Jian Liu unlocked the compartment and answered the phone.

"We can't wait any longer, Jian. The US Government will be issuing an edict preventing the code from being on public computers within days." The voice belonged to Ken Kwong, a newly-appointed attaché at the Chinese Embassy in Vancouver. A man whose impatience had proven beneficial for gathering information during his assignments at other embassies. But Ken Kwong and Jian Liu's relationship went back to the years in Taipei.

Jian's father had started a small calligraphy school once he'd gotten his bearings in his new city. Jian worked most days in a small restaurant, standing for long, hot hours stacking buns that one of the bakers had just popped off the side of a kiln-like oven. The buns used to make a sandwich eaten at both breakfast and lunch.

At night Jian worked as a tutor in his father's school. One of the students he'd been tutoring for a number of weeks asked him about his history. Jian Liu had lied and provided a story of how his father, a Beiping scholar, had come to Taiwan and taught in a small town in the southern part of the country. He took a wife and started a family but found it difficult to feed his family, so he'd moved them to Taipei a few months earlier. Because of the isolation and his father's incessant teaching, he'd grown up sporting a Beiping accent. The story worked for most of the people he told it to. This student seemed not to think twice about it, until one night when they were the only two in the room.

"Jian," the student addressed his tutor as his tutor demonstrated a stroke. "Do you remember drinking yellow wine with Commander Zhang?"

Jian's hand stopped. He stared at the end of the brush hovering over the paper, his ears beginning to pulse with the thump of his heart. "I'm not certain. I don't recall a Commander Zhang coming to our village."

His peripheral vision detected an intense glare from the student but he dare not look at him. He waited a long time, wondering if the student would provide information of how he knew of the yellow wine.

"Not in the village, in Beiping, the night you left for this country."

Jian waited, then said, "Will you tell me who sent you?"

"My brother. But that's all I know."

"What does your brother want?"

"He wants to know if you drank wine with Commander Zhang."

When the contact played out, the brother turned out to be Lo Chu Peng, who became Ken Kwong when he worked in certain embassies.

"Mr. Kwong, I've passed your concerns on to my daughter. She insists that if the code isn't available she is hardly in a position to insist that it be produced on your schedule," Jian Liu said.

"Are you saying that the great Jian Liu is capable of failing? I may have to change the report on you. After all of your assurances, it seems we won't be succeeding in acquiring a most important piece of code."

"I'll be seeing my daughter this afternoon. I'll pass along our concerns and hope she fulfills her duty."

"Jian, our relationship aside, there will be hot heads who have also provided assurances further up the chain. I don't know how much influence I have when one of them wishes to place blame."

"Let's let Yanmei work it out. This is more than we've asked of her in the past, but she's committed to the same goals we are."

Now, with Yanmei in the small basement apartment, he had to test her commitment.

"Yanmei, you're going to have to press. There are time constraints," Jian Liu said, his complexion reddening.

"I won't be seeing Mr. Henberlin until next week," Yanmei responded. "He's off on a trip to Vancouver on short notice. He says he doesn't have a system he can access at this point, but will for sure when he gets back. Does that fit your time constraint?"

"No, but when next week? Has he told you how he plans to copy the code?"

"Not important how he gets the code to us. He mentioned the name of the code and that it is accessed by what is called a system call. The code sits in some encoded area of the system. When a programmer inserts the two or three commands in a program where he wishes to use the code, the call includes a copy of the encryption code into the program when it runs. He told me the system call is named DIVZY." Yanmei sat silent, letting her father wait for something he could understand. "It's the first time he's indicated the code actually exists."

Jian Liu sat up straight then slapped the table top.

"Good. It would make everyone happy if you can get it as soon as possible. On Monday when he returns from Vancouver, you have to press."

"I can't press."

"Yanmei, if you need to speed your friend Henbrin, tell him that I have his father. Maybe he'll move faster."

"You want me to threaten his family?"

"You're close. Now we know the code is real. Move him anyway you can. Get it when he returns on Monday."

As Yanmei thought about where her father's increased desperation to get a copy of the code had taken them, her cell phone chimed Henberlin's message tone. She pulled out her phone and confirmed it was him but she didn't mention it to her father. She clicked on the message.

"Vancouver cancelled. At the apartment waiting for you."

She typed in a quick response without thinking about or caring why he hadn't completed his trip. The thought of an hour or two talking and relaxing with Henberlin created a comfort that surprised her with the level of eagerness that overcame her with each successive meeting. Safe, isolated friendship. Although he participated in the information exchange that caused her tension, he only participated as an innocent prop. He made no demands and in fact sympathized with her situation, even though he didn't know all there was to know about it. After all, he was in the same boat.

14

—

With Yanmei gone and not able to deliver the sabotaged code to her father, the job now rested in Henberlin's hands. Delaney updated him on the information they had already passed to Jian Liu—information that Yanmei credited Henberlin with providing—and what to expect from the next meeting. They were interrupted when they received simultaneous texts from Kyle:

→ Data glitch fixed. Ready again.

Both men thumbed their cell phones.

"That Kyle's message?" Henberlin said.

"Yeah."

Henberlin sighed as he placed his cell phone back in his jacket pocket. The dread of taking the next step began to build. He was the real go-between now. He would finish Yanmei's work. "When do I call Jian Liu?"

"In the morning. I'll get with Kyle tonight and let you know how you'll move the data." Delaney made notes on his small computer.

Henberlin waited as the other man typed for a long time. Wondering if he'd been forgotten, he said, "Sounds good. Am I supposed to know anything about this data?"

Delaney looked up above his computer screen at Henberlin. Henberlin thought he seemed annoyed at the distraction.

"Only that there was a problem when you presented it to Shield and that your analyst fixed it. Plead ignorance about everything else." His attention returned to his typing.

"Okay. Shouldn't I know why they want it and why you're faking it?"

"No. Best if you don't know."

"Does Kyle know?" His voice dropped off, "He's such an important cog in the gear box since he's supplying fake data to Jian Liu. "

"Everyone is important in this. And, if he knows, he didn't get it from us."

Frustrated, Henberlin decided to extend a theory. "Does it have anything to do with the Chinese wanting to buy into the Shield play, and maybe they don't trust the data Shield has been showing them?"

Delaney again looked up annoyed, but this time smiled after a few seconds.

"Nice try. You can ask me all the questions you want about this if you're intent on wasting your time. Trust me Neil, you not knowing their motives might work in your best interests."

Feeling untrusted, Henberlin asked, "What happens if I ask Jian Liu the same question?"

"He'd be thinking what I'm thinking, you're nosing around where you shouldn't. Just make it seem like all you care about is the money. You'll be doing yourself a favor."

"Okay, it's about the money. I'm glad to help you out, but if some cash comes my way I'm going to take it. What do I do if he says he's not willing to pay for my help?"

"He's got nothing else that can make you give away corporate secrets. Tell him Yanmei using you for information purposes hurts, and only money can make it better. The Shield data is another source of income. What you're after is money for the operating system's encryption algorithm. Kind of a revenge for his daughter pulling the wool over your eyes. Make that your only motivation and don't say anything about the US Government trying to prevent your company from selling your new operating system to the general public. The Chinese know that."

Realizing that Delaney wanted him in the dark about Jian's motives, Henberlin dropped his pursuit of an answer. "Okay. You'll call me in the morning?"

"Yeah, around ten," Delaney said. "Say, do you know a reservoir simulation analyst named Roy Warren? He wants to know if I'm going to have spare cycles on the new system that he can pay to use. Says he wants to do some testing."

Henberlin looked up in thought, twisting his lips to one side. Then he returned to putting things back in his PC case as if he hadn't heard the question.

"Neil, Roy Warren. Do you know him?"

"No, I said."

"Sorry, I didn't hear you. You okay? You've been through a lot the past few days. How's your wife doing? She was in the hospital for a while, wasn't she?"

"I'm fine. My wife is fine," he said with no inflection.

"Good, but when you talk to Jian Liu you have to be perfect. Do you want to wait another day?"

Henberlin tilted his head forward, rolled his eyes under his eyebrows, and shook his head to a slow beat. Then he straightened, squared his shoulders, and squinted at Delaney. "You can't lend your system to anyone. That would be a different contract, a data services contract. Your system would have cost more in that case. This Warren guy would have to buy his own system or you'd have to change your agreement."

Delaney looked at Henberlin with a curious twist of his head. He nodded at Delaney. "That's right, you can't do it."

"All well and good Neil, but have you forgotten that I'm not in this to run fast computers? I didn't even care if you hooked the thing up until now. I'm not trying to screw you out of any commissions. This guy just came out of the blue. How does he know I have a system? Maybe he's working for somebody. Maybe I have a chance to trap whoever is trying to gather information about the system. Your contracts have no meaning. We want this guy on the system so we can watch what he does. He may be another approach by Jian Liu or another company or country trying to find out about the encryption code. We have to show interest in his proposal and see what he does with any information he gathers."

"Right, right. Sorry. You told me to be a salesman through all this, to make it all about the money. The project is gathering steam, systems are going to start moving to the install phase and money is going to start rolling in soon. Sorry, I forgot about your end of it. I'll let Kyle and the field engineers know the system has to go live." Henberlin nodded and there was apology in his tone.

"Good, I'll call you tomorrow. Can you tell Kyle I'm going to need terminals installed in this office now and have him call me?" Delaney asked.

"Will do." Henberlin was about to reach the door.

"There's one more thing. We think we know who killed Yanmei," Delaney said.

Henberlin's hand froze as he reached for the doorknob. He spun, pulling his hand up and placing fingers splayed across his chest.

"We've been looking into who's been in town dealing with Jian Liu for the past few weeks," Delaney said. "There's one guy, a big guy, from the Chinese embassy in Vancouver. You know, the kind with a job title that means he does just about anything? He wouldn't have caught our attention except that we checked to see when he'd been here in the past. It coincides with the time Jian Liu's son disappeared."

"So you think Jian Liu knew his daughter fed him bogus information and they used the same guy to kill her?"

"That could be. We're going to have to proceed on that assumption. That means he may think you're the source of the bad data."

"If I'm the source, then why kill Yanmei? She just passed bad data." He tried to act afraid because he was about to go face-to-face with the man CSIS thought had killed his own daughter. In reality, knowing the wrong man was suspected of the murder washed him with waves of guilt.

"Maybe to scare you. We're going to discuss it, but we'll proceed with our current course."

Henberlin looked up, staring at Delaney, then nodded. Setting the record straight was out of the question. He left to walk back to his office.

The possibility of Delaney deflecting the direction of the murder investigation away from his wife danced in his head as he walked. It would be great to take the pressure off of Leyna, but putting the blame on an innocent man slowed the music. Though, if that man had killed Yanmei's brother, perhaps he deserved to pay the price. Did that also mean they would investigate Jian Liu for ordering the killing of his own daughter? It didn't take much thought to figure out what Jian Liu would do to get himself off that hook.

————

Melanie Jackson picked up the call and went straight into a tirade about lack of communication. Henberlin envisioned her sitting at her desk in Phoenix, one arm flailing in anger, the other wanting to but barely managing to keep the phone held to her ear. Their first meeting in Phoenix, not long after he'd purchased the apartment building, produced an adversarial relationship and somehow he comfortable leaving it in that state. He could tell she was married to her job and he wanted the person responsible for the management of his property to be serious about the work. She'd sold him on her dedication, all the time gesturing with her arms in wide arches, then tiny movements of the wrists, as if she sculpted her thoughts about servicing buildings.

He didn't know if it was due to the upper body activity or the heat outdoors, but Melanie's short round body perspired to the point of a shining forehead and moisture marks at the neckline of her blouse. His retained image included a short skirt making persistent attempts to roll up her thigh. She constantly tugged it lower, but it obeyed a force stronger than gravity to ascend her pink legs.

He apologized, then told her about what had been going on in his life for the past four days. The effect created a stunned calm in Melanie, giving Henberlin a chance to address the reasons he had called her.

"Now that there are systems to delivered, install, and bill I can improve my cash flow a little. I appreciate what you've done during this time when I quite frankly let some things slip by without getting the attention they required. And you are at the top of that list.

"Thanks again for taking the helm of the situation with the water tank. It's a sign that we're both on the same page with regard to the property. I'm sure the five thousand I sent you is gone, so I wanted to have you go ahead and charge another five to my AMEX. Use it for anything else needed for maintenance, and of course to catch up on the fees I owe you."

"I will, and thank you very much. I'm sorry to hear about what you've been dealing with," Melanie's sweet soft voice said.

"We'll get through it. Also, I'm thinking of coming to Phoenix for a visit, you know, to get my wife away from all this for a while. Soon maybe. Can you find us a place for a week or so?"

"Of course. That's never a problem in July. My owners are dying for a little revenue in the summer."

"Great. I'll be back to you soon and I'll do a better job of staying in touch."

"Okay. You said five thousand, right?"

"You bet." He smiled. The call had gone better than expected.

Later, when he finished his call to the order-scheduling department, things were a little different. 'Count to ten,' he told himself, 'do what Leyna does. Stay seated, take deep breaths, and count to ten. This can't be happening.'

He knew he couldn't make his follow-up call until he had control of his anger. The call was going to be a brief request for an immediate meeting. He had to keep his cool. One final deep breath, a long exhale, and he dialed the VP of Sales.

"Can I come see you?"

He listened.

"Yeah, right now."

He listened.

"I'll tell you when I get there."

He hung up.

Geneva told him to go right in, and he spent no time aggravating Brady by delaying with his usual check of the awards on the wall. He went straight and sat in the chair across the desk from the VP. Brady had spun his chair so Henberlin peered at his back. A thinning head of hair rose above the back of the leather chair. Henberlin paid no attention to the muffled words Brady spoke into his phone.

Finally Brady spun around and hung up. "What's this about, Neil?" he said in an abrupt fashion.

"I was just trying to expedite the systems for Contract Geo and Shield, and they told me they hadn't received the signoff from you. What's the holdup?"

"I don't know. I'm sure it's something in the normal process of things. What's the hurry?"

Henberlin wanted to keep his personal issues out of the discussion. "The project is the hurry. You know how much pressure the US is putting on us to get systems installed. Have you seen the orders?"

"Yes. There were some financials missing. When they come in, the process will move forward. You know what paperwork has to accompany an order. I think you were missing the financing options selection. In both cases, we need to know if they're buying or leasing. And if they're leasing, who's holding the paper."

"Payment options have always been a follow-on step. We've always been able to back-fill the process with those forms. Why are you switching it up now? You pissed off because I beat your time constraint?"

"Just trying to light a fire under your ass. Congratulations on the first sales of the new system, by the way. You broke your slump. We knew you could do it." His smile was nowhere close to genuine.

"It was a pleasure to get the monkey off my back. Now could you quit fucking around and get those orders moving? It's Shield Oil for Christ's sake. They have their own financing company. At least get that one moving. Contract Geo's agreed to take the demo machine that arrived yesterday. His paperwork will be here this afternoon. Let's not make a stunned-ass impression on our first customers with blatant assholishness."

Brady's smile perked up a little. "Well, since you put it that way, I'll see what I can do to assist you."

Henberlin knew he'd accomplished nothing.

15

—

The two police detectives stood outside Brady's office to greet Henberlin as he emerged.

Geneva smiled at him and sighed in empathy.

Henberlin greeted the men. "Gentlemen?"

"Could we have a word with you, Mr. Henberlin?" Sweetland requested.

"Sure. My office?"

The two men took seats in front of the desk and Henberlin asked how he could help them. His eyes wandered to the round scar beside Sweetland's right eye and froze there. His stare lasted a few seconds. Then, thinking it obvious that he was staring, he deliberately made eye contact with the detective, who sported a knowing smile.

"Hard not to look at isn't it?" Sweetland asked.

Henberlin looked away and cleared his throat. When he looked back, his eye migrated back to the scar. "Sorry," he said, then cleared his throat again. "Do you mind if I asked how you got that scar?"

Sweetland's eyes bore in on Henberlin without reaction. "An ex-wife gave it to me."

"'An' ex-wife? You have multiple exes?"

"I do."

Henberlin nodded. "Hmm. I'd heard policemen had high divorce rates."

"From what I've seen, all professions do," Sweetland said matter-of-factly.

"Yes, well, I didn't mean to imply anything."

"Mr. Henberlin," Detective Richie started, "do you mind if we get on with our questions?"

"Yes, of course. Sorry."

Sweetland reached into a report-sized envelope and produced a photograph. He slid it across the desk, placing it in front of Henberlin. In the picture was a person in a dark hooded sweatshirt, dark sweat pants, and a dark safari hat. There appeared to be a gun in the person's right hand. Richie asked him if he recognized the woman.

"How do you know it's a woman?" he asked.

Sweetland reached across the desk and pulled the photo back, spun it and looked at it for a few seconds before nodding in understanding. He then stated, "Hmm, I admit it's difficult to tell from the still photo, but in the video it's unmistakable. This person's movements are those of a woman. Do you recognize the woman in this photo?"

"You have a video? From where?" Henberlin responded.

Jian Liu had told Henberlin the police had seen the video but he didn't want them to think he knew of its existence. His mind raced. Had it been in the papers that a video had been the reason for his release from jail and his removal from the list of suspects? How much of the video had they seen? With movement, he probably could identify his wife. In a still picture with no facial features, it wasn't misleading to say he couldn't identify the person.

"Just tell us if you know who this woman is."

"I don't think I can tell from that picture."

"How about the clothing? The woman's height or body shape? Anything?"

Henberlin took his time, wanting to display a small measure of willingness to contemplate the figure in question. He tilted his head to one side then the other before sliding the photo across the desk and shaking his head.

"Nothing?" said detective Richie.

"Can't tell."

Sweetland adjusted the photograph so that it aligned correctly for Henberlin to see. "Did your wife know about your affair with Mrs. Albin?"

Hearing a reference to his wife in relation to Yanmei's murder shot cold bolts of electricity crackling up the back of Henberlin's neck. 'Are they fishing or do they have some reason to think she could have killed Yanmei? Have they had time to investigate Leyna's activities this past Saturday? No, of course not. Are they trying to get me to implicate myself beyond what I know now?' He found his eyes locked on the shiny pink skin of Sweetland's scar.

"Did your ex-wife give you that scar because she caught you in an affair?" Henberlin asked.

Sweetland sat up taller in his chair without taking his eyes off of Henberlin. "That's not pertinent to what we're discussing here."

"No, you're right. It isn't. But now you can feel what it's like to have people imply you did something immoral when, in fact, you did no such thing."

"From all the accounts of the witnesses we asked, it sure looks like you did. Did your wife suspect that you were having an affair?"

"She never said anything, and I didn't notice anything different about her behavior toward me."

"You spent Friday evening with your wife in Vancouver, saw her in the morning as she left your room and then you didn't see her again until Saturday evening, correct?"

"Yes, that sounds right."

"What time did she return to your room from the conference?"

"She arrived at the room just before I did, at six thirty."

"And when did she leave you in the morning?"

"It would have been before nine because that's when I ordered breakfast. She'd left sometime before that."

The two men looked at each other and shrugged. Then detective Sweetland said, "Okay."

119

They started to rise. Henberlin asked, "Why are you all of a sudden interested in my wife?"

"Any time there's an affair..." Richie held up his hands to calm Henberlin as he began to object again about the affair. "Or, uh, suspected affair, jealousy could be the motive. When we thought it was you lying dead in the apartment, we suspected Stephen Albin. Now the jealous person could be your wife. We have to look at everyone involved."

"But she was obviously in Vancouver."

"Right."

The two men left Henberlin alone in his office. Alone and concerned about the sudden change in direction the investigation had taken, his thoughts circled around his wife and her emotional health. It didn't take much imagination to know what would happen if the police found out Leyna killed Yanmei. Both their lives would be shredded. She would need help to get her mind back together, whether she went to jail or not. Therapy would be the only way she could stay sane if she was in custody with no day-to-day access to him. If she evaded detection, she'd need their relationship to get over what she'd done. 'But then, *should* she evade detection?'

She committed the worst possible crime. How could he let her remain free? Allowing her to be caught, to rightfully pay for what she'd done, would get Jian Liu off his back and would free him from his duty to Delaney. But how could he let her be caught? It was Leyna. His wife, the woman he loved, who helped him change his ways. Ways that, by previous indication, could have had him going to jail. Her love for him, his desire to preserve their life together, had saved him more than once. Now he had to save her. Yet, Yanmei deserved better.

There appeared to be no one left to notice that Yanmei had been cheated out of the rest of her life. Her husband was also dead, no trace of her brothers, her colleagues looking for promotions, and her father not interested in his daughter's end because of his quest for the encryption code. She deserved justice. Henberlin knew how to get it for her, but all he could offer was remembrance of the respectable person she was. Her intellect, her integrity, and the kind and loyal friend she had become.

The cell phone Delaney had supplied him rang. He answered and heard Delaney say, "Okay Neil. Everything's ready. Go ahead and call Jian Liu."

"Okay. What about the murder investigation? Are you sure Jian Liu ordered the job? Should I be worried about meeting with him?"

"I don't think you need to worry."

"Why? Do you know if he knew about the bad data?"

"We'll have to meet. I'll tell you about it then."

"You want me to call you after I talk to Jian Liu?"

"Please."

Henberlin hung up and dialed.

————

Following Jian Liu's instructions, Henberlin took a seat at the lunch counter of the Double Greeting, a street-level food court off Third Avenue and Center Street. It was straight across Center Street from the building with the worn wooden door where Jian Liu had first grabbed his attention. At least he'd been told to meet at a good lunch spot. Even during Stampede Week, with the city's emphasis on all things Western like eating beef, the usual crowd appeared at the Chinese lunch counter. Henberlin placed his hat top-side down on the counter.

He order a bowl of seafood conjee, a plate of Shanghai fried noodles, and some dried shrimp rice rolls. He loved to mix white pepper, chili oil, and vinegar in a small side condiment disk and drip some into the rice soup and on top of the noodles. Best hangover lunch he'd ever discovered.

Bowls clanged together, knives chopped, and cooks yelled in fast Chinese a step beyond the short wall that separated the kitchen from the seating counter. Order takers called in food orders and cooks fired up burners, then stacked plates ready to receive the customer's orders. Metal spatulas chimed on woks and woks crashed on burner rings as the cooks tossed ingredients and sauces to make the fresh, hot delicacies. The hunger-generating smell of savory fried food, garlic, onions, noodles, and chicken with the sauces beginning to caramelize on the hot steel reached out of the kitchen to crank up the customers' appetites.

Shortly after the food arrived Jian Liu, sat on the round stool beside Henberlin. He grabbed a small cup and reached for the pot of tea. Henberlin stopped his reach, then lifted the pot and poured for Jian Liu.

Jian Liu tapped the countertop. "How you, Neo Henbrin?"

"There's room for improvement."

"Ha! Always."

"I have something for you. What's all this stuff I'm giving you about?"

"It's about save your wife."

"That's why I'm here, but I think this is a little bigger than it seems. I know what this data is but I don't know what you're doing with it, and don't care. Also, I think it's worth a lot of money."

"To a lot of people it's worth more than money. To you, it's worth your wife. Your wife is free. She's with you every night. I lost my daughter but your wife is still free. You think I don't want to punish your wife? I do, and I can. If the time comes, it will be my pleasure to make her pay."

"But this data isn't what Yanmei wanted most. This is business. When you said you wanted what Yanmei had promised you, you were talking about something else you wanted from me. That's what I thought was going to save my wife. What I have for you today is new and it's business. I should be paid for that."

Grey, vacant eyes stared back at Henberlin. The darkened craggy skin soft and thin. It stretched tight over a flattened nose with outward openings. One or two grey nostril hairs visible over one or two grey whiskers on his upper lip. Nothing in his features moved for a long time but then a slow smiled appeared in the grey eyes and thin purple lips.

"Maybe so, but not today. We have agreement to save your wife and you didn't bring what I wanted?"

"We need to flip it, data for my wife, money for the encryption?"

Again Jian Liu stared.

"Give the data to the waiter and call me tomorrow." Jian Liu stood to go.

"Wait a minute, please. That's it with regard to my wife? You never mention it again?"

"No, no, no Neo Henbrin. I only don't mention it now. We'll see when the other things come around if I have to mention your wife again. Make them come around soon. Your wife doesn't deserve peaceful life. She should live in fear of jail."

"But..."

Jian Liu shook his head and walked away.

Henberlin turned back to his conjee. It had the bland texture of the white porridge broth, the small shrimp and the tentacles of squid between streaks of the chili oil that he knew would burn the way he liked. But after the threats, his appetite had vanished. He sought the waiter, made eye contact, then placed some bills on the counter. Under the bills he placed the flash drive. After seeing the waiter scoop up the bills and palm the hidden drive, he tossed his napkin on the counter and walked out.

16

—

Kyle Badgerclaw waited at the entrance of the tunnel leading to the infield of the famous rodeo and chuck wagon races. He wore well-worn cowboy boots, experienced jeans, a long-sleeved cream white shirt, a red neckerchief, and an immaculate brown straw cowboy hat with eagle feathers stuck in the rawhide hatband. What Henberlin noticed about his native friend was how natural he looked in his cowboy clothing.

Henberlin had on boots he wore only during Stampede Week, jeans, a golf shirt, and a standard white cowboy hat like most of the tourists were wearing. Leyna wore red boots, a denim skirt, Western-cut denim shirt, and a black felt cowboy hat with a shiny red belt hatband, including buckle.

"We were just saying that we've never been inside the track. This is going to be interesting," Henberlin said while reaching out to shake Kyle's hand.

"Hi Leyna. How are you feeling?" Kyle asked.

"Great. Long time no see. Gosh, was it last Stampede?" Leyna had no memory of her ride home from the hospital in the back of Kyle's car. "Thanks for inviting us to join you. You watch from inside all the time?"

"Yes, it's part of the native access."

Kyle had invited Henberlin to the chuck wagon races so they could have a short business discussion and then enjoy a Stampede Week outing. He would have suggested meeting in the apartment, except the police had only returned the apartment to Henberlin that afternoon. Returning to the location of the murders so soon would be a distraction to their discussion. Kyle didn't know if the cleanup crew had done their work and didn't want to be first to see the state of things in the apartment. A meeting at the chuck wagon races offered Henberlin the opportunity to bring Leyna along, as well.

They walked through the tunnel and took positions along the rail on the south side of the infield behind the calf-roping release chutes.

"You wanted to talk to me about something," Henberlin said, leaning against the rail, his back to the outside track.

"Yeah. I've been working on a reservoir simulator in my spare time."

"You have spare time? What's that like?"

"No different than work time when you do the same thing. Anyway, the simulator's coming along. I'm going to be going out on my own pretty soon. I wanted to let you know."

"Well, I know your work is respected, so I imagine you'll do okay. But for the record, you don't have my approval... for purely personal reasons. I won't have an analyst as good as you when you leave."

Kyle smiled. "You could leave with me."

At this statement, Leyna turned from watching the crowd arriving in the grandstand to listen to the conversation.

Henberlin crunched his eyebrows. "What?"

"We have a great opportunity here. You do the sales, marketing, and project planning while I take care of all the development and technical work. We keep it small, a few key clients. We both know at some point R.E.S. is going to allow dealers to sell the new system. You get to stay involved with the machine you're bringing to market, and you make money for yourself, not for Owen Brady."

"Making money always sounds good," Leyna said, turning back to grandstand viewing.

"How soon are you thinking this has to happen?" Henberlin asked, his interest growing.

"Still at least a month or two away. I want to get the first few systems installed with R.E.S. and see how they perform in the real world. The whole opportunity depends on the success of the new gear. You're going to want to get a few of them under your belt before stepping away, as well."

"Plus I'm not letting that prick Owen Brady get his hands on my commissions." Henberlin's voice heated up a touch. "Sounds interesting. I wouldn't mind saying goodbye to R.E.S. at this point. What about our other friend and the work were doing over there?"

"We should have that wrapped pretty soon, don't you think? I need his machine to test my simulator. I'm designing it for optimization in a parallel processing environment. It needs the new system's architecture and power. I can't run this type of code on R.E.S.'s conventional product line. Delaney won't know what I'm doing on it, or won't care."

"Good, use his system as long as you can. I'd sure like to be through with him," Henberlin said with a vacant look, thinking of the problems that his association with CSIS had caused.

"Agreed. Listen, there's another reason I asked you here tonight. I want you to meet someone."

Henberlin scanned the area to see if someone appeared to be waiting to join the conversation. Sure enough, a man wearing flat shoes, slacks that matched a suit jacket left in a closet somewhere, a striped shirt and a tourist's one-size-fits-all Stetson pushed off the rail and walked toward them.

Kyle made the introduction. "Neil Henberlin, this is Roy Warren, an old friend and coworker. And this is Neil's wife, Leyna. Tip your hat to a lady."

Roy lifted his hat an inch off his head and smiled. "Nice to meet you," he said.

Leyna smiled.

Henberlin looked at Warren for a few seconds then said, "You're the analyst who approached Delaney about getting access to the new workstation."

Warren smiled but Kyle answered, "I sent him over there. Roy is one of the best mathematicians I've worked with, and he understands reservoirs. I've asked him to help me with my work. The simulator he approached Delaney about is mine. I need it to run many times more than I can handle in my spare time. Roy can keep it processing when I'm not available."

"Well, that eliminates one mystery. You've got Delaney doing a little square dance over this guy. Your smoke-screen appears to be working, but if you guys worked together in the past, Delaney's going to find out."

"We can smooth that over with your help. If you let on that it appears to be normal, then maybe he'll let it go," Kyle said.

"I'm just here to lend my friend a hand," Warren said. "I'm a consultant who's curious about this system, like everybody else in the business. This could give me an advantage in my own work. But let's leave all that to another discussion. I can't believe what I'm seeing in this city. Is it always dressed up like this? And what are we about to watch here?"

Kyle looked at Warren, mystified by the question. He shook his head, then responded as if the answer were obvious. "The chuck wagon races. I told you that's what we we're here for."

Warren smiled. "I know what you said but that doesn't tell me anything."

"Okay, it's four chuck wagons in a race. They run around the track once. It's a throwback to old-time trail drives. When the cowboys moved camp, the cooks would race to the new site. First wagon to get a fire started at the new site won."

"Oh. What did they win?"

"Who knows? Back then, an extra plate of beans? Today they could win a hundred-thousand dollars."

"A hundred grand for racing around the track one time?" Warren said in amazement.

"No, not one time, they race every night. Best time gets to the final." Kyle turned to look at the infield where the teams prepared for the first race. He concluded his history of chuck wagon races talking back over his shoulder. "Of course it's changed a bit from the old days."

They all watched the teams of horse clamoring into position as they leaned against the inside rail of the track.

Four teams of horses stood wide-eyed, lips sputtering, nostrils snorting, hoofs dancing, waiting for loose reins and freedom to run. The drivers strained on those reins holding the lead horses, pulling back tight on the leather. A claxon gusted a loud rasping squawk. Movement erupted as one man behind each wagon held the reins of his horse in one hand while tossing a small barrel—symbolizing an old camp stove—into a basket suspended from the back of the wagon. This gesture, being the only remaining resemblance to the "old days" style of racing, simulated the breakup of camp.

The drivers released their teams, snapping the reins to start the horses weaving in a figure-eight path marked out by orange, plastic barrels, to make their way out to the track. There were sixteen horses in teams of four, four wagons with drivers standing in their rigs whipping the reins to get their horses moving, plus eight single horses with cowboy outriders. All this spilled onto the track at the same instant, not fifteen feet away from Henberlin and his group.

The thick sound of hoofs tromping the earth, raising dust, mixed with the sound of leather reins slapping the solid, thundering horse flesh. Then, at the speed of sound, the deep base rumbling of the action shattered as a loud crack of wood snapping cut the air with splintering clarity. The third wagon's wooden shaft holding the pin that harnessed the power of the horses to the wagon frame disintegrated, sandwiched between two of the other rigs.

The force of the collision moved the wagon out of alignment with the force of the horses. It lifted the inside rear wheel off the ground, twisting the frame and causing the shaft to break. As the wagon's rear end began to rise and lean toward the inside of the track, the driver must have realized imminent danger. If the jagged remains of the wooden shaft were to stick into the ground, the already-rising back end would jam the front of the wagon and cause it to tumble forward. With perfect timing he jumped, using the momentum of the upending wagon to catapult himself onto the back of the fourth wagon, just then passing by. All this action happened in a matter of seconds. The three remaining wagons kicked up dust and clots of dirt a hundred yards away before anyone uttered a sound.

In front of them, the carcass of the upended wagon laid tilted like a shipwreck on a reef.

"What the hell is this?" Roy Warren asked. He tore his eyes off the wreck to look at the back of Kyle's head. The back because Kyle had turned and continued to follow the race. Kyle flipped his head back for a brief look at Warren, then returned his gaze to the race, trying not to miss any of the action.

"He was lucky."

"Yeah, I'll say." Warren nodded at the back of Kyle's head.

"If that wagon hadn't broken clean away that driver would have lost some of his horses. That's terrible when they have to come out onto the track in front of thousands of people and shoot horses. Those horses cost a lot of money too. They're ex-racehorses."

Leyna turned away at the thought of shooting and they all remained silent as the race finished. The remaining teams passed the finish line on the far side of the track so they could drive around the broken rig.

The remaining nine races didn't have quite the action of the first.

17

—

After a lengthy lunch, Owen Brady munched on antacid tablets while brushing his sparse stringy hair, attempting to remove the hat ring. The hat was the only thing he could do without during Stampede Week's ten-day interruption to business. He looked down at the propped-up mirror in his desk drawer, angled so he could see himself. The object of his discontent, his cowboy hat, rested on the corner of his desk. As he grimaced to check his teeth, he heard the familiar door tap of his secretary, Geneva. He called for her to enter, then flipped down the mirror and closed the drawer.

"I didn't see you come back," she said. "Raymond called a while ago, looking for you."

"Raymond?"

"He said to have you go to his office when you got back."

Brady stood and smoothed the front of his shirt, then pinched and jerked the creases of his jeans. A move he made countless times daily, to make sure the cuffs of his suit pants weren't hung up on his shoes.

"Did he say what it was about?"

Geneva shook her head, her lips pressed in a hard smile.

Brady started to walk to the door but stopped when Geneva asked him if he intended to take his clipboard, something he always carried. He contemplated a minute then said, "No, it's Stampede Week." Then he returned to the desk to grab his hat.

Brady entered Raymond Lerner's office. Raymond, as the President of R.E.S. Canada, occupied a corner office overlooking the train tracks, which benefitted from a northwesterly view of the mountains. He joked that the view at sunset was included in his compensation package. Brady noticed a food services trolley with the remnants of a meal, including wine, sitting off near a wall. At the back of the office, Raymond stood talking with a man wearing a suit. When they spotted Brady they shook hands and the other man left from a rear office door without acknowledging the new arrival.

"Owen, come in, join us," Raymond said, indicating the small table sitting on the other side of the room.

When Brady looked at the table he saw Henberlin sitting in one of the chairs, a post-meal cup of coffee in front of him.

All three men wore cowboy hats, jeans, and boots.

Brady nodded a greeting to Henberlin as he took a seat. As Raymond sat, Brady asked, "Was that Pelle?"

"Yes, here for a brief visit," Raymond said.

"Your boss has been here twice in the last three years and it's usually a big deal and I usually get some face time with him. Why wasn't I told he'd be here?" Brady asked in sincere bewilderment.

"Twice that you know of," Raymond said with eye contact. "He makes special trips for specific reasons and this is one of them. And you don't need to let anyone else know that you saw him."

Brady nodded, maintained eye contact with Raymond, then pointed to his left at Henberlin. "Why is he here?"

"Neil told me that you're dragging your feet a little on the system orders for Shield Oil," Raymond began. When Brady tried to say something, Raymond raised his hand. "This system is Pelle's baby. I don't know if you know that but now you do. He had some concerns about why those systems weren't on the schedule yet, so he left Houston early this morning to come and find out."

"Why didn't you call me and ask me?"

"Neil told me about the delay. When Pelle showed up I told him and he asked to see Neil. He wanted to discuss the progress of the project with Neil, so we had a meeting."

"Again, why wasn't I asked to attend?" Brady's voice grew stern.

"Okay, I'll tell you. Pelle wanted the introduction of the new systems to be Neil's exclusive project from the outset. I insisted that you should be informed of progress since in the future you're going to have responsibility for the product. Somehow, I didn't make it clear to you that you had no responsibility in the project phase.

"At first, keeping you informed wasn't a problem. But Pelle said if you getting in the way to cut you out completely. Pelle asked me to tell you, and these are his words: 'Neil is in charge of this product line. He reports to me,' meaning Pelle, 'in this regard. Anything he says needs to be done is the same as me saying it needs to be done,' again meaning Pelle. Owen, do not let paperwork delay any of Neil's efforts."

"That's not right. If I'm not in charge of the sales of these systems now and in the follow-on phases, then I don't want anything to do with the project."

Henberlin spoke for the first time. "Okay. Then I no longer have to keep Owen in the loop."

"Now wait," said Raymond. "I still inherit the products when they hit general release. You're going to be part of International when that happens, so I need someone in management here who knows what's been going on."

"Yeah, let's not be hasty here, Neil," Brady said. "Now that I understand the importance this project carries with Pelle, I guess I can work that way."

"In my opinion, it's a waste of time updating Owen. Pelle said if he threatened to drop out, let him," Henberlin said, seeing his opportunity to be rid of Owen Brady.

"I know," Raymond said, "and if he'd stuck to his guns about not wanting anything to do with the project I'd have left him out. But..."

Henberlin refused reaction and they sat in silence until Brady said, "I'll get the orders signed off right away."

"No need," Henberlin said. "Pelle gave me signing authority. I'll make sure Geneva gets copies of my reports."

———

Henberlin stopped by Kyle's office. He expected a call from Brady and didn't want to be in his own office to receive it or put up with Brady's eventual drop-in. He closed the door, lowered the blinds in the window beside the door, then sat forward in the visitor chair and spoke in a low voice. "How serious are you?" he asked.

Kyle shifted his eyes to the door then back to Henberlin. "Serious."

"You've got something tangible?"

"I think so."

"At project's end I'm scheduled to move to Houston to become international marketing manager for the workstations. That means I'll be in charge of any dealer networks that R.E.S. sets up. I wanted you to come along but if you're serious you need to set up your operation and be ready to go. If you leave before the project ends we'll hire you back as a consultant. Then, when the time comes, you'll be a dealer."

"What about you?"

"When you made that offer at the races everything got more complicated. I'm still working on it. I'll tell Delaney that I met Roy and I'll smooth things so he gets access to the system."

"Okay. The Contract Geo system had first boot this morning. The machine engineer is still tweaking the operating system. I may have hands-on tomorrow."

Henberlin sat up and smiled. "Great, but listen, I'm going to be gone tomorrow afternoon and for the rest of the week. I'll be connecting via VPN so I'll be in touch. I'm doing a gin breakfast with Shield, then I'm gone. I'll be back for their barbecue Saturday. You going to that?"

"I wish. You think they're going to be in a party mood after the loss of both Albins?"

"No, not at all. It surprised me when they told me the event would go ahead as planned. Maybe it's what they all need, Stampede Week diversions to help forget. I don't think that's going to work for me. Time away might, that's why I want to get Leyna out of here for a while. And she can work from a remote site, too."

———

Back in his own office, Henberlin ignored the messages from Owen Brady. Instead he got online to Air Canada where he booked a flight to Los Angeles. After, he rented a car at a different website. If they attempted to track him, he had no intention of making it easy for them. He took a deep breath and relaxed a touch at having his travel plans in place. Then he called the police to see if he could have the apartment cleaned. The operator transferred him to Detective Sweetland.

"We're done with it so have at 'er," Sweetland said. "By the way, we've been talking about your wife's attendance at the conference the Saturday in Vancouver."

"What about it?" Henberlin asked.

"We have a few questions we'd like to ask her."

"I don't think that's necessary. I told you when she left me and when we met again. Where is this leading?"

"We don't know, but we'd like to hear her story from her. How's she doing anyway? Could we drop by tonight?"

"She has bouts of inward turning. At those times I don't seem to be able to get through to her. I don't think tonight is a good idea. I need to prepare her for your visit and what you want to talk to her about. She's been coming along, but she's still not right."

"Call me tomorrow. And Henberlin... we're going to talk with her tomorrow if we hear from you or not. Call and let us know when, and it will all go down easier."

"That almost sounds like courtesy, Detective."

———

During the early evening, Henberlin decided to tell Leyna about the changes to the trip they were taking the next afternoon to Phoenix.

"About tomorrow, a colleague of mine in the Los Angeles office has asked me for some information regarding some analysis we've been conducting on the new system. I had to make a slight change to our flight plans tomorrow," Henberlin said.

Leyna's shoulders slumped and she turned and looked away.

Henberlin thought, 'Does she know I'm lying?' He needed a reason to explain why they were travelling to L.A. He wanted to hide their real destination from anyone who might try to track them, and feared telling her his intent to avoid the detectives because he didn't want her to panic.

"It's not that bad. Nothing really. Instead of flying to Phoenix we go to L.A. The guy meets us at the airport, I give him the data and we're on our way again. We'll rent a car and drive to Phoenix. If you're tired, we can spend the night in Palm Springs. Kind of like adding on to our adventure."

Leyna's smile returned. He walked to her, took her in his arms and they held each other for a time. As they stood in their kitchen, the weight of her body pressed down on his arms and shoulders as she became dependent on his support. He led her to the bedroom so they could lie down on the bed and hold each other for the comfort of possessing each other's bodies.

With their bodies warming to each other, he asked if they could talk about what happened in the apartment. A long silence followed. He didn't want to press her, but he needed to know her state of mind. He wanted her to express a degree of remorse, not retain the arrogance of how well she'd performed her crime. Did she think she had a future of freedom? When he finally broke the silence, her response surprised him.

"I know I did it. I know I did something awful, something that is the worst thing a person can do to another person, but I'm starting to have difficulty remembering the details. I don't understand what state of mind I could be in to make me want to kill someone.

"I mean, I love you Neil, I want to be with you more than anything. But I don't remember thinking it would be the worst thing if I lost you. There was no desperation. I didn't think that no matter what it took to keep you I would do it."

"Then what triggered it?"

"I don't know. It scares me, though."

They lay in silence again. He remained wide awake thinking of her words, thinking of his own fear. From her regular breathing, he knew she too remained awake. Surprised at how late it had become, hunger got the best of both of them, and they knew they had to go out.

Whenever Leyna and Henberlin had a craving to go out for a bite, but had no idea what would satisfy their appetites, they always ended up at a small trattoria in the Flatiron Building of the Kensington district. Darkness hung ready to drop, which in July meant near ten-thirty.

In the restaurant, he ordered spaghetti in a marinara cheddar sauce that the restaurant's chef had created and had gained a reputation for. The balance between the fatty sharpness of the cheese and the acidity of the tomato sauce verged on perfection. He overlooked the fact that the dish violated the rule of no cheese with seafood. Three large shrimp garnished the top of the pasta, cooked with the deserved attention needed to preserve the delicate flavor of the sea. Leyna ordered the Caprese salad, ate the cheese, basil, and tomatoes joyously, then mopped up the remaining dressing with toasted bread.

When they finished the main course, they ordered coffee, knowing they wouldn't sleep whether they consumed caffeine or not. He knew this would be especially true after he broached the detective's request to talk with her.

"Leyna, another reason why I'm taking you away is to hide you."

Leyna swallowed. "From?"

"The detectives want to ask you about your attendance at the conference."

"They're not that smart. What made them think I could have slipped away?"

"I'm not sure they do think you slipped away. They came to see me and asked about when you left the room on Saturday morning and when you met with me that evening. Do you feel up to talking to them?"

"Do I have a choice? I'll talk to them, they won't get anything they can use from me."

"Why take the chance? Why stay in Calgary? If we leave and work from Phoenix we can avoid them for a while. We can then determine if you can ever come home."

"You mean I could be leaving for good? Going into hiding? They think there's a chance I did it and you think they're on to me, or you wouldn't be taking me away." She became quiet. The joy she'd displayed while enjoying her food wilted in an instant. She polished the end of her fork without knowing she had her fingers on it. "That's what you said, you were taking me away to hide me. Oh Neil, what do I do?"

"What do *we* do? I'm going to be with you."

"Do I need a lawyer? I don't want a lawyer. Won't that make the police think I'm trying to hide something?"

Henberlin had been thinking along these lines for a few days now. Shielding his wife behind a lawyer could be perceived as a defensive move indicating guilt. Without a lawyer, they would appear to be cooperating, doing what they can to help, shedding suspicion. If his wife's timing with the travel and her visibility at the conference were enough to make the police think she couldn't have made the trip, why get them thinking they had something to hide?

"I know, but I think it may be the right thing to do." He finally said.

"Wouldn't we have to tell a lawyer the truth? Wouldn't he then change his strategy with regard to what the best defense would look like? What if a lawyer says we should attempt a plea bargain? We'd be giving up."

Henberlin's relief that his wife still had her wits about her bolstered his confidence. She knew her situation and wanted to keep her crime between her and her husband as long as possible. Still, were they doing the right thing? He held his belief that punishment needed to be dealt to those who commit a crime and the most serious crimes deserved an equal punishment.

18

—

Marlin Walker became the interim department manager of Reservoir Simulation for Shield Oil, taking over for Stephen Albin. He told Henberlin at the gin breakfast that Shield wanted to increase the number of systems they wished to install in the first wave to fifteen. Henberlin thought he heard chimes at the news. His first instinct—to return to his office and process the new orders—took some concentrated effort to staunch.

Relationship building with Walker was Henberlin's reason for doing the gin breakfast in the first place. It still had priority. He worried that the current production level of the systems wouldn't allow him to make a definite installation date commitment to Shield. He knew he could have that information to Walker by mid-afternoon, but also knew, after a gin breakfast, Walker wasn't likely to care when he received the information. Hell, after a gin breakfast, he hoped Walker would remember he'd increased the order.

Next, he wondered about his trip to Phoenix to avoid contact between his wife and the detectives. The timing couldn't be worse from a business standpoint. Still, he had to go. Working over the internet wouldn't be a problem, dealing with customers would. A price he had to pay since he had to buy his wife time before allowing her to deal with the detectives. Now that their interest in her activities at the conference indicated they were getting on the right track, he had to make sure she could handle their questions. Leyna's freedom—taking her away to preserve her freedom as if she were guilty—dominated his thoughts as the gin breakfast progressed. But then he had to check himself. Leyna *was* guilty. The detectives would think her leaving was a sure sign of guilt and they weren't going to be happy.

Walker didn't mention the systems again for the remainder of the event. He seemed more interested in how many pitchers of gin and orange juice their party could consume. Henberlin tried to make it look like he enjoyed the festivities, but made sure to limit his alcohol intake.

By late morning, the inebriated imitation cowboys poured out onto Eighth Avenue looking for a place to enter stage two of a day-long drinking marathon. Beef-on-a-bun and a switch to draft beer seemed to be the desired pursuit among them. Henberlin remained with the group until they arrived at the door of the next establishment, then made his apologies, turning down request after request to have just one beer. He departed for his office to make a few arrangements before leaving the city.

A few minutes later, in his office, he had his answer regarding system production. Kyle had the information on Henberlin's desk thanks to a text from Henberlin he'd received earlier. Delivery dates looked favorable for the additional systems, so he calendared himself a note to work on the pricing when he got to Phoenix. On top of that good news, two of the first systems ordered had arrived in Calgary and would be staged the next day. Kyle would be spearheading the process. The American system engineer had suggested Kyle be the hands-on analyst in order to gain more familiarity with the systems. Installation of Delaney's system would take place in R.E.S.'s data center, the other system would be delivered to Shield before Henberlin returned.

Included in his list of messages were two from Detective Sweetland. His cell phone had a couple from the detective as well. One surprise message came from American Express. Missing last month's payment and charging close to fifteen thousand dollars in the past ten days had set off some alarms in the receivables department. That call would have to wait until he arranged a commission loan and had something positive to tell their collections group. Also on the waiting list, Jian Liu and Delaney. He didn't want to let them make any demands until he settled in Arizona. He did plan on calling Sweetland.

The next hour he spent sending emails to other members of the project team—updating them on time frames and upcoming new orders. He sent a brief email to Raymond regarding Shield's interest in additional systems, and that the production schedule could handle the additions. He knew Raymond would want to grandstand a little by forwarding the email to Pelle in the US.

Before he finally packed up his notebook and the files he needed to take with him, his phone rang. The display showed Raymond Lerner's name.

"Hold for Raymond, Mr. Henberlin," Raymond's secretary said.

Seconds later Raymond's voice sounded through the headset. "Neil, Pelle says thanks for the update. He doesn't know how to send email so he called me and asked me to express his appreciation."

"Oh, well thanks for letting him know."

"My pleasure. Take care." And Raymond hung up.

With additional sales beginning to mount up, it was going to be easier to beg forgiveness for leaving town during the critical first installations.

Now, the detectives. The confidence-building call from Raymond had come at the right time. He dialed Sweetland.

"Is there any way we could put this off for another day or two? When I told her about your insistence on an interview, she almost regressed to the state you put her in when you arrested me," Henberlin said.

"I'm sorry to upset her but this is important. It's well within reason to expect her to be able to address the matter after this passage of time. I'm afraid I'm going to insist on meeting her today."

"You haven't told us why it's so important. She's accounted for her time that entire weekend. You can't just maraud over people's emotions without supplying some reasoning behind your intrusions. We want to cooperate, but at this point, we don't know what we can add to your investigation. Bullying us without providing reasons is making us less willing to talk with you."

"Your wife is a person-of-interest in the case."

"Does that mean she's a suspect?"

"Not yet."

"So we're under no obligation to talk to you?"

"Correct, but that makes it look like you have something to hide."

"We have nothing to hide. I have someone to protect. You haven't seen how all this has affected my wife and you are the cause of most of her stress. If you hadn't hit the affair side of the situation so hard, she would have been in better shape to address your concerns."

"Don't try to make investigative procedures the villain here, Mr. Henberlin. Here's what I'm willing to do: We meet tonight with your wife. If she helps us do our job, we'll try to get it done in fifteen minutes. If you don't agree to that, we'll arrest her and interrogate her as an uncooperative witness. Your choice."

"I stay in the room while you interview her."

"No way, we want her alone."

"Why? She's not going to do very well on her own."

"You know why. Seven o'clock is good for us."

Henberlin thought for a second or two. They weren't going to be happy when they arrived at a dark house. "Okay, seven o'clock."

———

Tickets and passports passed inspection without a hitch. They were through Immigration. Henberlin lifted their luggage onto the US Customs conveyer belt and they cleared Customs. Just like that, they were officially in the United States. With little time to spare, they still agreed that a quick drink in the bar would help get them settled for the flight. Both drank in silence until the phone Delaney supplied Henberlin rang. He looked at the display out of habit, shook his head, and powered the device off.

He looked up, stared at a distance, and not meaning to speak out loud said, "He's tailing us."

"Who?"

"Nobody who can't wait until tomorrow. Don't worry. Let's go, our row has probably already been called."

Then the disposable phone that he used to contact Jian Liu rang. He turned it off as well saying, "He's tailing us too."

"Who? You're making me nervous," Leyna said as they showed the gate attendant their passports before entering the jetway.

19

—

Kyle toggled between the virtual screens he had set up to monitor the system installation of the two new workstations. He'd also setup virtual screens to monitor his access to the main R.E.S. system where he had test programming going forward, and he had a virtual session monitoring the company email distribution system.

Raymond had asked him to figure out a way to process the email accounts through the new encryption technology that would be inherent in the new operating system. The way corporate email systems were being hacked these days, Raymond stressed the need for as much security on internal communications as they could lay their microchips on. Until Kyle had an email server on a computer utilizing the new encryption-based operating system, there wasn't much he could do except familiarize himself with the system structure of the current email server.

In general, these pedestrian-type applications bored him. Incorporating the genius of the encryption software with the email service provided the only motivation he held for the project.

His toggling from screen to screen and the brief attention he directed to the new information on display annoyed detectives Sweetland and Richie, who sat across the desk from him.

"Mister Badgerclaw?" Richie said to get Kyle's attention.

"Oh, sorry. No, I don't know where he went."

"We've established that. Why don't you know where he went?"

"He and the other sales guys leave town a lot. Sometimes even when they tell me where they're going, I don't know where they are."

"Do you think he'll contact you?"

"Yes. I'm sure he plans to work remotely. At some point, he'll log in to one of our systems. I'm supposed to put pertinent files in a shared project directory so he can see them whenever he wants."

"Can you tell if he's logged in now?"

"I've been checking the whole time you've been here, and he's not."

"Can you tell if he logged in earlier?"

"His last remote login was yesterday afternoon at two forty-eight. I presume before he left his home."

As Kyle responded to the detectives, the tab on his email screen began to blink. He toggled to the email system and saw that he had a chat request from user OB1, whom he assumed to be Owen Brady. He ignored it and it stopped blinking. Seconds later the blinking started again. Best to let Owen know he would have to wait. He accepted the chat and began typing the conversation while the two detectives sat frustrated at another of his toggled interruptions.

BADG-> Sorry, tied up for a while. Contact later.

OB1-> Kyle its me N. OK 2 chat?

BADG-> Not now. People here want to hear from
  you.

OB1-> What people?

"Mister Badgerclaw?" Richie's voice had a little less patience.

"Sorry. I've got stuff running that needs my attention."

"If you could just hear us out for a minute, we'll let you go."

Kyle looked down at his screen.

OB1-> You still there?

BADG-> Detectives. Give me 10. Call back.

He disconnected the chat before Henberlin could respond, then killed the email virtual session.

"Okay, let me check one more thing, then we can finish." Kyle toggled.

"When Neil Henberlin does dial-in, will you be able to tell where he's located?" This time it was Sweetland speaking.

"He won't *dial-in*, but I know what you mean. He'll be connecting via an R.E.S. Virtual Private Network or VPN. This is a security mechanism that can only be accessed by people who have security clearance for our VPN. The VPN then changes the IP address of the requesting computer masking the access to an IP address assigned to our VPN. It's the same sort of setup that allows people abroad to watch American television on streaming sites when they're in geographical territories where the local IP address blocks the foreign content. The streaming site that's supposed to reject transmission believes the requesting system is in the proper geographic territory. When Neil connects, his IP address will be valid within our VPN and one that we can tell is remote. But we can't tell its originating IP address, therefore its location."

"I don't know what all that means but you're saying no?"

"Correct, no."

"If you don't mind, I'm going to have one of the computer specialists from the force call you to get clear on that."

"Fine."

"I'll call you later today to see if Henberlin has called in. If you talk to him, tell him it's important that he call us."

"I will."

―――――

Delaney still hadn't recovered from the appearance of Roy Warren baring gifts. He had been dialing Henberlin's personal cell phone as well as the private one CSIS supplied him. He'd been on the verge of putting in a trace with the CIA, but decided not to have them think he couldn't control his assets. Then Warren showed up in his lobby.

"I wanted to thank you for allowing me to have a little processing time on your new workstation, and to talk to you about the arrangements," Warren said.

Delaney looked at him a little dumbfounded and shook his head. "I'm sorry, you're going to have to remind me."

"Did Neil talk to you?"

"I've been trying to reach him all morning. Did you talk to him?"

"No, not since Saturday night at the wagon races. But he said he would talk to you about me testing some reservoir software on your system. I'm here to find out when that can occur and to give you a small gift of appreciation." Warren held out a small bag stuffed with bubble wrap.

"Well this isn't at all necessary. Why don't you come back to my office?"

As they sat down Delaney asked again, "You haven't talked to Henberlin today? Do you know where I can reach him?"

"Sorry. I expect you've tried his office?"

Delaney nodded.

"I asked him if he'd ever heard of you and he said he hadn't. Now you're saying he intended to contact me on your behalf?"

"Yes, Neil's analyst Kyle Badgerclaw and I go way back. I'd contacted Kyle recently to kind of stay in touch, and he told me about his current project involving the new R.E.S. workstation. He told me about your system and the possibility it would have some idle time. Lights went on for me, and that's when I flew up here and approached you. You didn't seem too keen on the idea, so I asked Kyle to introduce me to Neil and then I asked Neil to talk to you about letting me access your system. Sorry to spring that on you. I thought he would have talked to you by now."

Delaney sat quiet for a moment, then picked up his phone and dialed.

"Kyle Badgerclaw please."

He kept his eye on Warren while waiting for Kyle.

"Kyle, Delaney here." Silence from Delaney while he listened. "Nothing? Make sure to have him call me. I've got something else for you. There's a Roy Warren sitting in my office. He says you go way back. That true?"

Another silent waiting session.

"Okay." Delaney finally said and hung up. "Okay Mr. Warren, Kyle says it will be a day or two before you can access the system from this office. Stay in touch with him, then let me know when you're coming. How do you know Kyle?"

"Well, we met under similar circumstances to what we're going through now. Back in college, we crossed paths in the mathematics department here at the University. I needed access to a vector-processing computer and the only ones available came from commercial data-servicing companies. They cost money and I couldn't afford the rates. But native students received a grant that they could use for outside services. I asked Kyle if he planned on using his and then worked out a deal for him to set up an account with the computer service company. His creativity and playfulness while setting up the account went a long way toward us remaining friends."

Back then, Warren had explained the grants to Kyle and convinced him to go along with the plan. One day, Kyle found himself entering the offices of Continental DP Timeshare, the owners of a Beta-Vec supercomputer. He stated to the receptionist that he wanted an account to do some processing on the Beta-Vec. The receptionist looked across her desk at him. A clean-cut native with long black hair, not combed but not messed up, either. A checked brown shirt, worn jeans with a large round turquoise buckle, scuffed work boots, and a large padded computer carry-case over his shoulder. Her first thought was to get rid of him.

"I'm sorry but we don't set up accounts for individuals, only companies." She smiled.

"Oh. Well, I'm native. I have a grant."

"Sorry, I don't know anything about a grant, so..."

"It's okay. Your manager will know about the grants. Just tell him I'm a native."

"It's a she. Our manager is a she. And I'm afraid I'll have to take a message and have her get in touch with you."

"Excuse me."

Kyle and the receptionist turned to face a blond woman, well dressed and confident. She made eye contact with Kyle, ignoring the receptionist.

"Are you speaking of the Native Affirmative Science Endowment grants?"

Kyle didn't know the actual name of the grants but he went with it.

"Those are the ones," he said, giving her one nod.

Even though reservoir simulation applications were the perfect target for Continental's Beta-Vec business, new accounts had proven difficult to acquire. The manager had no intention of letting someone who walks in the door asking for access to the Super-Computer to walk away without being heard.

"Okay, please come with me Mr...?"

"Badgerclaw, but you can call me Kyle."

"Kyle, I'm Shelly Brant. It's nice to meet you. I want to introduce you to our Beta-Vec specialist."

They walked down a hall. At an open door, Shelly asked him to grab a seat while she fetched the specialist. The specialist was currently performing busy work, straightening up the documentation room. He welcomed the interruption when Shelly summoned him. A short time later, they'd returned to the meeting room and Shelly introduced Kim Parnel to Kyle. That done, she said she'd leave them to their discussion and turned to leave.

"Wait," said Kyle, "don't I get to talk to you?"

"I'm sorry Kyle, but Kim here knows a lot more about the Beta-Vec than I do. I'm sure you'll find it a better use of your time to talk to someone who can answer your questions." Shelly's disarming smile could gain agreement from anyone after mere seconds of exposure. Kyle developed the symptoms of agreement and nodded, happy at having the smile aimed his way, though he'd rather have her stay.

Kim settled into one of the soft brown ultra-suede chairs that surrounded the long wooden conference table. The walls of the room were spotted with watercolor prints depicting Western scenes, all produced by Western artists.

"What is it that you wish to use the Beta-Vec for Mr. Badgerclaw?"

Kyle preferred to be called Kyle, though he enjoyed hearing a white man call him mister. Gratification for the a small amount of perception change of Native Canadians he would facilitate in the eyes of the white establishment.

"Analysis," he replied.

"Would that be financial or scientific?"

"Scientific."

"Good. What type of scientific analysis is it that you do Mr. Badgerclaw?" Kim's voice took on a testy element due to Kyle's short answers.

"Petroleum."

"Ah… is it reservoir- or seismic-oriented?" Kim perked up a bit.

Kyle knew that petroleum analysis meant bigger budgets and bigger commissions. His next answer would have Kim's internal compensation calculator tap dancing.

"I do reservoir simulation." Bingo. That brought out Kim's smile.

"I see. Do you work for one of the oil companies?"

Kyle thought that Shelly must not have told him about the Native grant and how he could afford to ask for time on a supercomputer.

"No," he said, then waited while the smile faded from Kim's face before continuing. "I work for many oil companies, in many countries." He used a sly tone and turned his head, keeping his eyes on Kim.

Kim hesitated a moment.

"Tell me about these companies you work for."

"Some of them are governments, but I won't say which ones." Now he entered full leg-tugging mode.

"But it's all petroleum-related analysis that you perform, right?"

"Sure, let's say that."

Kim looked down at the table and nodded several times.

"How is it that you get these work assignments from companies and governments?"

"They call me and arrange a time for a data transfer. It's dropped onto a shared server and I copy the data to a flash drive. I move it to the processor I'm going to use, do the simulations, and send them the results."

"And then they pay you?"

"If they like the results I send them, they pay. I give them a money-back guarantee on my work. Like a discount furniture store."

"What? A furniture store?"

"That's the way to keep customers coming back. That and huge limited-time discounts or buy-one-get-one free sales, or nothing down and no interest until next year." Kyle held a straight face and entered the ensuing staring contest intent on remaining locked in for as long as it takes.

Kim took up the challenge for about half a minute then twisted his head and scrunched his face on one side before saying, "You're shitting me."

Kyle laughed. "Yes, I take it that Shelly didn't tell you about the Native grant accounts?"

———

Warren leaned back in his chair in Delaney's office and said, "He's always had a subdued sense of humor. Not up front all the time, but it's there and you never know when it's coming."

"He's always so serious when I talk with him, but I detect the spirit of a jokester from time to time. He clowns around a bit with Neil," Delaney said.

"Anyway, Kyle introduced me to Neil. I assume he gave Neil the background between us and then he asked Neil to intervene with you so I could get a little work done. I wanted to get started right away but this Stampede Week thing keeps getting in the way. Have you ever stayed at the Indian Village?"

"Where, down at the Stampede grounds?"

"Yeah, you get to sleep in a real teepee. Kyle set me up with a family to stay one night, said it was quite an honor. They sleep on a thin blanket laid out on the ground—my back hurt the entire night. The kids and dogs get up really early and were staring at me like I fell asleep in the wrong place."

"Did Kyle stay with you?"

"Yeah, kind of. He said he was in another tent."

"Right, I'm sure it was his own 'tent,' the three-thousand square-foot bungalow teepee that he owns in Shaugnessy. Did you at least get breakfast?" Delaney chuckled.

"That son of a bitch," Warren said.

The two men shook hands and Warren asked for the shortest route to Kyle's office.

20

—

Hummingbirds attacked each other with buzz dives, feather-seeking missiles trying to gain domain over the blood red sugar water contained in the feeder. Henberlin, up since sunrise drinking coffee on the patio, immersed himself in the action for the last hour. From time to time, the brave little birds checked out his human figure sitting close to their prize. They took turns hovering a few feet from Henberlin's face, a few quick position shifts up or down, a head turn or two checking their perimeter, their wings a beating blur. The curious bird currently monitoring him and the surrounding sky expected a rival to launch a head-on dive bomb attack any second in a mission to acquire some of the sweet liquid. A flank attack came out of nowhere and both birds blasted off in a chase, around and through the leaves of an olive tree, over the row of bougainvillea, then disappearing behind the tennis courts. Again and again the persistent mini avian battlers returned. Never giving up, always wanting complete control of the food source.

The welcome diversion ended as Leyna slid the patio door open. He wished Leyna would sleep longer; she needed the rest. They both knew early morning was the best time to sit outside during July in Arizona. To make the best use of their time during the trip meant getting up early. If he rose first, being alone allowed him to get his thoughts in order. Fleeing Calgary may not have been the best plan but, it's what he came up with in the short time he had to find a way to protect his wife. Time to think didn't exist back home right now, and it wasn't until the drive from Los Angeles, Leyna asleep beside him, that he tried to appraise their predicament.

A few realities set off sirens he wondered if he could handle. The first reality being that it seemed they were on the run, trying to get away with murder. Once they were safe, away from Canadian law enforcement, he thought of setting Leyna up where no one could find her. Then he'd go back to Calgary to straighten out the situation. What could the best outcome of a murder be? For the murderer: Never getting caught. For the victim's family: The murderer paying a heavy price for committing the crime. For society: Fair application of the law. For the victim: Justice.

The second reality that set off sirens was the fact he was obstructing justice. What was that going to cost him? How much was he willing to pay?

The detectives would soon commit to Leyna being the number-one suspect. He had to make sure they thought he still didn't know and never did. A spouse always wants to believe in their counterpart's innocence. He had to convince them he couldn't bring himself to believe she could do such a thing. Not a real stretch, he had to admit. He still couldn't believe it was true.

"It scared me when I woke up and couldn't find you inside. I thought you left me," Leyna said.

"I'm not going to leave you. But we may have to separate for a short time."

He watched Leyna deflate. "I can't... I can't let you leave me."

"Leyna, the detectives are asking about your time on that Saturday of the conference. They're referring to you as a person-of-interest, and soon they're going to consider you a suspect. I'm going to talk to them this morning to set up a meeting. I'll go back and talk with them to arrange for you to come back and give them an interview."

"You would leave me here alone?" Her tone changed to accusatory.

"For a day. They're desperate to talk to you, they'll want you back as soon as possible so they'll make some kind of deal with me to get you back," he said, detecting his wife's genuine discomfort at being left alone.

"What kind of deal could you make? We have nothing to offer."

"Crime of passion."

"But then I'd be confessing." She looked at him as if he'd lost his mind. "I'll go to jail or to an institution. I thought you were trying to protect me, to keep me free so we could still be together. You can't let them lock me up."

"Leyna, I'm not saying that's what we're going to do, but it may end up being the only way we can get out of this. Then you'll get a few years in jail or a hospital. I'll visit and be waiting for you. We'll still have time together when you get out."

"No." Her voice was firm, anger creeping in. Her neck muscles tensed and she held her hands on either side of her head. "I'll lose you. You're trying to get rid of me. You're mad at me because I killed your girlfriend."

"No, Leyna, listen. It's horrible that you killed someone for no reason. You should have confronted me with your suspicions instead of acting out on them. I would have told you everything, even though I'd sworn not to. I wouldn't have let you get into this position, but now that you're in it, I'm going to get you out of it." For the first time Henberlin entertained thoughts of his wife slipping away from him.

"If I'm who they're going after, there's no getting out of it unless we run. I'll go to jail if they catch me."

"I think we can justify our coming here based on you having a mental breakdown. They won't like it, but so what. That will buy us time to put your explanation together. You have to provide information that proves you were at the conference.

"Remember when you told me about the timing and how it worked out? You were almost proud of the way you pulled it off, saying they couldn't prove you weren't at the conference." He saw

Leyna sit up straight in her chair, gathering herself. "You have to follow through with that level of confidence. You have to give them enough concrete evidence of how you spent that day to make them doubt you had the time to make the trip. Even if they continue to think you did it, their only hope is solid proof that you travelled back to Calgary. If your contacts with people at the conference that day show the tight timeline you set up, then they'll never be able to prove you left, flew to Calgary, committed the murder, and returned to Vancouver by the time you were with people in the hotel bar."

"Why can't I go back with you?" Her eyes were clear and alert as she asked.

"Because they'll arrest you and take your statement in jail. I want them to agree to leave you free while they investigate. You'll cooperate because you have nothing to hide." He had to sound convincing.

"But I think I'll do okay in an interview. I know I can handle them if I stick to my story, like you say."

"I do too, but there's also Jian Liu. He's been sounding a little more threatening. Now that he sees I can take you out of his reach, he may get a little jumpy. I want to figure out his level of annoyance before you return."

"Neil, I killed that man's daughter because I don't want to be without you." Excited at first, her eyes dropped again. She stared at her coffee mug and spoke in monotone. "I can't let you leave me."

He watched her, noting her eyes didn't blink and her chest made scant movement when it rose to breathe. He touched her hand and said, "We'll figure out a way. We're going to be together."

He convinced Leyna to lay down and rest. He had to make some calls, then he'd talk with her again after she woke up. He made sure she took a tranquilizer so she'd be out for a while.

With Leyna in a deep sleep, he called Kyle and got an update on the detectives. Not much there except they insisted that he call them. As far as the workstation implementations, everything remained on schedule. Communications to Delaney's office were up and working, so Roy Warren would be accessing the system the next day. The system for Shield Oil configured as planned and would be on site the next day. Their analysts would be logging into the station by Thursday. Kyle reminded him to call the detectives and Delaney, then they said goodbye.

Delaney blew a gasket when he recognized Henberlin's voice. Henberlin had learned at an earlier time in his sales career that, when a customer got angry, the best thing to do was let them vent. To not try to defend your actions until they'd laid all their frustrations on the table. Then you had to show that you understood and had your reasons for doing what you had done, but you had misunderstood the customer's wishes. Now that you knew, you would act according to those wishes. Customer relationship restored.

He listened as Delaney threatened him with putting everything they'd done at risk, called him an amateur, accused him of being unreliable, and reminded him that, as long as he was part of the effort to find out what the Chinese wanted with the new system, he reported to Delaney. When Delaney threatened to end Henberlin's involvement, Henberlin suggested that would be a great solution. But he bet Jian Liu wouldn't stop pressuring him for the encryption code.

"Do I tell him I don't have to give him the code any longer because CSIS fired me?"

Jian Liu was the one who said whether or not Henberlin was no longer involved.

"So where are you?" Delaney asked in acceptance.

"That doesn't matter. I'll be back in a couple days. You can get me on the same phone by leaving a message. Then I'll call you back."

"You're still in L.A.?"

"Sure. Now I have to call Jian Liu. I plan to tell him that the code he's after is in machine language form on the workstations. The only way to see how it works is to decompile it from a system dump after it runs. It'll take a few days to make sure the decompiler is ready.

Kyle's onboard with this. Has anything happened, or is there anything you want me to say to Jian Liu?"

"No. Does he know you've left the country?"

"Probably. I don't know why he'd care except he wanted to meet with me to get the code. He'll be mad that it's still not available, but that's tough. He's still desperate to get his hands on it."

"We've had eyes on him the past two days. He's looking for you everywhere. He's got people in front of your house, outside your office building, at the apartment. They want the code yesterday. Whoever's putting the pressure on him has some big chops. He's run things however he wanted up until now, so I expect he's going to be pretty hostile."

"I'll let you know."

"Say, Neil, why did you leave in such a hurry?"

Henberlin took the phone away from his ear and cocked his head looking at the device, wondering what to tell Delaney about the murder investigation and the imminent development he wasn't looking forward to.

"My wife is having some issues with regard to the murders. I thought it best to get her out of that environment for a few days' rest. If I tried to clear it with you, Jian Liu, and my boss, it likely wouldn't have happened."

"Yeah, probably not. I wondered when you were going to address your wife's involvement in the murder investigation. You never mentioned she's the prime suspect."

'How does Delaney know that? He's talked to the detectives and they're calling her the prime suspect,' he thought.

"She won't be for long. Those detectives only have a theory that they can't get off their minds. She's told me where she was that whole day and I believe her. And she's not capable of murder. Besides, it's impossible to travel between Calgary and Vancouver within the time frame required."

"We told them about our investigation into Jian Liu taking out his own daughter. They listened, thanked us, and then said they didn't think we were right. They told us about their thoughts on your wife. I hope they lose their commitment to their idea and look into ours."

"Is the big Chinese guy still in Calgary?"

"No. He's back in Vancouver, but it doesn't take long to travel to Calgary to kill someone."

———

Jian Liu spoke in Chinese for a full minute after Henberlin said hello. When he finished he seemed to be waiting for a response.

"I'm sorry but I didn't understand any of what you just said. You don't have to repeat it in English, I caught your tone," Henberlin said.

"Why did you run? Why didn't you answer when I called?"

"I'm not running from you. I found out what you're asking me to deliver won't be available the way you're expecting it. It's going to take until at least Friday. Since there's nothing I can do for you until then, I decided to take my wife away from everything. She needs a break. I couldn't return your call because I was in transit. I'm returning it now."

Henberlin explained the technical difficulty with the machine language code, but said he'd figured out a workaround. He just needed to talk with an analyst to work out the details.

"You're in Los Angeles. When are you coming back?" Jian Liu asked.

"Friday. I'll call you late that day to let you know where we stand. If I can."

"What do you mean?"

"I may be arrested when I return. The detectives investigating your daughter's murder think my wife did it. Now that I've taken her out of the country, they could charge me with obstruction. You don't know how they got that idea do you? If you put them on her trail, you won't be getting what you're after."

Silence came from the other end of the call.

"We have a deal, Neo Henbrin. You do your part, I do mine. Your wife safe as long as you deliver."

"Good. I'll be back Friday."

———

Henberlin dreaded, yet couldn't wait for the next call. Knowing the way things stood with the detectives would shed considerable light on what he would do with Leyna. Detective Sweetland remained calm after Henberlin identified himself.

"Mr. Henberlin, you're obviously not cooperating."

"How could I when you aren't cooperating yourself?"

"We requested an interview with your wife through you because we didn't want to barge in on her. You set up a meeting with no intent to be there."

"I requested that you give her a few days because you have an adverse effect on her mental condition. She understands that she has to talk to you and she's looking forward to clearing up your misconceptions."

"Fleeing isn't looking forward to an interview."

"I'm calling to clear up any misunderstanding. I couldn't risk her having an anxiety attack like the last one you gave her. You didn't know her mental state then and you don't know it now. I do. You wouldn't listen when I said she wasn't ready for your questions, so I had to take her away."

"Mr. Henberlin, you need to bring her back."

"Soon, I promise. I'll be back Friday and I'll get in touch with you then. I want you to know we aren't hiding from you. You left me no choice but to protect my wife in this way. She has always been willing to cooperate, and will come back to meet with you."

"We know you took a flight to Los Angeles and that you rented a car. Where are you now?"

"After my wife is strong enough to withstand what you'll subject her to in an interview, she'll meet you in Calgary. I have to go."

Henberlin disconnected.

21

—

Leyna slept for two days, aided by the block-out blinds on the sliding glass doors, he figured. He also thought that she had to be taking something extra to make her stay in bed so long. The tranquilizer he'd given her earlier wouldn't have affected her to this extent. He'd been watching the prescriptions she'd brought along and noticed that they weren't diminishing in quantity. Finally, she opened the sliders and joined him on the patio.

"Hello," he said, "I was just coming in to check on you. Are you okay?"

She smiled. Even her eyes turned up and he hadn't seen that in a week. She nodded in short little jerks showing, no intention to speak.

"I'm worried. You haven't been taking any of your medication and all you've done is sleep. Do you have something else I don't know about?"

Again the smile and the quick nods.

"Do you remember me getting you to eat yesterday?"

She tilted her head and pressed her lips tight. "Nope. Sorry."

"Do you remember me trying to get you to walk a little? I dragged you around the living room a few times, then made you some toast."

She looked down at the floor then shook her head.

He frowned for a second, but then perked up, not wanting to give her the impression he was disappointed.

"Do you remember coming out of the bedroom naked, standing in profile and beckoning me in with your eyes and your fingers?"

"You're making that up, but I wish I did."

"That's the thing, you did, and I followed you back to bed."

"Oh, what happened?"

"I met with a hungry, talented, sexual athlete who wanted everything she could imagine. Everything, all at once and for a long time. I feel quite exercised."

"My muscles are little sore as well, but I thought that was bed stiffness. Sounds like I missed out. Wish I'd been there."

"Oh, you were there. And you demanded and encouraged more motion, more pressure, more use of strength, and more creativity. I thought we were dating again."

"Now you're embarrassing me. Really? Creativity?" Leyna stood and walked to her husband. She bent down and kissed him, then opened her robe and pulled his face into her belly. He placed his hands on her hips and began kissing her skin. She allowed him to cover her soft tissue with his lips until the heat inside her built even higher than when he'd described their ambitious lovemaking. Then she turned away, grabbing his hand, pulling him behind her to the bedroom.

———

In mid-afternoon, he awoke from his post daytime-sex nap and found Leyna sitting up in bed, wide awake. Not reading, not watching television, but staring at the opposite wall.

"Hi," he said. "You're awake."

Leyna blinked, turned her head, and smiled. "Yes, for a change."

"Do you remember the recent past?"

"Of course. I didn't want to miss out again."

He pulled her down to lay beside him and she snuggled in, her head on his shoulder, her hand on his chest.

163

"What would you like to do on my last night with you here in Phoenix?"

"Last night? What do you mean?"

"I'm going back to Calgary to see what the detectives plan to do about interviewing you. I want you to wait here or in L.A. until I know how mad they are at me."

"No, that's not necessary, I'm okay with seeing them. I'll go back with you."

"I don't think so. I want it to be as easy on you as possible. Tomorrow, I want you to wait until I call you from Calgary. It will probably be fine and you can catch a flight in the late afternoon. I'll meet you at the airport."

Leyna sat up, then leaned over him, staring into his eyes. "I can't let you leave me. I won't let you."

"We've gone over this. They'll throw you in jail and probably me, too. The media is all over them because they haven't made any progress on the murder investigation. They'd love to make an arrest just for show. You have to stay until I call you back. Jian Liu is mad too. He's been following us in Calgary. He knew we were at the airport before we left, and that didn't make him happy. I want to make sure there are no surprises waiting for you, so you have to wait until I know. Is that understood?"

Leyna rolled over on her side, her back to Henberlin. She reached down to her bag on the floor and retrieved a prescription bottle, took out one of the pills, and swallowed it.

"What do you have there?" Henberlin asked.

"A relaxant."

"Let me see it."

"No. I said it's a relaxant."

"Leyna, I need you to be awake tomorrow and for as long as you stay here while I'm gone."

She nodded, and he could see cloud cover drifting into her eyes.

————

After landing in Calgary the next day, Henberlin couldn't think about anything except getting through Customs. Then he could use his phone again to call and check in with Leyna. She'd been awake when he left, awake but drowsy. She understood what was taking place, which was a good sign. But still, if she took another pill after he left, she could be out-of-touch all day. Maybe that would be okay too.

When he walked out of Customs, his hopes of using his phone diminished to zero. Detectives Sweetland and Richie waited a short distance outside the security barrier. Two television news crews and a newspaper reporter stood off to the side. The detectives approached him as he passed through. He lifted his hand to shade his eyes as the camera lights switched on.

"Where's your wife, Mr. Henberlin?" asked Richie.

"She has to take a later flight."

"Okay, you're coming with us down to the station. We have some questions for you."

"Can it wait? I have things to do. I'd planned to contact you a little later."

"No, it can't wait."

The reporters fired questions at him as he walked away. Sweetland and Richie flanked him on both sides.

———

At the station, he sat in a cold interrogation room by himself for a number of minutes before the detectives came in to talk to him. They began by asking for the location of his wife, and he stopped them before they could even get started.

"Are you going to arrest her?"

"Until we talk to her and get her side of the story, we don't know."

"Do you have a reason to arrest her?"

The detectives sat silent.

Henberlin started speaking again. "You're fishing. You have a theory that you can't prove. For some reason you think my wife came back from Vancouver and murdered the Albins. I assure you she didn't. She doesn't have even the slightest degree of malice in her body. I understand you have to investigate your theory. But why should she have to suffer because you two are on a fishing expedition? She was pretty adamant last night about wanting to return with me today but I wouldn't let her. I suspected you two weren't going to be nice. When I have your assurances that you won't do any grandstanding, like making sure the press are waiting, she'll come back. She could be on a plane later today, but you've made that possibility go away. When you decide to treat her like the cooperating witness that she is, you'll get your interview."

"Is your wife well enough to give us an interview?"

"No. I'm still worried about what your questions are going to do to her. You insist on insinuating that Mrs. Albin and I were having an affair. Although Leyna believes me when I say there was no affair, she has to live with the stares, and the questions, and the insinuations of others. These are the things that hurt her."

"We believe the affair is the motive. We have to question her in that regard."

"Do you? You've already made your own conclusion that the affair existed and that it drove her to commit murder. Why not just perform your investigation considering that to be the motive? What could she possibly say that would convince you otherwise?"

Sweetland lowered his head and stared at his hands as they worked against each other, as if being washed. Richie glared at Henberlin. They said nothing.

Henberlin intended to watch them in silence, hoping to increase their discomfort over their forgone conclusions regarding his wife. When he realized he had his eyes fixed on the odd round scar beside Sweetland's right eye, and that Sweetland knew what he focused on, he turned to Richie and said, "I'm leaving. When you assure me you won't brow-beat my wife and you *both* give me your word on that, she'll come back."

Henberlin walked out of the police station to be met by the same pack of reporters that had been waiting for him at the airport. He ignored their questions and left the area in a taxi.

The taxi dropped Henberlin off on the Ninth Avenue side of his building. Before he made it to the entrance, two men walked up to him. Both Chinese.

"Mr. Henberlin, would you please come with us? You've been invited to a short meeting."

He made a feeble attempt to pass by the men, but they blocked his way.

"We don't want to put hands on you, Mr. Henbrin, but we will if that is required. This will only take a few minutes and we'll bring you right back," one of the men said.

Henberlin sighed, smiled, and nodded. The men led him to a black Lincoln Continental, and one of the men opened the door for him. They drove half-a-block and turned right off Ninth onto First Street, went under the railroad tracks, and made another right a block later on Tenth Avenue. Half-a-block up Tenth, a similar black car sat parked in front of a boot factory. The driver of the car Henberlin rode in double parked beside the other Lincoln. Doors opened on both cars and Henberlin moved across into the other back seat. An old man in old clothes but tidied hair, dark with dull silver streaks and separating waves, sat in the passenger side of the back seat. It took seconds for Henberlin to recognize his own father. Then he heard the voice of Jian Liu.

"You can't protect your wife by hiding her, Neo Henbrin. I'm not having much patience left for you, so you better start doing as I tell you and not doing anything on your own."

"What are you doing here?" he asked his father, ignoring Jian Liu.

"I don't really know, but he said I was going to meet with you," his father responded. He smiled, though his expression displayed confusion at seeing his son. "How have you been?"

Henberlin scanned his father's features, then checked out the condition of his body. Thin but erect, the skin tone weathered but healthy.

"Good, I've been good."

Henberlin turned to Jian Liu sitting in the front passenger seat, whose tiny body didn't make it up past the headrest. He leaned forward to speak and saw the straight, grey-streaked hair.

"I wasn't trying to avoid you. I told you that when I called. What is my father doing here?"

"Doesn't matter. I'm taking care of him. He works for me." Then, turning a slight degree, he raised his voice. "Okay, father Henbrin, you can go now."

"But I want to talk to him for a minute," Henberlin's father said.

"Call him yourself. You can talk then. You go now."

Henberlin's father's eyes drooped, but he lifted the corners of his mouth. "How's your mother? She okay?"

Henberlin twisted his face. "Fine."

"Okay, good." His father looked down and turned to the door and opened it. He hesitated, half-turned his head back, but then ducked his head out the door and left. Henberlin turned toward Jian Liu as he heard the door shut.

"What are you doing with him?" he asked Jian Liu.

"I'm taking care of him. I've got him. You save your wife and you save your father. That's all I'm doing with him."

"I don't care about him. You think you can make me give you what you want by threatening him?"

"We do what we want. We know what you do from now on. Don't forget. Now you have one day to get me the program code. No excuses."

"I can't guarantee that I can get it. When I get to the office, I'll find out where we stand as far as the code being on the systems. I'll update you later today."

"No, Neo Henbrin, you bring me the code tomorrow. I don't trust your stories. You have the code, now bring it."

"If I don't have the code, I don't have the code. If I give you a bunch of fake code to get you off my back what good will that do me? You'll get mad and take it out on my wife. You do that and I have no more reason to get you what you want. When I have the real code, I'll get it to you. If it's tomorrow, then it's tomorrow. And you better have cash waiting for me. One hundred thousand dollars sounds right. When I deliver the file you'll get half the code. When I walk out with all the cash, you'll get the other half."

"We have your wife video and we have your father."

"You can keep my father. Cash gets you the code."

Jian Liu looked out the front windshield for a moment without saying a word, then broke his silence. "Your wife isn't important to you anymore, you just want cash?"

Henberlin hesitated a second then said against his better judgment, "Your daughter's death isn't important to you anymore. You just want the encryption code?"

"My daughter wanted to help her China. Her death will be remembered and your wife will pay." His words we short stabs. "It better be tomorrow. My men will take you back now."

He reversed the car transfer and the driver took him to Eighth Street, turning right to cross over the train tracks this time. Right again on Ninth and back to where the taxi had dropped him about seven minutes earlier. Without saying a word, the man in front pointed at the door and Henberlin climbed out.

———

Owen Brady's business analyst trailed him back to his office, cowboy boots clomping all the way. He'd jumped on Henberlin's tail when he saw him pass down the hall. Henberlin didn't acknowledge Owen's pest even when he'd sat at his desk and the analyst continued to demand that he report to Brady's office.

Henberlin sifted through his messages, kept one to one side of his desk, then looked up. "Tell Owen that Pelle has asked for an update. I'll get in touch after I finish that call."

"Listen Neil, you have a responsibility to keep Sales informed about your activity. Owen is just doing his job. Part of doing his job is seeing that you do your job. Word is, Shield is increasing their initial order. We need that information so we can make our forecasts."

Henberlin smiled, held up the pink message slip, and said, "Do you mind?"

The analyst left, shaking his head.

First he called Leyna's cell phone, but she didn't answer. He feared she might not and mock pounded his desk when her voice mail message came on. He left a message asking her to call. He didn't want to tell her via message that it looked like she may have to wait another day before coming.

Next he called Kyle.

"Neil, you're back." Kyle answered. Caller ID had forever changed the formality of answering a phone call. "You need to call Delaney. Something's happened with the situation. He wants to give you a heads-up."

"What happened?"

"Call him. I'll let him tell you."

Delaney didn't answer. The phone he used for Henberlin's calls was exclusive, and there had never been a time when he didn't answer. He wanted to hear from Delaney before he called Jian Liu. He had to wait.

'Business,' he thought. 'Take care of a little business.'

Henberlin put in a call to Marlin Walker at Shield Oil. He wanted to touch base and let him know the additional systems were moving along through the queue and should be delivered in the next ten days. No answer. Then Henberlin remembered it was still Stampede Week, and that Walker would be in the thick of it.

He called Kyle again.

"No answers. So what's up with Delaney?" Henberlin asked.

"Two attempts to call DIVZY. One on each of the systems."

"DIVZY?"

"The system call to execute the encryption code. Roy Warren tried it on Delaney's system and someone in Yanmei's group uncommented the call on the Shield system."

"Remind me of DIVZY."

"It's a Trojan Horse we put in the code. When it's called, a message is launched through the maintenance port. It's filtered to send the message to us. It lets us know someone has accessed the code. The fake call has functions that don't actually do anything, but the inserted code is meant to look like the new encryption method. It also alludes to a complicated decryption process that uses a series of inverted matrix calculations. It looks like a new method of making encryption unhackable. Yanmei explained the process to her father. He's the only person to receive that information, so he must have passed that information to Warren and the person at Shield. I'm a little disappointed that it's Roy trying to get the information," Kyle finished.

Henberlin nodded, letting this development sink in. 'They now have evidence of Jian Liu trying to acquire corporate secrets and potentially national secrets,' he thought. 'They'll arrest him and he'll do whatever he can to protect himself, including bargain Yanmei's murderer to keep his freedom. If that happened this morning and they believed they had their hands on the code via one of these sources, then why did Jian Liu stop me to demand the code by tomorrow?'

22

During the walk from his office, Henberlin tried Leyna's cell again, and again wound up speaking to her voice mail. He wondered if he should get back on a plane to go find out why she didn't respond. Also along the way, Detective Sweetland called to see when Leyna would be back. Henberlin told Sweetland the truth: He didn't know because he couldn't find her.

"You're lying," the detective said. "Just like you lied about meeting us before sneaking off to Los Angeles. You don't intend to bring her back. What's she hiding?"

"Believe that if you like. I'm trying to find my wife and bring her back to answer your questions. I still haven't heard you or Richie say you would go easy on her. Until you do, she's not available. Even after I find her."

Delaney's communal receptionist sent Henberlin straight back when he flew through the door. A number of reports, oil-related graphs, and printouts with columns of numbers were splayed on Delaney's desk. His printer shot out more pages that he immediately placed under one of the piles. When he had a true oil industry analyst in his office, he had these files to make him look the part. He looked up at Henberlin and smiled a rare smile. Henberlin stopped in his tracks when he saw Delaney beam.

"I thought you'd be pissed at me," Henberlin said.

"Pissed? Why?"

"Roy Warren. You suspected him at first and I vouched for him."

"Oh that. Well, even though you vouched for him we weren't going to trust him. That's not what we do."

"So what happens now? Am I done?"

"Not sure. We have some people to watch for a while. We didn't think the attempted access would happen so fast. That just goes to show how worried Jian Liu is about the code getting locked up for good. He wants it fast. Now we know we're right about what he wants. We also know two guys who are working for him. Now we watch."

"Why are you not sure about me being done?"

"Jian Liu may still expect the code from you for confirmation. I think he will. We may also want you to give him some other information."

"When? Aren't you going to arrest him? You have proof of corporate stealing." Henberlin dreaded what he thought the answer would be.

"Oh no, we aren't going to arrest him. We've watched him for a long time and he's mostly been involved in some petty stuff all along. When China bought into the Oil Sands project, we started seeing a different group of Chinese operatives showing up in town. We spotted them because we were watching Jian Liu. We weren't quite sure what they were after until he started putting some pressure on his daughter to provide oil patch information. Your company's new technology created an uptick in activity and an opportunity for us to gather information. That opportunity is just getting started."

Based on his recent contact with Jian Liu, with Jian Liu trying to increase the pressure on him by threatening his father, and from Delany's words, Henberlin knew he wasn't done. "Jian Liu picked me up before I got to the office this morning. He does still want me to deliver the code. He also had my father in the car with him."

Delaney, after a slight reaction of surprise, said, "Your father? Jian Liu mentioned your father the first time he approached you. So how is your father involved?"

"Jian Liu says he's taking care of my father. He said if I wanted to protect him, I need to provide the information he's asked for."

"I'm sorry to hear that. Hmm." Delaney's eyes peered at the floor, his fingers pinching his pursed lips. Then he caught Henberlin's eyes. "We'll keep a watch on him. It does show the Chinese still want code supplied by you so they can compare it with what he got from the system call. Giving him matching code will make him think he got what he's after. What we let him pick up through DIVZY this morning looks like it's the key to an encryption system. It's embedded code but set up to look like it could be modified to extract any encryption encoded seed string, reverse process it, and unscramble the data.

"If we see future system breaches utilizing any of this code, we'll know who's behind the attack. For that plan to pay off, we have to let them think they got what they wanted without us knowing. If we arrest any one of these people, they'll know not to use the code."

A vacuum pulled at Henberlin's chest and stomach. Jian Liu may never be arrested. Good for Leyna to maintain her freedom, but bad because he and his wife could be at Jian Liu's mercy for a long time. They'd be forced to wait and see if he'd send her to jail, doing whatever he asked to keep their freedom. But could they live in that kind of freedomt? They had to figure out a way to get off of Jian Liu's hook.

"What about Roy Warren? He's working for the other guys, do you just leave him alone?" Henberlin asked.

"Not for a minute. We'll keep a close eye on him to see if he has other involvements with Jian Liu. We'll want to find out when he first made contact and how, then we'll save all that evidence until we need it. If he's a regular for this sort-of-thing, we may want to turn him and use him ourselves."

Henberlin twisted his face, trying to understand. Then he asked, "These guys like Warren work for the Chinese, selling American technology, and you let them get off without punishment? How are you protecting our interests?"

"We look at the long term and what we can discover about how our enemies operate." Delaney smiled. "Warren's in the terminal room right now. It wouldn't hurt for you to go in and talk with him about normal activities."

"He's still here?" Henberlin said, surprised.

"Yeah, said he's working on a new simulator. Looks like he's putting the system to a test. Kyle said he's running legit simulations on some historical production data. When you finish in there, I'd like you to go over to Shield and meet the guy from the sucker rod department that performed the DIVZY call. Get a feel for him. Call me after and let me know what you think." Delaney then did something he hadn't done since their first meeting. He extended his hand to shake Henberlin's. "And, Neil, I mean it, we'll try and keep an eye on your father."

Henberlin nodded as he shook hands, then marched off to meet Warren. He found him leaning back in his chair in the terminal room staring at numbers step-laddering up his screen one line at a time. His suit jacket hung over the back of the chair, the sleeves of his shirt rolled halfway up his forearms. He reached forward to pick up a brown plastic coffee cup holder holding a white plastic disposable cup. Noticing it had no weight, he looked into the vessel to see the bottom. Then he nodded and stood to go get another cup of coffee. The life of an analyst waiting for the completion of long-running programs. He stopped when he saw Henberlin entering the room.

After greeting each other, Henberlin asked for Warren's first impressions of the system and its performance.

"It's quite impressive so far. I couldn't resist running a few of my own benchmarks to see what I was sitting in front of, and your systems blew everything away. I thought the program had failed, so I retried it about four times before I checked to see if it created a results file. I found four of them. It finished so fast I thought it was a failure rather than a completion."

"Good. How's the coffee here?"

"Industrial strength. I like it. What brings you here?"

"That's my machine you're working on. You're the first to give it a taste of the real world. After hearing Kyle's plan for future processing, I wanted to know how you were doing with the new simulator."

"That's what's running right now. I had to straighten out a few compile time errors, but not much. I'm looking forward to the optimization suggestions from the runtime module. It will be interesting to see how vectorizing the data will take advantage of the parallel processors. I'm pretty sure this system, with the right optimized software, is going to be leaps and bounds better that what's been available so far."

"Good. How long do you think it will be before you've got it all together?"

"This stuff can be tweaked forever. I'm willing to stay until Kyle or Delaney kick me out."

"Sounds good. How are you keeping Kyle informed?"

"He's watching the same way I am, and we screen chat."

"Great. Well, I have to go visit the people at Shield and see what their first impression is. Take care."

Henberlin left Delaney's rent-an-office and headed to the Shield office a short distance away. Being the last Friday of Stampede Week, he expected to find his contacts in the Reservoir Simulation department absent. Instead, most of them were standing in front of the main terminal of the new R.E.S. workstation. They'd uploaded some of their own software to do some preliminary benchmarks and were curious to see the results.

Henberlin stood nearby and watched as they tried to execute the program. They looked confused as the screen indicated run completion as soon as they entered the run command. Cursing and wondering why the program didn't run, they looked at each other and threw hands up in frustration.

"Have you checked for output?" Henberlin asked.

The man sitting at the terminal turned to look at Henberlin and said, "It's not even running, how can there be output?"

"Maybe it's that fast. I've seen it before," Henberlin responded.

The man turned back to the keyboard and typed a display command. There was a list of output files. He did a file display on one of them, and they all saw the columns of data representing iterations of large prime number multiplications and divisions, plus the timings of each of the calculations. It took a second or two for them to realize that they were looking at the normal results of the program. They just couldn't believe that the program ran instantaneously.

"Holy shit. This thing is fast," one analyst said.

That got the entire group suggesting what they should run next and all hands began to reach for the keyboard, trying to shove the man in the seat out of the way.

With all these reservoir analysts fighting over his machine like he wanted, Henberlin made his way to the sucker rod department, stopping at Gordon Venzi's office first. Gordon was acting as department manager since Yanmei had been murdered. Henberlin seemed tongue-tied trying to carry on a conversation with Yanmei's replacement. He couldn't bring himself to congratulate him for his promotion, so he got straight to the new system.

"What are your first impressions?"

"Well, I haven't looked at the initial results yet. I'm trying to figure out a processing schedule for machine use at this point. I had one of the guys run a few things on it this morning, then let the reservoir group have a go. I'm trying to figure out how Yanmei planned to go about using the system. It looks like I'm going to have to come up with my own schedule."

"Why's that?"

"I can't find any notes on her implementation plan. Either she didn't make one, which seems highly unlikely knowing Yanmei, or she never expected to have a system installed."

"Hmm. I'll see if she copied me on anything like that but I don't recall a department-specific implementation plan," Henberlin said. "Do you think it would be possible for me to talk to the analyst who worked on the system this morning?"

Venzi stood and led Henberlin down the hall to introduce him to Peter Fowler.

Henberlin thanked Venzi for the introduction, then turned to Fowler, who appeared to be a recent graduate. Young, pale skin, brownish hair that hung off his forehead as he read the reports in front of him. He didn't hold eye contact and preferred to talk while seeming to continue his reading.

Henberlin asked Fowler if he thought the system would be a valuable new tool for analyzing sucker rods.

"I don't think there's any doubt about that. I only ran a few compiles this morning and this machine is fast. I'm going through the results and the system recommends a number of areas where we can improve our code to take better advantage of the system. The thing is, though, even if we don't make the improvements, our code's going to run faster than it's ever run before. We don't have the extensive data that some of the other departments have. For us, it doesn't really matter if the jobs run in a tenth of a millisecond or a hundredth. We don't have that many jobs to run, so no job is time sensitive."

"Yanmei had commented on the cost and maintained the department would get a good return on the machine. She also thought it likely the group would come up with other processes they could apply to the analysis that would provide even more benefits."

"Well, that's a decision for the people I report to. They give me the code and I run it, then analyze it. I don't know why they chose these programs to run this morning. I took the files I was given and ran them."

"Who gave them to you?"

"Gord. He brought me the files on a flash drive and asked me to run them. I left the output where he could get to it in case he wanted to see it. I'm going over the results now."

"Right. Can you tell if Gordon has accessed the output files?"

"I don't have those kinds of administrator capabilities on this system, but he did comment on the processing time of the compiles. I assumed he'd looked at the results."

"Well I'm glad that the system is faster and seems like it will help the department out. I'll let you finish what you're doing."

As he walked past Vinzi's office again, Henberlin stuck his head in to say goodbye. "Thanks. I'll check to see if Yanmei gave me any planning documents and I'll get back to you. I'll probably be dropping in regularly. I hope you don't mind."

"Not at all. See you soon," Venzi said.

Henberlin knew he had to get home so he could spend some time trying to contact Leyna. He also wanted to let Delaney know what he'd found out about the DIVZY access. He called Delaney and, when he explained that Gordon Venzi had supplied the files, Delaney had something to keep him busy for a while. Now Henberlin had to find out if he needed to fly back to Phoenix.

23

—

Henberlin had perfect timing with the automatic garage door opener, hitting the button as he turned the corner at the end of his block. By the time he got to the front of his house, he could pull right into his spot beside Leyna's car without having to stop until he was inside. No waiting for the door to rise all the way. Then he hit the button to close the door before shutting off the engine.

After retrieving his case from the back seat and walking around the car to the door into the laundry room, the garage door would be coming to rest, closed. Normally he smiled a little, pleased at his perfect timing, but today he heard a car pull up and park across the street before the door touched the floor. He put his case on the kitchen table, then hurried into the living room to look out at the street. He stood in front of the sofa, far enough back that he didn't think he could be seen. Sheer drapes, left closed when they weren't at home, clouded his shape from view. They still allowed him to see a grey, late-model Toyota with a man sitting behind the steering wheel.

He moved a little closer to get a better look at the driver. His lips moved as he spoke the license plate to help him concentrate while memorizing the number.

"What the hell are you looking at?"

Henberlin jerked upright. His skin tingled, then contracted as blood rushed to his brain. Lightheaded, he turned to find the voice. His heart slammed against the inside of his rib cage. His hands rose, palms outward as protection and his wide-open eyes looked at the body standing in the doorway.

"Leyna!" Henberlin relaxed, bending over to take a few deep breaths. "Jesus, you scared the shit out of me."

"I can tell."

"What are you doing here? Why didn't you call me?"

"As you can see I was trying to surprise you." She spread her arms to show off her body.

Then Henberlin noticed that she wore a black teddy that rode high on her hips. The bodice wrapped tight, pressing her breasts up and in to display a strong curved line of cleavage.

"I thought you'd enjoy being seduced. The reaction I got isn't what I expected." She smiled, then exaggerated her hip movement as she walked to him. She slipped her hands under his arms, placing them on his back and pulling him into her body. "I couldn't stay away from you."

Henberlin's head spun.

The car outside, his wife here when he'd asked her to wait until he determined it was safe to come home… Had the police met her flight the way they'd met his?

Finally, he acknowledged his wife in his arms and leaned down and kissed her. Her face made up, except she wore no lipstick. She smelled of exotic fruit, tasted of mint.

"You shouldn't have come home. Did you have a welcoming committee when you arrived?"

"None that I know of, but we'll talk later." She raised onto her toes and nuzzled into his neck—the thing she knew would pull him into a sensual state.

"No." He hooked his thumbs in her elbow joint and pushed her arms down while pushing her away. "You have to take this seriously. The detectives met my plane. They took me to the station, and I spent a long time trying to find out what they intend to do to you. They've called me three times since then to find out when you'll be back. I've been telling them it may be a couple days. I still think they're going to arrest you, just to shake you up. We can't have that after all you've been through. I don't want you admitted to the hospital again."

"It's okay. I've been going over it a lot. There's nothing they can do to prove—"

"Whoa, whoa, whoa..." Henberlin interrupted and put his finger across his lips. He pulled her close again, placing his lips beside her ear. The exotic scent making his head light again, he whispered, "Don't say anything about what happened. There were cameras in here before, someone may have put them in again. Get dressed, we're going out into the yard."

"Aren't you being a little overly cautious?" She nibbled his ear.

"Not at all. There's a car parked across the street that I don't recognize. They said they were going to watch me from now on but this car... I don't know if it's the police or the Chinese."

While Leyna put on jeans and a long sleeve Western shirt, Henberlin opened a bottle of wine and put some snacks on a plate. They moved outside into the warm July evening and sat at a small table for two by a lattice. The table and two chairs were decorated in a tight wrought-iron pattern. They were heavy, hard to move, uncomfortable to sit in, always dirty, and needed a new coat of paint every spring. Not his choice. The lattice, though, he loved. It held back an overgrown lilac bush he would have had to trim more often if it hadn't been partially hidden. At times they could hear the traffic noise of the major thoroughfare down the hill behind their home.

"The detectives are getting angry. They threatened to throw me in jail until you returned. They want to talk to you real bad, and when they do they're not going to be playing it easy," Henberlin said.

"It's okay. I'm ready." She said swirling her wine.

"Jian Liu is angry too. When I left the detectives, Jian Liu had two of his bruisers pick me up and take me to a meeting with him. It didn't last long and my father was there."

"Your father? Which father?"

"My real one. Jian Liu threatened his safety if I didn't get him the information he's after, and said you would pay for his daughter's death." Henberlin watched as his comments took effect on his wife. He waited, letting them sink in. Then he said, "You can either say something or pull your jaw up off the ground."

"Your real father?"

Throughout their relationship, she'd tried to pry information from him regarding his real father. A subject he didn't care to talk about. He only told her now because now it affected her.

He intended to get his wife thinking seriously about what appeared to be coming their way.

"Soon, you're going to be sitting in a gloomy room with the detectives firing questions at you about that day in Vancouver. They're going to be direct and tactful trying to find holes in your timeline for that day. You need to be consistent on every detail regarding the events you attended and the people who can confirm they'd seen you.

"They're going to drill you about Yanmei, insinuating that it was a serious affair and that you knew all about it. They're going to be graphic and suggestive, and you better be prepared to hear some pretty sordid descriptions. None of which are true. They can lie to you and try and make you believe they're telling the truth. They want to make you angry at me. That's why you have to believe in your heart that I'm the one telling the truth."

Leyna listened. Her initial shock had disappeared. At times she smiled, raised her eyebrows and made funny faces. But when he mentioned the affair she tilted her head, steeled her eyes and pursed her lips.

"They've got the right idea. They're on to you and you have to get them off. I can't ask you if you think you can do it. I can only tell you that you have to do it or you're going to jail," he said, trying to get her to adopt a hardened resolve. Then he dropped his eyes to contemplate if having her fool the detectives was what he wanted. Or did he want justice?

Trying to protect her and retain her freedom was natural, but should he be supporting her deceit? How could he best protect her? What was in her best interest? Jail would keep her away from Jian Liu. Wasn't that in her best interest, too?

Leyna picked up her wine glass, swirled the liquid inside again, and placed her nose inside the rim to take three quick sniffs. Lifting her glass, she saluted her husband before taking a drink, swishing it in her mouth and swallowing. She smiled and said, "This is good."

They held a stare for a few seconds before Henberlin looked away.

She continued in a calm voice. "I heard you and agree with you. I've been going over everything I did that day, it's all come back to me. There's no way they can prove I made a trip to Calgary. People saw me do things in the morning and they noticed me later in the day. The timing to get to Calgary and back is so tight you'd have to be real good to pull it off. I did. But I set it up so it's too unbelievable to do. They know the only way it can be done is to fly. There are a few flights that meet the times needed, but they won't find any proof that I took any of those flights. I know I have to be consistent, I know I have to be believable, and I know I can pull it off."

"You also said you didn't think they would ever suspect you after they heard your alibi. You knew they'd have to look at you, but that their suspicion would be short-lived. That didn't work out. Your plan was based on them not investigating your alibi too vigorously. Now they're going to try to tear it apart. And they're not going to be easy on you." On one hand, he welcomed her confidence, it would contribute to her success at staying free. On the other, he regretted it because of the pride she displayed regarding the setup of her perfect crime.

She sat for a time, smiling. Once or twice she looked at her empty wine glass, then up at him, hoping he'd get the hint. He refused to budge.

"It's funny isn't it?" she said finally. "A lot of people are found guilty because of circumstantial evidence. In my case, the situation is inverted. The circumstances I've created are going to keep me from being arrested, let alone convicted."

"Why are you acting so smug about this?" he started, stunned by his wife's attitude. Then he lowered his voice to a whisper. "You killed two human beings. Neither one of them deserved what you did to them. There is nothing in this you can be proud of."

"I have to try and forget what I did. That's the only way we can have a normal life." Leyna's voice clipped and angry. Then she softened and said, "You have to forget it, too. You wait and see, in a month or two it will be like it never happened."

Henberlin looked down, took a deep deliberate breath, exhaled through his mouth. "Except for Jian Liu," he said. "Two months from now, he still has the video."

Her smile disappeared. With her mouth closed she stared toward her bare feet, focusing beyond them. She slapped at a mosquito that tickled her neck as it landed, snapping her out of her remorseful thoughts. "Time for me to go in."

Henberlin remained sitting, looking through the neat angled slats of the lattice into the tangled mess of branches on the other side. He heard the rubber squeak of the refrigerator door opening as Leyna retrieved the wine bottle. Then he heard the doorbell ring.

Leyna appeared in the window above the sink, leaning into it as close as she could. "Neil."

As he looked at her a hard knock came from the front door. Leyna snap-turned but pressed herself back against the counter. He rose and walked into the house to answer the door.

"Detectives, hello. What brings you here?" he said.

Outside, beyond detectives Sweetland and Richie, two police cruisers and a police truck blocked the Henberlins' driveway. Detective Richie held out a search warrant and said, "You should read it. I hope we'll have your full cooperation."

Stepping forward into the living room, they met Leyna as she entered from the kitchen. Both detectives came to an abrupt stop.

185

"Mrs. Henberlin, we didn't know you had returned," Sweetland said. Then he turned his gaze to Henberlin. "You said you would call us when you knew when she would be returning."

"I..." Henberlin shook his head, fumbling for words. "I didn't know. She was here waiting when I got home."

"Mrs. Henberlin, I'd like you to go with Detective Richie down to the station. We have a few questions. Mr. Henberlin, we'll need you here while we conduct our search."

"Search? What are you looking for?"

"It's all in the warrant." Sweetland paused and, shaking his head, added, "You should have called us."

Henberlin had to take a seat on the sofa. A search might turn up the flash drive with the video, taped under the drawer of his nightstand. It didn't matter how well Leyna's planning had gone. If they found that flash drive it would be over for both of them. He'd already removed the copy from his PC. The video proved he'd known of his wife's guilt for some time.

Leyna's hands gripped his shoulders. He looked up into her clear, knowing eyes. "Don't worry, it'll all be okay. I'll go down and explain it all to the detectives. They have to do this. There's nothing to worry about. Nothing."

24

—

The greyish foam egg-crate walls of the interrogation room had been damaged in places where previous occupants had nervously picked chunks of the crumbly material. Three steel and black plastic chairs and a white plastic table were the room's only furniture. Leyna sat straight in one chair at one end of the table. Detective Richie sat at the corner of the table, crowding her position while Sweetland sat farther along its length. Sweetland had arrived earlier after completing the search of their home. His stern, even expression when he arrived gave no impression of how the search had gone. The only acknowledgement he had provided of his having been at their home was when he informed Leyna that her husband waited outside.

"Who did you meet at that time?" Richie asked.

"Haven't we already gone over this?" she said, then waited for them to respond. They knew she would sit in silence until one of them spoke.

"We have, and we need you to tell us again."

"Bob Parry from Mackie-Boudreau. They're a competitor of ours. He's a technical coordinator and part-time director for television commercials. I've seen him at previous conferences. We always spend a little time together before or after a session we're attending."

"You also met him after the conference?"

"Well, we hadn't planned to meet. We had a brief conversation."

"You spilled coffee, then went to the back of the room to watch the first part of the presentation, and then left. What time would that have been?"

"The session started at nine. I presume it started on time and I left after fifteen or twenty minutes."

"How long did it take you to check your coat, then go to the presentation that you joined in progress?"

"I'd say five minutes. I chatted briefly with the girl at the counter while she hung up my coat. Then I walked to the last room in the hallway, to the session."

"That would have put you near the exit from the basement to the street at nine twenty-five, let's say nine-thirty. Who saw you in that presentation?"

"I don't know that anyone saw me. I sat in the back row. The lights were low for the projector. I was looking at the back of heads. At the end of the session I got up and was the first person out the door."

"So no one can put you in that room?"

"Not that I know of."

"So you could have gone out the exit and never gone to that presentation. You could have left the conference and made your way to the airport and back to Calgary. Half-hour to the airport, you time it right and have a short wait before catching an hour flight to Calgary. You could have been here by, say, ten forty-five."

"I wasn't. Do you think that's possible?"

"Even if you're a little later, it's possible. You still had the whole afternoon to commit the murders and then return by...What time again did you say you were at the cocktail hour?"

"When the sessions ended for the day at five or so, just like everyone else."

"Who did you see at the cocktail hour?"

"Everyone."

"You really aren't cooperating, Mrs. Henberlin. Why can't you answer the questions?"

"I have answered the questions, all of them, a number of times. Have any of my answers changed?"

"We're not trying to catch you in a lie, Mrs. Henberlin. We think of other elements related to the question, and ask it again keeping those new elements in mind as you answer the question."

Leyna listed a few of the people she had run into in the bar at the conclusion of the conference. The same ones she'd listed the first and second times she'd answered the question. She ended her answer the same way as the previous times, "…and Bob Parry, the guy I spilled coffee on. Oh yeah, I remember asking him what he thought about the lunch they served. That morning he'd indicated he came to the conference for the food, so I wanted his take on the mysterious entrée. A weird chicken dish. All the pieces of chicken were formed into the same shape. Served with a bland port sauce with a touch of licorice flavor. A little sweet, served beside carrots. There was too much sweet on the plate."

"What did he say about the meal?"

"He laughed, said the only way it could have been a bigger disaster was if they served larger portions. Then he said he ate it all."

"Did you eat it all?"

"I ate the salad, tasted the sauce, and crossed my utensils on the plate." She stared at them, then smiled. "I'm glad I remembered talking about lunch. How could I have arrived in Calgary at ten forty-five, made it downtown, killed two people, and travelled back to Vancouver in time for lunch?"

"Now you're saying you were back even earlier, that you were back for lunch?"

"No, as I've always said, I never left. If you don't leave, you don't come back, because you never left."

"We think you left. Obviously you couldn't have made it back for lunch, but you could have made it back by the end of the last session."

––––––

Henberlin sat in the hallway waiting area where they said his wife would come through—if they released her. Shiny tile, stained orange fabric sofa, cork boards on the walls filled with pins and ragged paper. He heard a door open in the direction that he had come from, so he knew it wouldn't be Leyna. When he looked up, he recognized the expensive suit, well-groomed hair, and stained teeth.

"Neil, I thought I'd find you here. Any idea when your wife will be coming out?" It was Hec Taylor.

"I haven't been told."

"Do you think we could step outside for a few minutes? I'd like to talk privately."

Henberlin didn't think Leyna would be walking out of captivity in the too-near future, so he stood and let Hec lead the way. They walked the few blocks to the Eau Claire area, then down to a bench overlooking the river. The water raced by, a little high for July but, after the rains of June, it was to be expected. Henberlin found the unusual rush of the water calming, so much so he didn't care if Hec Taylor bothered to start a conversation. Nor did he care what came out of his mouth when he did.

"Jian Liu has offered to have me represent your wife if you need my services."

Henberlin kept his eyes on the racing river as his mind clicked over the idea. The man blackmailing him with his wife's freedom, making a grab to take her freedom further into his control... It made sense and it showed Jian Liu's desire to continue to extract information about the computer system.

"At this point, I don't think that will be necessary."

"Well, the offer's there. He also wants you to know he still expects to get that item that you've promised to deliver. He wants to know when he'll get it."

"Soon, maybe. It's not at the top of my to-do list right now."

"That's understandable, but he wants to know when it will make the top, and he hopes it will be soon. Also, if your wife should get charged with his daughter's murder, that doesn't let you off the hook. He can still make sure she's found guilty. If she is, he can still turn you in for handing over the information."

Henberlin turned to look at Taylor but didn't respond for half-a-minute. Then he asked, "Wouldn't he be turning himself in at the same time if he did that?"

"He'd be long gone when he handed over that information. And still free while you go to jail for life."

"Man, he's cold."

"There's one more thing: The data you provided to him before, the reservoir data, there are no geographical data points indicating where the reservoir is located. He thinks you're trying to fool him."

"It happens. Companies sometimes want outside consultants to look at some data, but they don't want the consultants to know any of the information, like the reservoir's location. The consultant might sell it. If other companies find out the location they'll go and try to lease land in the areas adjacent to the reservoir. The company with the data does all the analytical work and the leaches do some directional drilling and exploit some oil. Withholding GPS data is a method of protection."

"Yeah, well, he wants you to get that information. You're going to be doing a lot of work with the Shield people, so you're going to be in a position to find out the location."

"I wouldn't know the first thing about where to look to get that information."

"Your analyst Kyle does. Make sure he finds it."

Henberlin turned away from Taylor and fixed his eye on a small island that the river had created. The smaller trees and bushes at the water's edge bent at a slight angle with the press of the river.

"I don't think I gave you my card last time," Taylor said, holding out a card sandwiched between his index and middle finger. "Call me if you need my help."

Henberlin remained on the bench as the high water continued to flow by.

———

Leyna sat slumped in her chair. Fatigue began to work its mind-busting ways. Her thoughts wandered from the current situation. The detectives would ask a question and she would start to answer, but after a short time her response became unrelated to what the detectives had asked. She shook her head trying to clear her thoughts. In a moment of clarity, she decided she'd had enough and needed to get out of the interrogation room.

"You finished your search at my home a few hours ago, didn't you?" she asked looking Sweetland in the eyes.

He hesitated for a few seconds then said, "Yes."

"Did you find anything interesting? Something that would cause you to arrest me?" She tilted her head as she asked.

"We're still going through what we confiscated."

"I don't think you found anything, or you would have asked me some new questions, or you would have arrested me. Don't you think you better let me go?"

The question caused the two detectives to look at each other. Sweetland twitched his head at the door. They both stood and walked out of the room. Alone now, fatigue and the chill pushed Leyna close to panic. She took in slow, deliberate breathes, reminding herself to keep her wits about her. She needed to know what was going on at all times. Especially now.

She didn't know how long the detectives were gone, and she started when she heard the door handle turn.

They walked to the table but remained standing. Sweetland said, "Your husband is still in the waiting room. We took a number of items from your home that we'll continue to analyze, and we'll provide you a list of those items. We'll also notify you when you can pick them up. One thing we will be keeping is your passport. Your husband's, too. The search warrant outlined that we were to confiscate the passports and keep them until we think you aren't a flight risk. Unless you have any questions for us, you're free to go."

Leyna didn't say a word. She stood, stared at the two men, and caught herself staring at Sweetland's scar. Breaking off her mesmerized glare, she turned and walked out the door.

Not knowing which way to turn in the hall, she looked both ways and chose to go right. She heard a voice from the room she'd just left, telling her it was the other way. She turned and marched down the hall, lips pursed, nostrils wide to accommodate her deep breathing.

The hall turned right after a short distance and she spotted her husband sitting in the orange sofa. He jumped up when he saw her and walked to her. She allowed him to envelope her in his arms. She sunk deep into his body, his warmth, the comfort of him. She said nothing, nor did he. They stood and stood and stood, silent. He must not have realized she was crying until he heard her sniffles.

"Are you okay?"

She nodded against his shoulder.

"Let's go home?"

She lifted her head, wiping the tears from her cheeks. She looked him in the eye for the first time and nodded, then waited for him to lead the way.

————

Once they were in the car and a few blocks away from the station, Henberlin told her, "When the police searched the bedroom they looked at the underside of the drawer in my nightstand. The flash drive with the video was gone."

"I know. I destroyed it as soon as I could. I told you we had nothing to worry about." She looked at him and smiled with pride.

"That was the only thing I worried they would find. I thought that would be the end of this, that we'd be spending a long time in jail."

"I knew that video had to be gone, so I took care of it. We're safe. They don't have any evidence they can use to charge us with those murders."

"Well, the worst is over for now," he said. "Do you need something? I have your pills in the glove compartment."

Leyna didn't respond. Her smile disappeared and she stared out the window as if unaware of her surroundings.

"Leyna..." he said again, but received no reaction.

They remained silent for the remainder of the drive home.

25

—

Delaney fist-pumped when Henberlin told him that Jian Liu still wanted the encryption code.

"What about your father? Did he mention him again?"

"No. I've emphasized the money. He thinks I couldn't care less about my father."

Henberlin hoped Delaney still believed Jian Liu bought the money motive and wondered how long that would remain the case. But now it looked as if there was an additional reason for Henberlin to play along: His own freedom. Freedom that could disappear in an instant.

Delaney smiled and said, "If he only knew you're working him."

Then Henberlin explained why the coordinates are often left out of the data, and suggested that the Chinese might be actively purchasing leases in the area of interest.

"How would they acquire these leases?" Delaney asked.

"Send their landmen out to negotiate the rights."

"Landmen?"

"Oil companies have a department called Land. They acquire the right to go onto certain areas of land to explore for oil and gas, then extract it if it's found. Some landmen spend their time analyzing old production data from shutdown wells. If new techniques will bring them back to production levels that make them economically viable, they'll go out and negotiate a lease.

"Other landmen go to where they're told to go by the exploration department. Exploration may have discovered something or is reasonably sure they will, and they'll try to acquire land leases without notice by other oil companies. Some landmen watch the activities of competitive landmen to see where they're buying leases. Then they try to get their company to buy in the same area.

"It's a weird department in an oil company, the closest thing to a sales department you'll find in oil and gas. Lots of personalities in the Land Department. They need to convince landowners, usually farmers, to allow the oil company to operate on their land. The offers can get competitive."

"So I need to find the Chinese Land Department and watch what they get up to. How does one watch leasing activity?"

"Can't help you. I've never been involved in Land. But like I said, a lot of the lease agreements are with farmers. They may not want to sell the rights to a foreign oil company."

Delaney nodded. "I don't know if that helps me, but I'll start looking into it once we decide what type of location data we want them to have."

"They mentioned Kyle to me, said I have to make him get the data. Were they testing to see if I know about Kyle's involvement with them?"

"Could be. What did you say?"

"Nothing. I turned away and ignored it. He didn't bring it up again."

"Okay. I'll get to work on what we want you to deliver. We'll have it soon so you can set up your next meeting with Jian Liu. In the meantime, I want you and Kyle to actually try to find the GPS data from within Shield. That way you can provide Jian Liu with real updates on your progress. It'll be harder for him to think you're cooking something up when you're doing what he asked. We also don't know how many people he has inside Shield that could report to him on your activity. He'll get similar reports of Kyle's activities if he does. Keep me posted on how difficult it is to find the GPS data."

––––––

The little restaurant where Henberlin and Jian Liu were meeting to transfer the confirmation copy of the encryption code had its usual crowd during the lunch hour. People lined the street to come in for their salt-and-pepper squid. A common dish on most menus in Calgary's Chinatown, this restaurant's squid stood above all other offerings. Elevated beyond the norm due to the thin, crisp batter, or the temperature of the cooking oil, or the mix of onions and bell peppers, or the amount of red chili flakes, or maybe it was as simple as the salt and white pepper blend they applied immediately after frying. It didn't matter, the squid was always tender, always hot, and always delicious.

Jian Liu's distant manner discoforted Henberlin. Maybe the old man's patience had grown thin. He didn't know if a lack of patience would be a good thing or dangerous. Jian demanded shorter timelines in order to get his hands on the GPS data. "Your wife is going to jail soon."

Henberlin looked long at the unflinching eyes next to him, then said, "We've had our access limited on the Shield systems and they appear to be hiding the data. They want to know when Kyle is logging in. When he does, there is limited data in his view."

"You need to get more view or you lose your wife. That's always the deal."

"We have to get rid of that part of the deal. I want more money. You don't need to use my wife if you pay me enough money.

"I haven't given up hope that Kyle can find the data you want. He's a smart analyst, and he's created backdoors that can get him into the system without the Shield people knowing. I've expressed the urgency, but he's getting suspicious, wondering why the hurry.

He may need some financial motivation himself. Can you get more money?"

"Maybe."

Customers streamed in and out of the random spaces between tables laid out in no particular pattern. They came and went with regularity, dancing with the staff who used the same random spaces to clear away dishes, change table cloths, replace teapots, and serve customers who had already ordered. All to a low, noisy din making it impossible to eavesdrop on another table's conversations.

The squid arrived at the table along with a plate of ginger beef—the other staple of Chinese restaurants in Calgary—and a bowl of steamed rice. Jian Liu looked at the plates and asked, "How can you eat that?"

"You don't like these dishes?"

"Like the squid. Beef taste like candy." He grunted. "You give me bunch of excuses, but you said you got something for me."

"Yes."

"Okay good. Leave it with the waiter." He stood to leave but Henberlin placed his hand on Jian Liu's arm.

"Wait. You're supposed to give something to me."

"Forget that, Neo Henbrin, just think about your wife, not money."

"I carry considerable guilt over what my wife has done. It's possible the police are going to figure things out. She may go to jail and perhaps she should. If she does, Yanmei gets justice and you lose your leverage with me. Then you lose your access to the kind of information I can provide. Blackmail doesn't build trust, commerce does. Things can really slow down without money."

He took his arm off Jian Liu and turned to the squid. He swore Jian Liu's eyes were leaving scorch marks on his neck. He heard the old man clear his throat, then the intense force walked away.

———

Detective Sweetland spent his afternoon once again looking at the Saturday flight schedules for airlines flying between Calgary and Vancouver.

He'd developed a liking for analyzing logistics. When a case required that someone look into how or if a crime could be committed, he volunteered to do the analytical work—work that indicated whether or not the investigation followed a viable course. In most cases, the work only required one man to dig into the details. He had nothing against working with a partner, but working on his own increased his productivity. He also liked the fact that, when he worked alone, no one stared at his scar.

At first the look of shock on people's faces made him a little uneasy. As he got used to it, he realized it didn't bother him as much as it bothered the people looking at him. He let them have their fill, waiting until they realized they were staring. Then he acted as if they hadn't been.

Because he was a cop, people always expected to hear he'd been shot in the line of duty. But when he told them it came from his ex-wife, they usually cracked an innocent joke and changed the subject. The fact that his ex-wife had actually shot him made it all seem like the joke was on those people curious enough to ask the question. He cursed his ex every time he caught someone staring. But he also remembered that the bullet that grazed the side of his face had been the exact message they both needed to let them know their marriage had ended years before.

It burned like hell and required skin grafts to fill in the hole where the flesh above his cheek had disappeared. The graft hadn't healed as expected leaving a roundish depression in the skin with a slight overhang around one edge. The scar meant his sideburns had to be trimmed even with the top of his right ear, where an aspirin-sized chunk of skin and cartilage was missing. He loved the long sideburns he used to have.

So had his ex.

He worked at his desk looking for a schedule that could get Leyna Henberlin to Calgary and back the weekend of the murders. First, he checked that exact Saturday's flights and discovered that the schedules hadn't changed. Their preliminary review two weeks earlier had indicated the distinct possibility that travel between the two cities could be completed in the time Leyna had that day. It didn't matter that they hadn't found her listed as a passenger on any of the flights—she may have travelled under a different name. They could dig deeper into that element if they found something more concrete, but what about travel within the cities? Did the time and traffic density, to and from each airport, eliminate the probability of completing the trip?

Detective Sweetland checked the vehicle traffic data in both cities during the times Leyna would have been in a car or bus travelling to and from the airports. He concluded it would be close, but it could be done. Only one way to find out: He would have to recreate the trip.

He spent some time choosing the air route: The major carriers or the small regionals? The non-stops of the majors allowed for more time on the ground in Calgary, but they had more scrutiny during passenger boarding and more security cameras in the terminals used for their flights. The regionals meant a stop along the way, costing close to an hour that would best be used in Calgary. But it would be easier to board these regional flights with shaky identification.

Then he tried to think like Leyna. She may not know Vancouver very well, so it's likely she relied on taxis there. He would do the same. In Calgary, Leyna would know the transportation system better and had more options. How would he try to get to the airport without leaving a trace?

Cab drivers are good with faces, so in Vancouver he would have to go a day early to talk with some drivers and to people in the hotel. He hoped a cab driver would remember picking Leyna up outside the hotel around the time she left the conference that morning.

In Calgary, she could've taken the train out of the downtown area using an untraceable train ticket, or used the bus system with cash, or caught one of the hotel shuttles that travel non-stop to the airport and again paid with cash. He chose the train to a Northeast shopping mall because it was on the way to the airport. From the mall, she could've walked to a chain hotel in the area. That hotel ran a shuttle to and from the airport.

Now he had to wait until Friday to travel to Vancouver, interview some of the hotel staff, then get up the next morning and recreate Leyna's trip.

Two days later, Delaney called Henberlin into his office. They had to set up a meeting with Jian Liu to deliver GPS data related to the reservoir Jian Liu had his eyes on.

"I want to bounce something off of you," Delaney began. "Kyle's modified the GPS data so the Chinese won't know the real location of the oil field. The fake land has no potential of oil production. Once we send this data to Jian Liu, how do we watch to see if he's taking the bait?"

"The most likely place you see them make a move is at the lease registration office. Monitor the areas you're sending Jian Liu and see who begins to show an interest. Anyone who thinks they know where Shield is making a play will start registering leases in the same or adjacent area."

Henberlin let his comment sink in for a moment, then said, "I have news. Jian Liu contacted me about something else he wants to know about. He said since Kyle and I had access to Shield's systems, he wanted us to find out what other areas Shield is exploring. He seemed to know that Kyle had found the GPS coordinates he wanted. That's interesting because I didn't know Kyle had found the coordinates until just now. I couldn't have indicated to Jian Liu that we were close to getting the data, yet he acted as if he knew we had.

Someone inside Shield must know Kyle's been fishing around their files," Henberlin said.

"If Jian Liu has someone inside, why doesn't he get that person to supply the GPS data?"

"My guess is Jian Liu's contact is someone from IT. A person that doesn't know which data pertains to the specific reservoir data Jian Liu is interested in, but knows where the data is stored and who's looked at it. They could be watching what Kyle's user ID has done on the system. If Kyle downloaded a file, the IT guy would be able to tell which file."

"Why wouldn't he make a copy himself and deliver it to Jian Liu?"

"I'll bet He did. It's possible Jian Liu has an original copy and he'll be able to tell that the file we deliver has been modified."

"Shit." Delaney turned and looked out the window for a moment. "Can Kyle tell if the file he downloaded has been downloaded by someone else?"

"I'll ask him."

"Don't call Jian Liu until we know. We may have to give him a copy of the unmodified data."

–––––

Walking north from Delaney's office up Fourth Avenue, Henberlin passed a small service alley that led to the delivery docks behind a hotel long-time Calgarians referred to as the Calgary Inn. As he passed, strong hands gripped both his arms and pressed them behind his back. Two men prison marched him down the alley and into the loading dock. They pushed him up against the old brick wall, face first so he couldn't see them. They didn't speak. Their hands wasted no moves as the ranged over his body and into his pockets. They threw the contents of his pockets on the ground. Then they grabbed the small case he carried, dumping its contents out on the concrete pad of the loading dock—all the time pressing him hard into the brick wall.

One of the men told him to take his shoes off. He did and one of them reached into the toe of the shoes, then tossed the shoes behind him. Henberlin heard their hollow sound as they bumped and rolled a short distance. Without saying a word, the men pulled Henberlin away from the wall, pointed him at the loading dock, and shoved him hard. He lost his footing and ended up skidding on the concrete. When he gathered himself and looked back to see who had forced him into the alley, the men were gone.

He stepped back to where his possessions lay spread on the ground. Putting his shoes on first, he then took his time gathering everything from his pockets and his case, catching his breath and letting the tempo of his racing heart slow down. He checked to see if his phones were broken, glad he only had two of the three with him. He never carried the phone he used to contact Jian Liu when he visited Delaney. The men who accosted him didn't find someone having two phones unusual, but three may have caused alarms to go off.

When he got back to his office, he closed the door and reached into his drawer to get his third phone. He dialed the only number in the phone's memory and Jian Liu answered.

"That's going to cost you," Henberlin said then hung up.

26

—

The mosquitoes became unbearable after Stampede Week. Prior to and during the event, the city sprayed in order to make the annoying bloodsuckers as unnoticeable as possible. They didn't want itchy welts to be one of the lasting memories tourists took away from their party in Calgary. But the locals who had to live in the city afterward were allowed to be sucked dry.

With the additional aggravation of the bugs, the Henberlins were reluctant to sit outside for their private conversations. Instead, they left their home to sit in a restaurant or lounge when they needed to talk about their situation. Always making sure they weren't too close to any other patrons who might overhear them.

Leyna had suggested going for Chinese food but, these days, Henberlin preferred anything but Chinese. They ended up eating perogies, sausage, and sauerkraut.

"It's getting scary Neil," Leyna said as a shiver wracked her shoulders.

"I don't think it's out of control, though. I think Jian Liu is showing signs of desperation."

"And you don't think that makes him more dangerous?"

"Maybe. But I want him to see that I can get the information his people are pressing him to get. I want him to think I'm more motivated by money than I am by him blackmailing us. He'll calm down once he starts getting more of what he asks for."

Henberlin concentrated on his food for a few minutes, cutting his perogy. Then he spread a little sour cream on top and a sprinkle of bacon crumbles. The mix of smooth, creamy dough with cheese and potato filling topped with the savory salty crispness of bacon made his taste buds rejoice.

"I don't know if these little dumplings are simple or complex," he said, looking at his plate. "I only know they're a real treat." Expecting confirmation from Leyna and not hearing it, he looked up to meet Leyna's expressionless gaze. He stopped his knife and fork work and said, "What?"

"We have to get rid of Jian Liu."

He placed his utensils down on his plate while gathering his thoughts.

"What do you mean? Not…"

"I can't live like this, Neil. How long do you think you can?"

"No. I'm not listening to this. It's bad enough as it is. We can't pile on to what's already been done. You have truly scared me. I'm worried about who I married, but toss it off to a snap of jealousy developing into temporary rage. Now you're startling me. I can live under this cloud forever rather than do what you're suggesting."

"Then how do we get this man off our backs?"

"I'll think of something," he said. "I have to."

He knew Leyna would never get over this episode in their lives. How could she? How could he?

———

Kyle had left himself enough access on the Shield computers to be able to monitor the system's activity. Once he identified the busiest usage period, he knew when to access the system via the backdoor he'd created. He logged in with a user ID that had medium security access, but he'd placed a high-security leapfrog program in a directory that this medium security user ID could execute. He entered the program's unassuming name, 'timespan', and in a flash the super-user prompt appeared his screen.

He intended to see which analysts on the system, if any, had executed the binary editor that would allow them to read and modify the access settings of all files on the system. Other than the super-user ID, there were four other analysts with the capability. Bad news. This meant someone could see if a file had been copied, then edit its settings to show that it hadn't. Kyle looked at the GPS files he'd copied. He hadn't gone in and erased the access indicator when he copied them, and saw now that the copy indicator was set to one, the one copy he'd made. No way to tell if someone else had seen this. No way to tell if someone else had made a copy, then reset the indicator back to one.

CSIS decided to go with the original data file after Kyle indicated that Shield's IT personnel were capable of deleting indications of file access. If Kyle couldn't tell if the file hadn't been copied a second time, it didn't mean it hadn't.

Delaney, accepting the additional risk of providing Jian Liu with the real data, gave Henberlin the go-ahead to contact Jian Liu to make the exchange.

Henberlin called and arranged a time to meet, insisting that Jian Liu meet him on the street, not inside a building. He added that Jian better have a package of money or he'd be walking away without getting what his people were after. He and Jian Liu would transfer the items personally, no waiters this time. Jian Liu agreed.

Henberlin watched from a window inside a bank as the old man shuffled along on his cane toward the agreed-upon food stand on the Stephen's Avenue Mall, what older Calgarians still called Eighth Avenue. He let Jian Liu stand and wait in wind that bent the trees. Lunch hour on the mall on good weather days meant crowds wanting to take their meal outside, hectic business for the food stands and crowded outdoor seating areas. With the wind blowing cold like today, the crowds didn't show.

Henberlin left the bank and walked up to Jian Liu.

"Is that for me?" Henberlin asked.

"Yes." Jian Liu jerked the hand holding the small bag out to Henberlin. Henberlin took the bag then reached in his pocket to retrieve the flash drive for Jian Liu.

"This works much better for me," Henberlin said.

"This better be the right data, Neo Henbrin. I can trust you?"

Henberlin held up the money. "Keep this coming and you can trust me. I've got a line on more of what you want. It's a little more risky to get my hands on, so more money next time."

Jian Liu raised his chin in acceptance, then turned and shuffled back in the direction of Chinatown. Henberlin crossed the mall and entered the Glenbow Museum. He rode the escalator down to the ticket entrance, then stood and watched who came down behind him. After the escalator cleared, he walked to the up escalator and returned to the lobby where he'd entered the museum. He laughed at himself—a computer salesman taking precautions as if he lived a dangerous life. Then he left by a door that exited onto Ninth Avenue.

———

"You don't get to keep it," Delaney said. "It's evidence."

"But..." Henberlin said in a half-hearted protest.

"It's great evidence too. There are people who want to put an end to Jian Liu's activities. With the money, the pictures we took of you receiving it, his possible actions with the man from Vancouver, his increased interest in information from Shield, along with your testimony, we can put him away for a long time."

"Any time in jail is life for Jian Liu. The guy is ancient. I almost felt bad having him walk four blocks to meet me... but that didn't last long."

"We've continued looking into the man from Vancouver as a suspect in Yanmei's murder. He looks good for killing her brother but not for her. He came to Calgary a few weeks before she died and then arrived back here the day after the murder. It turns out there's been a lot of contact between Jian Liu and the embassy personnel. Our thought is the big guy that had been coming to Calgary has gone back to China. We can't find any trace of him. Makes him look guilty, but not in the Yanmei killing. That doesn't help your wife out. Any developments on the case?"

Henberlin shook his head. "We haven't heard from the detectives at all. It looks like they realized they were wrong, but they don't want to admit it to us."

"Don't be surprised if they never give up. That way they don't have to let you know they were wrong.

"I hate to say it, but the Shield installation seemed to heat up and move along at a quicker pace without Yanmei. Her death was tragic, but it got you more involved and that allowed us to make a stronger case."

"What case? I thought you said there would be no arrest."

"I hope there isn't, but I'm getting a different read from the people upstairs. I think taking him in is a mistake. If my superiors decide to make a case of it now we shut down, lose the future intelligence of continuing to monitor Jian Liu and his network. But you'll be free of this thing, sooner than you think."

Did Henberlin want to be free of it? He had no choice. It looked like Jian Liu's arrest would come soon. At that point, the walls crash in on him and Leyna.

———

Detective Sweetland walked from a modest hotel on Robson Street in Vancouver down the ever-so-clean streets to the Bayshore Hotel on the waterfront, where Leyna Henberlin had stayed during her conference. Arriving early for his unscheduled appointment, he stopped in the bar where the reception took place after the conference adjourned that Saturday. He showed a picture of Leyna to the few members of the bar staff preparing for another day of vending alcohol. One bartender, polishing wine glasses with a white linen cloth and holding each one up to a light, said he'd been on duty that night but had no recollection of seeing Leyna. Sweetland asked for directions to the conference center and strolled down to take a look around.

People crowded the lobby area in the second level basement floor. There were three different functions taking place, all beginning at different times to stagger the rush on the facilities staff. He walked the perimeter of the conference lobby looking for exits, then down the hallway that led to a few other meeting rooms. Down that hall, he found a set of restrooms and an exit. Stairs led up to the street. He stepped out, letting the door shut behind him, then checked it and found it locked. Back around to the front entrance and back down to the conference center he went.

When he returned, the lobby crowd hadn't thinned at all, so he made his way over to the backend catering door. Inside, he asked for two workers and a manager by name. All people who had worked the conference he had come to investigate. One of the women remembered Leyna because she had spilled an entire cup of coffee across one of the tables. She was embarrassed and wanted to clean the mess herself, but the hotel employee politely took over the task.

Next, he walked to the coat room and watched as two workers exchanged tokens for garments. They then placed the garments on a rack that stopped and started moving along a track to produce a new span of unused hangers and tokens. The women were able to handle the crowd with ease, the receiving half of the garment exchange being an orderly and efficient process. But the later return of the garments was always chaos. The motorized track being useless in a random distribution situation when the attendees showed up in an unpredictable order. So the hotel added additional staff who ran their feet off making trips into the back along the track to find the right garment.

Once the attendees were inside their meeting rooms, Sweetland asked for Laney Gilchrist, one of the women who had been on duty the Saturday morning of Leyna's conference. He showed her the picture of Leyna and asked if she'd seen her.

"I might have," she said. "We see a lot of people here."

"Yes, I'm sure. This woman checked her garment late. She said she'd taken her garment into a presentation due to the long line at your coat check. She left her presentation to attend the end of another one and on her way she checked her garment," Detective Sweetland explained.

"Oh, yes. I remember something like that." She reached for the picture of Leyna so she could have another look. "Maybe, I don't know. It could have been this lady. I remember it happening, but I'm not too clear on the face."

Sweetland nodded, knowing it could be argued that Leyna had told the truth regarding the coat check and could establish the approximate time she was definitely in the hotel. That, along with the coffee spill, supported everything Leyna had said. He would have to come back in the morning to retrace the trip to Calgary. It would start with a test of local traffic at that time of the morning. Would it allow her to make it to the airport in time for the flight Sweetland thought she had most likely taken? He had booked a ticket on the flight scheduled for the same time.

The next morning, he stood in the conference center lobby and waited for the new batch of attendees to clear the lobby and disappear into the conference rooms. When it cleared, he waited until the time when he thought Leyna had checked her coat, then started for the exit by the far restrooms he'd spotted the night before.

He didn't see a cab stand on that side of the building, but hailed one before attempting to walk back to the front of the hotel.

He told the cab driver his destination, then asked, "I believe the Highway Ninety-nine route is the fastest, is that true?"

The cabby rocked his head from side to side in thought, then answered, "Most of the time. Cambie Street can sometimes be quicker."

"What about now, and most Saturday mornings? Which way would you take if you were in a hurry?"

"I'd take a shot on Cambie. The circles at Pacific Street can get backed up and then crossing the island can be a pain. I find Cambie to be more consistent and sometimes even good. The only problem could be the backtrack on Marine Drive. That can get a little congested."

"Which route would most cab drivers advise?"

"Cambie."

"My flight leaves in an hour. Am I going to make it?"

"Depends on how quick you are when I let you off."

The stop-start of Cambie Street stretched Sweetland's patience. He confirmed that the driving skills lacking in Calgary were also absent in Vancouver. The people he saw driving outside the cab window drove with the same radical moves as Calgary drivers, but slower.

The cab driver commented that things generally moved faster. By the time they got to Marine Drive to backtrack the short distance to the airport, he had twenty minutes to make his flight. They cleared the left turn into the airport and he paid as they cruised along the access road. He jumped out and ran to find out which gate he had to get to. Then he relaxed when he saw the word 'Delayed' flashing beside his flight information. Luck played in his favor—but did it? The delay meant he'd have less time in Calgary, tightening the time frame even more.

The line at Security took twenty minutes. He caught the eye of a security officer working in the search area beyond the scanning devices and asked if Security on Saturdays at this time was always this backed up. "Like clockwork," the officer responded.

So now it didn't matter if he made the flight. If the flight he intended to catch hadn't been delayed, the twenty minutes in Security would have caused him to miss it anyway.

He sat on one of the benches used by travellers to put their shoes back on and pulled out his notebook to check his backup flights. The flight leaving in half-an-hour was his second choice. He turned to a page where he had sketched a number of timelines for the trip. He looked at the one for the flight in thirty minutes. That flight had one short stop on the way to Calgary, but the round-trip could still be done in time. It meant that everything in Calgary had to go without a hitch, and he knew that wasn't likely.

This development made him look at the timeline for the first flight again to see what the delay would mean. Even with the delay, and assuming the delay would be the indicated twenty minutes, he would still arrive in Calgary before the second flight would arrive. This added more variables and less likelihood to the idea of Leyna being able to complete the trip.

What if there had been no flight delay the Saturday she had flown the round-trip? She would have missed the flight due to the delay in Security. What if she'd been lucky with the traffic on Cambie and Marine Drive? She may have made the flight. Too many things could go wrong, and he had only attempted half the trip. He decided she couldn't have made the flight and must have taken the second one, which made a stop. He went to that gate and purchased a ticket. While waiting at the gate to board the plane, he went over the timeline for the second flight again.

He'd left the hotel at nine-twenty. The cab ride took thirty-eight minutes, but it didn't matter that much if he took the second flight. Twenty minutes for Security and he would have been at the gate in plenty of time. The second flight left at eleven-oh-five, stopped for twenty-five minutes in Kamloops, then arrived in Calgary at twelve thirty-seven. It remained to be seen if he could get from the airport to Henberlin's apartment by one-thirty, less than an hour from the airport to the downtown core.

The one-stop flight arrived in Calgary on time. The cab-stand line looked like about a fifteen-minute wait. Sweetland went to the front of the line to talk to the stand captain, and asked if this line was normal for this time of day on a Saturday. It was. Next, he asked if people ever jumped the line and was told it happens all the time.

"No apology, some assholes just think their time is more important than everybody else's," the stand captain said.

Sweetland then pulled his badge out and explained that he was timing a crime that had occurred and needed to jump the line. The person at the front of the line yielded to his mission and he found himself on the move, assuming that Leyna would have found a way to do the same thing.

The normal Saturday noon-hour traffic moved along at a steady pace, so they made good time down Deerfoot Trail to the Memorial Drive exit. They had some delay at Edmonton Trail, and then ground to a halt as they reached Center Street. The cab driver cursed under his breath.

"We should have taken Edmonton Trail. Center Street can backup in the afternoon," the cabby said.

Sweetland then saw the hopelessness of what he was trying to accomplish. There were too many ways she could have gone. One of them may have gotten her to the apartment on time, but the odds were against it. Regardless, he wouldn't be able to complete the round-trip in time on this occasion.

"Change of destination, take me to City Hall."

Sweetland walked into Detective Richie's office and slumped into the stainless steel and durable fabric visitor chair.

"No luck, huh?" Richie asked.

"Unless she knew of some magic route or got real lucky with the traffic, it's an impossible trip."

"You weren't that far off making it to the apartment on time."

"Yeah, true. And it's possible if the murder took place a little later that she could still return to the conference before the last session finished. But we know exactly when the murder took place thanks to the video. I can't be a little late making it to the apartment,

I have to make it before the time of the murder. I should go talk to the witness that places her back in the bar at the end of the day."

———

Detective Sweetland left City Hall to walk to Bob Parry's office. He sat down in Parry's visitor chair and waited while Mr. Parry finished up a phone call. After the call and a brief greeting, Detective Sweetland asked Mr. Parry if he could remember what time Mrs. Henberlin had arrived at the cocktail party after the last session of the conference.

"Her drink was half gone when I first talked with her at about five-thirty, so she probably arrived fifteen minutes before that."

"What did you talk about?"

"Oh, she always makes fun of me at these things because I take advantage of the free food and drinks. I had a plate full of appetizers in my hand. I'm sure she made fun of me about food."

"Can you remember what she said about the food?"

"She said she wasn't surprised to find me with a plate in my hand and asked me how they tasted. I told her she should try them, they were quite tasty."

"Anything else?"

"Yeah, she commented about how bad the lunch was. Said surely I couldn't have enjoyed it. I told her I ate it all so I must have, something along those lines."

"Did you see her during lunch?"

Parry thought about this for a few seconds before he answered. "No. I guess the last I saw her before cocktails was in the first session."

"But no other time during the day?"

"I can't remember seeing her."

"Okay. Thanks for your time."

27

—

Henberlin had been nervous about the news he wanted to break to Leyna over dinner. Hoping to make the information more palatable he'd taken her to one of her favorite places to dine. He watched as she attacked her plate, waiting for the right time to have the conversation.

"It seems the people I've been helping have enough evidence to arrest Jian Liu." Henberlin watched as his wife stopped eating and placed her knife and fork across her plate. "They aren't going to, yet. But it's a possibility."

For her to stop eating this food that she so looked forward to was unusual. He saw the color drain from her face.

"He'll turn me in won't he? He'll give them the video to keep his ass out of jail." Her look expressed acceptance of the inevitable.

"It's possible," he said, then finished eating in silence. A silence that continued in the car on the drive home—a long, drawn-out ride that took forever. Red lights never lasted so long, and it seemed they all conspired to turn red as he approached.

He welcomed the turn onto their street and the distraction of reaching up to press the garage door opener. They made the right turn, which within a short distance snaked back to the left along the high bushes that surrounded the public park. As Henberlin released the button and looked three houses down the street to confirm that the automatic door began to rise at their home, his eyes went blind with car lights coming out of nowhere. Before he knew the source, a large mass crushed his door and forced his car sideways. His body flew across the console between the front seats. An abrupt stop against his seat belt snapped him back to impact with the driver's door. The window crackled as it spider-webbed. Small crystals falling onto his lap. The car jumped the curb and carried on into the public park's row of caragana bushes, then whiplashed to a stop.

Henberlin looked up and saw the lights of the vehicle turn off. Then he saw a large man climb out of the driver's side door. He carried a square-edged wooden bat.

Coming to the front of Henberlin's car, the large man saw the passenger side pushed deep into the thick bushes. He couldn't get around to that side of the car.

Henberlin called to his wife, who answered as she released her seat belt.

"Can you get out?" he yelled.

Leyna tried the door. It opened but the bushes blocked her exit.

"Push hard. Climb out into them if you can," he told her while trying to get his leg free. The driver's side door had crumpled, pinching his leg to the steering column.

Leyna half-grunted and half-screamed as she pushed hard on her door—finally getting it open enough to attempt to get her body through. Henberlin saw the large man come from around the other side of the truck. He ignored Henberlin and went to the back of the car, trying to get to the passenger side.

"Get out!" Henberlin yelled at Leyna. "Get through the bush and run. Push through now."

Leyna leaned into the bush with her shoulder, pushing branches out of the way and moving to the center of the bushes. She must have been aware of twigs snapping and poking her through her dress. She lay suspended in the bush, but placed her foot on the car seat she'd just left and pushed hard with all the strength in her legs. Her upper body cleared through to the other side of the bushes. She kept pushing with her legs against the branches she'd cleared, and at last rolled onto her back on the other side.

The large man tried to push through the bushes but they were too dense for his body to penetrate. He started for the park gate some yards back down the line of bushes—the only opening on this side of the park.

"Run Leyna. Get down the hill away from these lights."

Leyna scrambled, her legs tied by the tightness of her dress. She reached down and grabbed the hem, lifted it up to her waist, then ran with full strides to the far end of the park. There, she climbed over the short chain-link fence and ran down the hill that led to a main thoroughfare.

Henberlin continued to struggle with his leg, trying to free himself. He stopped and pulled out his cell phone to call 911. When he turned it on, the glow lit up his face so he turned it away so he wasn't illuminated. Then he heard a voice yell in Chinese.

Within seconds the large man came running back to the truck. He jumped into the driver's seat, backed the vehicle up, and turned and sped off, leaving Henberlin alone in the car.

Henberlin sat in his seat, moving his legs and arms and rotating his neck. When he twisted to check his back, pain clenched the muscles of his stomach, back, and ribs.

"Are you all right?" Leyna asked, out of breath.

Henberlin tried to jump away from the window. When he saw Leyna he said, "Christ, you scared me. What are you doing back here?"

"I ran to our yard to watch from there. When I looked around the corner, the truck was gone. What are you doing with the phone?"

"I'm calling for help."

"No, you can't. Those men were after me. How will you explain they wanted to kill me? The police will want to know why they came after me."

"I'll report it as a hit-and-run, but we need to get someone here to get me out."

"Did you see who they were?"

"No, but they spoke Chinese."

217

———

The firemen arrived first and removed Henberlin from the car. He gave a brief statement to the police as the paramedics placed him in the ambulance for the trip to the hospital. They'd already given him something effective for the rib pain, it already seemed like he had no injury at all.

In the hospital, life after injury got a little more complicated. The doctors played with a little more vigor. They pushed at the injured ribs, trying to get an indication of the severity of the injury—the best indicator being pain.

Meanwhile, the police report had caught the attention of an alert desk sergeant who recognized Henberlin's name, and that he was involved in an ongoing investigation. The sergeant put in a call to Detective Richie. Before the doctors had finished poking Henberlin where it hurt, the two detectives arrived to add to Henberlin's discomfort.

"A dark-colored truck. That's all?" Richie asked.

Henberlin tried to take a deep breath but had to stop. He let the wave of pain pass, then answered, "The lights were in my eyes. I couldn't see anything."

"What about when they pulled away, the lights weren't in your eyes then?"

"That was when I saw it was a dark truck."

A doctor squeezed his ribcage with a hand in each armpit. Henberlin's lungs froze, unable to breathe in, unable to breathe out. The doctor pushed him back to lay his head on the pillows. He couldn't speak to let them know how much pain he was in.

"Those ribs are going to be sore," the doctor said.

Henberlin eyes widened. 'No shit,' he thought. He turned and watched as Richie addressed Leyna.

"What did you see Mrs. Henberlin?"

"I didn't know what happened. I heard a thud and something hit the other side of the car. I saw Neil in pain on the driver's side and I knew I had to get out. Somehow I got the door open and made it through the bush, ran around to the gate and came to help him. The truck drove by me but I didn't look at it. I was trying to get to my husband."

Henberlin listened. His eyes closed, his ribs burning. Then he heard Leyna's voice again.

"By the way, why are you here? This is an accident, a hit-and-run unrelated to your investigation. Are you guys following us?"

Detective Sweetland spoke up. "We have to check on everything Mrs. Henberlin. Your husband's name showed up in a report and we had to see if it had any bearing on our case. That's all. A description of the truck or the driver would be very helpful."

"We've told you what we saw," Henberlin managed to get out. "Now do you mind? I think I'm going to be sick."

The doctor looked up from the clipboard he'd been writing on to look at Henberlin's complexion, then looked at the nurse standing by. The nurse walked past the detectives to take Henberlin's pulse. When he finished, he smiled at the detectives, indicating it was time for them to leave.

The doctor finished up, then left the Henberlin alone in their curtained area of the emergency room. Leyna leaned in close to Henberlin's ear.

"They know. They think someone tried to kill me. Why else would they be here? This is starting to be too much. That old man is after me. He's getting dangerous."

28

For two days, from his bed, Henberlin tried every hour to reach Jian Liu.

No answer.

Leyna paced the bedroom looking at him with dead eyes—on the verge of speaking, but always turning away to pace some more. After each phone call he made, she'd ask, "What if he's already sent the video? What if they come back?"

Henberlin reached Delaney and stuck to the same hit-and-run story he'd given the police.

"What about Jian Liu? I've been trying to call him like you suggested. Do you know where he is?" he asked Delaney.

"No, we haven't spotted him for a few days. We're worried something has scared him and he might try to disappear."

"So what do you do?"

"Watch all airports with international departures, watch all the border crossings into the United States, watch the port in Vancouver in case he tries to get onto a Chinese freighter," Delaney told him.

"What would have let him know that you guys might be getting close to arresting him?"

"Don't know. They have pretty good intelligence themselves, you know. They may have been watching us, watching you... who knows. They may have spotted something in the fake code we gave them. You never know when you're made. They may also have been happy with what they got and pulled up stakes."

"So what do you guys do now?"

"We go over everything again and keep a watch out for him. Hell, we're still not sure we want to capture him. If he stays in Canada, we'll probably just watch him, see who he talks to. If he goes to a friendly country, we watch him there. Meanwhile, we build a case against him and try to see if any of the bait code we planted shows up in future cyber-attacks. We do our due diligence, keep an eye on his contacts, watch Roy Warren to see if he's up to anything else on Jian Liu's account, and watch Gordon Venzi at Shield to see who he talks to. And, of course, we work with the CIA as they do their own follow-up."

"Am I involved in any of that?"

"We want you to continue to call Jian Liu for a while, and there may be some reason for you to talk to Warren or Venzi. We'd like Kyle to keep us updated on any inappropriate access made to the systems at Shield Oil."

"Okay. I'll keep trying and let you know if I connect with Jian Liu."

––––––

As Leyna paced the room, she noticed that her husband had used two different phones. One to call Delaney and another to call Jian Liu.

––––––

On the third day, Henberlin could finally walk with a tolerable level of the pain of his ribs being ground and pried apart with a burning rasp. The frequency with which he called Jian Liu had decreased since he began to believe what Delaney told him about the old man disappearing.

He grew tired of trying to get things accomplished from his bed and decided he could make it to work. Leyna helped him pack his case and made sure to misplace the phone that he used to call Jian Liu. She helped lower him into her car and wondered if he would be able to get out on his own.

"I'll have Kyle meet me at the car when I get to the office," he promised.

Leyna returned to the bedroom and retrieved the phone from where she'd hidden it. She powered it up, keyed in the security code her husband always used, and checked the contacts list. Only one name to be found. Instead of dialing his number, she sent him a text.

➜   This is his wife. Can we talk? - SEND

She placed the phone on her end table and resumed her pacing. To get her mind off of the waiting, she tried to think of things at work that required her attention. It worked for a while. When she realized how far behind she had become in all things related to her normal life, she recognized the first stages of the slide into depression beginning. She couldn't allow that. She had to be thinking, sharp, and alert to whatever Jian Liu might say if he agreed to talk with her. She took another of her pills. After twenty minutes, with the additional clarity the drug provided, she decided to text again.

➜   I'm so very sorry. – SEND

She sat bent over on the bed with her face in her hands. Her skin pulled tight across her face. She didn't know how long she sat, but became alert to having remained in the same spot when she noticed her upper body rocking. She stopped. She walked to her living room and stood looking out at the street.

The entire time, however long it was, she didn't see a single person. Not even a car passed in front of her view. She walked to the door, opened it, and reached into the mailbox to retrieve the day's mail. She placed the envelopes and advertising on the coffee table without looking at them, then returned to the bedroom and picked up the phone to text once more.

→ I would like to settle things with you. Nothing can be undone, we both have to move on. – SEND

This time she held the phone inches away from her face in both hands. She shook it trying to get Jian Liu's attention. She stared at the small screen for a long time. She growled, screamed, and threw the phone onto the bed. She turned, went into the bathroom, and began to run hot water in the tub.

She soaked for an hour, always listening for an alert from the phone. Drifting off, her thoughts wouldn't leave the sense of urgency she maintained about contacting Jian Liu. He had to agree there could be no benefit to either of them if he turned her in. She would have to live with the fact that she took another person's life, and she didn't know if she could do that without going insane. Her life could never be the normal pleasant life she lived before the incident. Her husband looked at her with a constant expression of concern, her work suffered, she'd lost her focus on any of the goals she had set for herself. But, she wasn't going to let the old man prevent her from trying to rebuild. If she allowed him to disappear without settling this thing, she would be waiting, expecting the bars to close in on her at any minute.

The water had cooled some. She slipped down, her nose just above the water.

'He wants me dead,' she thought. 'How did I let myself get to the point where someone wants me dead?'

Wrapped in a thick aqua-colored towel, Leyna dried and styled her hair. Next she painted her toenails with the new color she'd picked up in the cosmetics section of the Bay. She didn't trust herself with her fingernails, so their current state would have to do. She powdered her body, then put on a comfortable bra and panties. A last check in the mirror and she left to go and check the phone.

Nothing.

Her hand gripped the phone. Squeezed tight. She shook it and began to type.

→ Tonight. Walking Path Riverfront Avenue under the Center Street Bridge. 7:00. We MUST talk. – SEND

Using her own phone, she dialed her husband at work.

"Neil, do you think you could stad the pain of grabbing a quick bite downtown. I need to get out of the house for an evening." Leyna's voice had a desperate tone.

"Well–"

"I don't want you to make the trip back and forth, so I'll make my way to your office and I'll drive home."

Henberlin smiled at her considerate thought. "Sure, what did you have in mind?"

"How about Eau Claire Market? It has easy access and we can order fast and get out of there before you wear down too much."

He agreed, despite the ache that had been building all day in his ribs. His wife's cheery state of mind made him willing to suffer a bit longer. Besides, he had enough Percocet to double up his dose and thought that would get him through dinner.

They sat in the food court at the east end of the Eau Claire building and chose their meals by scanning the lighted menus in various food kiosks.

He watched her during the ordering process, trying to evaluate her mood. She seemed upbeat and timed the ordering of their meals with two different kiosks perfectly.

Beaming, she arrived back at the table with his food.

"Perfect timing," he said.

They took their time eating, talking about the various stores in the mall and remembering some of the purchases they'd made here. Leyna left him alone at the table on one occasion while she walked to the other end of the mall to see if the Montreal-style bagel shop still existed. When he saw her carrying a bag of bagels, he knew that it did.

Checking outside through the glass walls, the shadows told her the sun remained high in the western sky and would until quite late. She often checked him to see whether his pain level had increase. So far, the drugs were a match for the pain. At six forty-five she acted as if a great idea popped into her head and suggested a quick run to the Hong Kong Bakery to buy some custard and coconut tarts for later. He smiled and nodded.

"I hope you won't mind if I don't keep you company," he said.

"I'll be fine. I'll get you more water before I go."

After returning with the water, she gave him a quick kiss before walking through the food court exit onto Riverfront Avenue.

Walking east on Second Street, Leyna made her way to the nearest pedestrian bridge that crossed the river. She stepped into a landscaped rock garden and hurried to pick out a round stone larger than her hand. She placed it into her bag—a bag she'd chosen based on the strength of its straps.

She turned east and walked down the deserted riverfront pathway. It forked at the Center Street Bridge. She stayed to the left to follow the path under the bridge, where she found herself alone. The water rippled past, fast moving only a foot or two from the path. She continued out to the other side of the bridge and, a short way beyond, stopped to lean on the steel rail fence. Behind her stretched Chinatown. She'd picked this location so Jian Liu wouldn't have to travel too far, should he decide to show up.

A few evening walkers and joggers made their way along the paths. She knew they would all prefer the upper level of the path to remain in the evening sun, since the area under the bridge was shaded.

A few minutes later, she returned to the shadows under the bridge. She spotted a short man with a cane standing in the middle of the asphalt path, his eyes fixed out over the river. She approached and stopped about five feet from the man.

"Mr. Liu?"

Jian Liu turned to face Leyna and nodded slowly.

Leyna reached to her left shoulder and, in one motion, slipped her bag down her arm to her left hand. With both hands gripping the straps, she twisted her body back to the left, coiling energy. Then, with swift recoil, she brought her arms up to shoulder level, extended them completely as if swinging an Olympic hammer, and brought the stone-weighted bag into the right side of Jian Liu's head above his right eye.

She heard a *twack* as the bag's momentum turned her in a complete circle. When she saw Jian Liu again, his body seemed suspended in air, head back, the cane leaving his hand and falling to the ground. Then one leg took a step back, wobbled, and stalled his body from falling. But then it dropped. His head cracked on the lower rung of the steel rail.

Leyna walked to the body and placed her bag on the ground beside it. She reached into his pockets darting her hand into each corner and along the bottom seams. When she found what she was after, she pulled her hand out with his cell phone in its tight grip.

'Good, a pre-paid,' she thought, as she placed it in her bag.

Then she pushed Jian Liu under the rail and into the rushing water. The small man's light body offered little resistance. She turned and grabbed his cane and threw it in the river behind him, along with the stone from her purse. After inspecting her bag and finding blood smeared on the bottom corner, she dipped it in the river and wiped it down.

Leyna looked down the river. Seeing no sign of the body, she walked up the path access to Center Street and found her way to the bakery.

'It worked,' she thought. 'Perfect timing.'

She'd counted on Jian Liu not being able to resist an unexpected chance to get at her again—even if he had to come for her alone.

The evening continued to cool. She noticed a chill at the edges of her hairline where she had begun to sweat. Her heart pulsed and fog obscured her thoughts. Inside the bakery she couldn't remember why she had entered, the warmth and humidity closed in on her.

The fast-paced beats of her heart swelled in her fingertips, her knees wanted to unlock and give in to gravity. She was going to go down if she didn't go back outside to the cool air. Outside, she told herself to breathe.

'Walk slow and breathe,' she thought, as she returned to her waiting husband.

He sat at the table, his complexion white turning to grey. He saw Leyna approaching without a white bakery bag.

"Don't tell me they were closed," Henberlin said, opening his eyes wide in disbelief.

"Yep, so I walked down to the bakery next to the Silver Dragon, closed as well, and then tried the Chinese Cultural Center and they were closed too. Sorry."

"You got me all excited about those tarts."

"I'll try to get some tomorrow."

"Your hair's a little messed up. Are you okay?"

Leyna nodded. "I was hoofing it so you wouldn't think I was gone too long."

Henberlin smiled. "You think we could head for home? My ribs are starting to bake."

"I'll get the car."

She leaned in and kissed him, then stood and hugged his head to her stomach. Her cheek rested on the top of his head. After a few seconds, in a somber voice she said, "Let's get home where I can take care of you."

29

—

Henberlin limped by Kyle's office intending on a short visit on the way to his own. He'd walked the longer route through the hallways only to find the office empty. Hobbling into Kyle's office, he looked for a pad of paper to leave a note asking Kyle to call when he returned from his mid-morning coffee break. Henberlin had overdone it on his ribs the night before with Leyna, but the welcome distraction of work brought him from his home this morning. Sitting in his bedroom with nothing to do gave him only one thing to think about: The pain in his ribs. At the office, he could check order status, call customers, and update project reports. He wouldn't have his mind occupied by the pain alone. But, so far, he'd begun to think he'd made a big mistake by coming in.

It seemed like a hard thumb pressed into his bruised and aching bones with each step he took this morning. The ribs screamed a reminder: "Still broken, still broken, still broken."

Fatigue rushed on him after limited exertion, and exhaustion spied on the fatigue, ready to take over. Taking a deep breath to increase oxygen flow only increased the pain. He feared the pleasure awaiting him when he reached his office and had to lower himself into his chair. Once there, during the seating process, the pain made him rethink the benefit of sitting down. In a slight panic, he stopped halfway to the seat and thought of standing again. But he knew his ass had to find that chair seat. It might as well be now rather than stand up and try again.

Constricting his stomach muscles hurt and shifting his ribs hurt more. Finally arriving at the seat cushion, he relaxed the muscles forcing his ribs to grind against each other. He realized he'd been holding his breath and had to take in a deep one to prevent himself from passing out.

Leaning back in the chair broke the pain level in the wrong direction, shooting spikes into the cartilage between his ribs.

He forced his muscles to relax and took short, deliberate breaths to settle himself. In this manner, he reduced the tormenting agony to severe irritation. Then one of the cell phones in his pocket vibrated, startling him, causing him to tense his upper body muscles. Sparks shot through his brain as it registered the minor shift in his chest cavity.

'It's the Delaney phone,' he thought. The Jian Liu phone, which he remembered this morning, lay quiet in his other pocket. Taking his time to retrieve the cell phone, he raised his face to the ceiling and closed his eyes while he concentrated on breathing through his nose.

"Hello," he squeaked out.

"Neil, how you doing? You sound like shit."

"Everything hurts, especially answering the phone."

"Cracked ribs are a bitch, and it takes forever for the misery to ease up."

"That doesn't help."

"Right, nothing helps. It's one of those injuries you just have to take your lumps and live with."

"Still doesn't help."

"Yeah, sorry. I don't know if this will either. They found Jian Liu's body snagged in some low branches down in the Bow River."

Henberlin jerked to sit up, but pangs of pain sent him back. He groaned in response.

"They're not sure when or where he went in. It's too early to tell. They're probably still putting him in the ambulance."

"Wow," Henberlin said. "No wonder he didn't answer my calls."

"Oh no, his body hadn't been in the water that long. He likely floated through the lower water side of the Harvie Passage. He snagged up after passing the final pool."

"So he stayed in town."

"I guess he knows where to hide."

"Now what?"

"We stay on the others, see if they start working for someone else, see if someone takes over for Jian Liu. Did you manage to contact him yesterday?"

"No. I tried a few times but no answer, and he didn't return my calls."

"Okay. You just need to sit and wait. Let us know if someone makes contact with you. We'll be in touch if we need additional input."

"Yeah, sure. Listen, there may be something you can help me with. Not right now but maybe soon."

"What's that?"

Henberlin picked up a note of impatience in Delaney's question.

"The detectives and their investigation into my wife. They're coming on a little strong."

"Neil, I can't interfere with a police investigation."

"I don't want you to interfere. I'm thinking there may come a time when I need you for a character reference. You know, if you tell them how I've cooperated with you, they might cut me some slack over the way I've been trying to protect my wife."

"Do you have a lawyer? And I don't mean Hec Taylor?"

"No, she didn't do anything. Why would we need a lawyer when we have nothing to hide? We've cooperated all along, but they don't know how this is affecting my wife."

"We'll see. I really don't want to get involved with the locals."

Disappointed, Henberlin said, "Yeah, well it hasn't come to that, yet. Let's hope it doesn't."

"Right. I should go."

The line went dead.

The Jian Liu phone began to burn a hole in his pocket. It had to go. But where? Was it slim enough to shove through the shredder he had over his waste basket? No, it had to go through the industrial shredder in the copy room. Before he self-inflicted another round of scrambling his pain receptors, he decided to delete anything he found on the phone in the privacy of his own office. He flicked it on, then clicked on the contacts. The only entry, Jian Liu. He highlighted it and a secondary menu popped up. He clicked on the calls box and deleted each of the calls listed. When he finished, he ended up back at the pop-up menu. Though he'd never sent Jian Liu a message, he clicked on the messages box anyway.

He had to shake his head to make sure he saw the displayed information. Messages sent. Based on the content, they'd been sent by Leyna.

He stared at the messages for a long time. When he awoke from his stunned state, he deleted the messages, stood, and, ignoring the pain, walked to the copy room.

Alone, he took a few sheets of blank paper from the supply shelf. He fed half of them into the shredder, then dropped the phone in behind. The shredder blades slowed and labored for a second, then buzzed a high-pitched buzz before falling silent. Small plastic chips sprayed against the plastic garbage bags in the machine's hopper. He placed another stack of paper into the feeder to clear any phone debris that may have stuck in the cutters.

Geneva's voice startled him. "What was that noise?"

"I fed an entire report folder to save time, one of those ones with the metal fold-over tabs for three-hole punch paper."

"Did it go through okay?"

"Noisy, but it wasn't much of a challenge for this beast."

"Kyle was just asking for you."

"Oh, he's back. Well, can you tell him I'll call him later? I'm a little done in. I shouldn't have come here."

"I was surprised to see you. I'll tell him. You go take care of yourself."

———

In the elevator on the way down, Henberlin's personal cell phone rang. He looked at the screen to see it was Detective Sweetland.

"Hello Detective."

"Good morning, Mr. Henberlin. Would it be okay if we came over to have a talk with you?"

"Actually, I'm heading home now. My ribs are acting up a little."

"Then could we come to your home?"

"I guess. What do you want?"

"Something's happened that I'd rather not talk about over the phone."

"Fine."

"Will Mrs. Henberlin be home?"

"Should she be?"

"It would be great if she could."

"I have to make a quick stop, so can we make it after lunch?"

"Great. See you around one."

Henberlin placed a call to his wife. When she answered, he told her about the detectives coming to the house at one o'clock.

"Again?" she said. "What do they want this time?"

"Well, you probably haven't heard, but they found Jian Liu's body in the river this morning."

"Jian Liu? The old man?"

"Yes. They didn't mention him, but I'm sure the detectives want to ask us if we know anything about it."

"Why would we?"

"Right. Are you at home?"

"Yes."

"Good. I'm on my way. We'll talk when I get there."

Sweetland and Richie arrived early. A short time after Henberlin had gotten himself seated and medicated, the doorbell rang. Even though they'd been in the home before, the two detectives looked around, checking the room with the same moderate taste they'd observed previously.

"When was the last time you spoke with Jian Liu?" Richie finally asked.

"Yanmei's father? I suppose it must have been after I was released when you arrested me. I called to thank him. Why?"

"And you, Mrs. Henberlin?"

Leyna bounced upright in her seat. "Me? I've never met him."

"Jian Liu is dead. Do either of you know anything about that?"

Both of the Henberlins sat wide-eyed and seething as they shook their heads.

"What are you saying? That because you mistakenly believe Leyna had something to do with his daughter's murder, she's somehow involved in this man's death as well?

"The facts clearly indicate my wife couldn't have murdered Mrs. Albin. Your refusal to believe that is now harassment. It seems that the only form of satisfaction you can derive from this misdirected investigation of yours is to make our lives miserable. We have no knowledge of anything Mr. Liu ever did in life. None."

"Certainly during your affair with Mrs. Albin, the two of you would have mentioned her father. You must know something about him."

"Do you insist on calling it an 'affair' deliberately to harass my wife?"

"Come on, Mr. Henberlin. Nobody believes you when you say there wasn't an affair." Detective Richie leaned forward. "I can even see in your wife's eyes that she doesn't believe you. You went outside your marriage. Your wife became jealous and put an end to the affair—and we're going to prove that she did. But that's not why we're here. We want to know anything you can tell us about Jian Liu."

Henberlin raised his body, ignoring the pain his ribs delivered, and leaned forward as Leyna drew back against the back of the sofa. "You're wrong," Henberlin said, "and my wife knows you're wrong. You're trying to shake her belief in me, and that's not going to happen. Why are you assuming we know anything about Jian Liu?"

"I'm only trying to piece together any information I can find about Mr. Liu. You have a connection to the family."

Shaking his head, he said, "No I don't. I had a business relationship with Mr. Liu's daughter. It had nothing to do with Mr. Liu and therefore nothing to do with his death. There's nothing we can tell you about what happened to Mr. Liu. If that's why you're here, then I'd say we have nothing more to discuss."

"Can you tell us where you were last night?"

"If you'll tell us what your motive is for asking us questions that imply we know something about his death." Henberlin's jaw dropped when he finished his question.

"Mr. Henberlin, we'll be out of your hair in minutes—if you'll tell us where you were last night."

"You're harassing us with your questions. We told you, we have no relationship with Mr. Liu. That should be the end of it, unless you are intent on disrupting our lives. You haven't said whether or not Mr. Liu's death was murder or an accident. You would only be asking us about our whereabouts if you suspected us of being involved with his death. Are we suspects in the death of Mr. Liu?" Henberlin's voice rose as he asked the last question.

"We're not at that point yet," Detective Richie said.

"Then you're harassing us. Get out." Henberlin indicated the direction of the front door.

He kept watch until their car pulled away from the curb, then turned to Leyna. He indicated with his hand for her to come close.

He placed his mouth beside her ear and whispered, "Please tell me you had nothing to do with Jian Liu's death."

Leyna pulled back and looked down at the coffee table. He could tell she hesitated while concocting something that she hoped didn't upset him. He knew of her texts to Jian Liu the previous day, and wanted to find out if she would be honest with him, if she would continue to trust him with her freedom.

'What if she denies contacting him?' Henberlin thought. 'What if she admits she had something to do with another murder? Could I still protect her or have I had enough? If she's involved in Jian Liu's death, then three people are dead because of her insecurity.'

After too long a time waiting for her reply, he signaled her close again.

"I heard you," she said in a soft voice but remained in place. "I couldn't help it. Something had to be done about that man."

"Nooo…" Henberlin moaned.

"He has the video and he tried to kill us. Were we going to sit around waiting for him to attack again? That threat's gone now, thanks to me." Anger built in her words.

"He was about to leave the country," Henberlin said. "In fact, they suspected he already had. He wouldn't have been a threat any longer."

"They were wrong, weren't they? He was still here and would still be a threat if I hadn't taken care of things. You should be happy I got rid of the problem. Now we can begin to live normal lives."

"How? Knowing that you've killed three people, how can we live normal lives?"

"We do, that's all. We just do."

"Do you think those detectives are going to leave us alone?"

"With time, yes. They have nothing. They can't charge us with anything. You're in as much trouble as I am, so you have to protect us by living as normal."

30

—

The VP of Sales' business analyst knocked on the frame of Henberlin's open door. Henberlin ignored the interruption and continued to read the project updates from the Shield Oil system implementation. In the past two months, R.E.S. had completed the installation of twelve systems in the Reservoir Simulation department and had taken orders for sixteen more. Once installed, they would complete the first phase of the project. Henberlin worked with two other salesmen in the Calgary office to begin sales campaigns aimed at other large oil companies—ones that were already trying to place orders to get on a delivery schedule. The Shield success rippled out to the oil patch to both local and international oil companies.

The analyst knocked again. This time Henberlin lifted his head and made eye contact.

"What does he want?" he said in a flat tone.

"Mr. Brady is wondering when the project report for Shield will be available."

"The updates haven't arrived. I'll let him know when they do."

"He doesn't understand why his name isn't on the distribution list so he doesn't have to keep asking you for the information."

Henberlin stared at the analyst with no intention of answering the question.

After an uncomfortable silence, the analyst said, "He also wants to know who's going on the trip to Houston and who from within R.E.S. will be at the meetings. He thinks he should be there."

"I don't see the point of him being in Houston. I'll provide him with all the information regarding the meeting. So he'll know what's going on, but there's nothing he can add to the meeting."

"You know he can travel whenever he wants and could be in Houston without your approval."

"If he wants to look that desperate, I can't stop him. If he shows up, we'll fake that he's welcome, but I'll let everyone know he's there because of his insecurities."

Henberlin smiled at the VP's analyst, then held up the document in his hand and turned his eyes to continue reading. He saw through his peripheral vision the analyst turn, hesitate to leave, then finally step away. Henberlin instinctively rubbed his hands over his ribs. The pain was no longer on his mind, but the habit of checking remained with stubborn dedication. Then he remembered that he had to get his passport back from the detectives.

———

Detective Sweetland stuck his head in on Detective Richie, who had the Captain of Detectives in his office.

"I just got a call from Neil Henberlin. He wants his and his wife's passports back. Seems he has a business meeting in Houston in a week or so. His wife isn't going. I don't see any problem giving them back, do you?" His eyes took in the captain as well as Richie.

Both men thought for a second, then shook their heads.

"Okay. Last I saw them you had them, Richie. You know where they are?"

"Yeah, I'll get them."

"Give them to me when you do."

Detective Richie nodded.

Sometime later, he dug into his filing cabinet and pulled out the file on the Albin murders. Sitting at the top of the file were the two passports. He pulled them out and slapped them onto his desk. Since Sweetland intended to return them, and they wouldn't be seeing them again, he decided to take another look through the booklets. Flipping through Henberlin's passport, he saw nothing unusual. He hadn't travelled internationally very often. In reality, the detectives didn't have any interest in his travel prior to the murders about three months earlier. All entrance stamps and re-entry stamps appeared to be in order.

He closed the passport and placed it back on his desk. In Mrs. Henberlin's, he flipped back a few pages looking for stamps from before the murders. He flipped back too far, to a stamp that came from a trip to Portugal the previous summer. He flipped forward and found a trip to the United States during February. Then he found nothing but blank pages where there should have been a stamp for her re-entry to Canada when she returned from the trip she'd taken with her husband to Los Angeles shortly after the murders.

He flipped back to the first page of stamps and went over each one—in case the immigration agent had used an earlier page and put the stamps out of chronological order. He studied each one. When he returned to the stamp from the February trip without finding the stamp he was looking for, he turned each of the remaining blank pages to ensure they were blank. They were.

The detective picked up Henberlin's passport again and found his return stamp from that trip. He wrote down the date. He then leaned back in his chair and began to pull up his memories of that day. Henberlin's wife had surprised everyone by returning on her own, not even telling her husband that she was returning.

What flight had she returned on? Where had it arrived from? He opened the case folder and looked over his notes. They'd never checked the exact flight, but in the notes she said she'd returned via Seattle. The detective turned to his computer and accessed a travel website, keying in a trip from Seattle to Calgary. He knew Henberlin had arrived from Los Angeles before noon and that his wife was at their home that evening. Richie and Sweetland got to the Henberlin residence around seven, so he looked for flights arriving in that interval.

The list included thirteen flights, all from Seattle. He did a screen print, then ticked off the ones most likely to be her flight. He took his list into Detective Sweetland's office and filled him in on what he'd discovered.

Detective Richie called the feeder operation of Alaska Airlines to acquire the passenger list for a number of their flights from Seattle to Calgary for the last Friday of Stampede Week. He expected he would have to let them know he was willing to get a search warrant, if they didn't cooperate. This type of reluctance he'd seen on television detective shows, the airlines always wanting to protect the privacy of their passengers. This airline didn't hesitate for a second. In a matter of minutes, they emailed him the lists he requested. His heart-rate rose a beat when he saw Leyna Henberlin's name on a flight that arrived at six PM on that date. She couldn't have been home long when they arrived after seven o'clock. Next, he booked out to the airport. It wasn't the practice of the people at Immigration to answer questions over the phone.

It took a few minutes to explain what he needed from the Immigration records and why he needed it. Once they understood, the Immigration people got behind his cause and printed out a list of returning citizens for the flight in question. When he reviewed the list of names, Leyna Henberlin's wasn't on it.

"Is it possible for a name that appears on a flight manifest to be missing from the list of passengers you processed through Immigration?" Richie asked the agent.

"Virtually impossible. She had to have registered."

Richie nodded. He couldn't afford to alienate the agent with his next question. "What do you think she did to get through the check-in?"

"Identification." She held Richie's stare, her face stern. Richie thought she was shutting him down until she said, "Wait here for a few minutes. I'll get the video from that night."

He waited what seemed like a long time before the agent returned and escorted him to another room. The agent operated the equipment, scrolling back and forth as Richie watched each line for Leyna to appear.

Within ten minutes, he spotted her in one of the lines.

"Wait, stop. That's her." Richie said.

"Okay, timestamp is eighteen-twelve and she's processed at desk seven." She wrote down the information, then matched the time and agent ID on a report she'd previously printed off. "The name with that agent at that time is Michele Reddig. She used someone else's passport."

"Reddig." Richie looked at the wall and rubbed his upper lip. "We interviewed someone named Reddig. Can you look up the passport and get me an address?" Detective Richie asked.

The agent copied the passport number with her mouse, then toggled her screen to another inquiry screen. She pasted in the number. Soon, the screen filled with what looked like the information page of a passport, including the picture.

"Oh, we did talk to her. It's Leyna Henberlin's sister. She goes by Louise, but I see that's her middle name. They do look pretty similar, don't you think?"

The agent looked at Richie, somewhat bewildered.

"Right, you've only seen her in the video. Take a look at her passport." Richie held open the passport for the agent.

"Very similar. Her using another person's passport is a federal offense. We're going to want to talk to her," the agent said.

"She's in more serious trouble than a passport violation, but we'll be glad to add your charges to what we're going to lay on her. Now that we know how she hid her identity once, we have some additional work to do. I'll let you know when we're getting ready to charge her, and we'll get your charges on the slate."

He left the airport and didn't mind once that the traffic into the downtown core stopped, started, and crawled, delaying the enjoyment he knew would flow free through his mind as he presented his findings to Sweetland and the captain.

Their next task was to take another look at the flights from Vancouver to Calgary on the Saturday of the murders.

31

—

The two detectives had to execute a flurry of procedural activities created by Michele Reddig's passport before they could request a search warrant to actually get the document in their hands. Letting Leyna and Neil Henberlin know that the investigation had advanced could be disastrous to their efforts, so they worked fast to minimize the potential for discovery.

Detective Sweetland contacted the regional airlines that Leyna Henberlin might have flown the day of the murders if she had made the perfect flight and executed all her movements with perfect timing. Again the airlines cooperated, supplying passenger lists for a number of flights.

To Sweetland's great pleasure, Michele Reddig's name appeared on one of the lists.

Next, he contacted Airport Security and made an appointment to review the closed-circuit camera video to identify Leyna Henberlin exiting the plane.

Two hours later, he returned to the office holding up a DVD and smiling wide as the prairie.

"She's there, moving as if she had all the time in the world. Even got her walking out to the taxi stand, but at that point she soon goes out of frame. I don't have a cab number."

"We don't need the taxi since we know where she went," Richie said. "Let's take a look at the video, so we can see what she's wearing. Then we'll get a search warrant for her clothes, too. One of us will go to the sister's for the passport, and one of us will go to the Henberlin's place."

"And an arrest warrant?" Sweetland asked.

"Captain?" asked Richie.

"Yeah, but hold off on the arrest until you actually find the clothing and see the passport with the re-entry stamp. We want this tight so the arrest sticks. While you're waiting, take another good look at the video of the murder. Try and find something we can attribute to Mrs. Henberlin."

Detective Richie knocked on the door at Leyna's sister's home. Michele Reddig answered the door. Recognizing the detective immediately, she paused in her movement. Her cheery expression became serious and flat.

"Hello Detective. I don't know what you could possibly be doing here. It's been months since you stopped bothering my sister, so now you're going after her family members?" Leyna's sister held her arms across her chest, leaning against the door jamb and blocking the entrance.

"Just need to search your house." Detective Richie lifted the corners of his mouth into a sardonic smile. "I have a warrant. If you cooperate, this won't take but a minute."

"Like I have a choice." She turned inside and cleared the door for Detective Richie.

He stepped into the living room and offered her the warrant. She took it, then placed it on the coffee table without opening it to take a look.

"First, I came here to get your passport. I'm going to want to take it with me. Is that going to present a problem?"

"Passport. Gee, I haven't travelled in years. I imagine it's in the desk, but I'm sure it's expired."

Mrs. Reddig disappeared down a hall, and Richie could hear what he presumed were desk drawers opening and closing, mixed with the shuffling of paper. He needed to be in the room, so he joined her. He stepped into the room as she laid her hands on the passport.

"May I see that?"

She handed him the passport without opening it. Richie flipped to the information page, read the expiration date and looked at the picture.

"You're right, expired." He pursed his lips. "This picture doesn't look much like your sister."

She tried to take the book from Richie to see the picture but he didn't give it up. He flipped to the pages intended for entry stamps and found no stamps at all. He handed it to Mrs. Reddig, who flipped to the photo.

"It doesn't look like me now, either. Back then, like now, we looked a lot alike."

The detective looked her in the eye. "You don't have a current passport?"

"No. I don't travel anywhere that requires that I have a passport, and don't intend to."

"Can you check and see if you're still in possession of your other forms of identification? Driver's license, Social Insurance Number?"

Mrs. Reddig moved past Richie and returned to the living room. Her purse sat on a small table by the entry. She searched through it and found both documents and showed them to Richie.

"Can you recall before and after the weekend that your sister went to Vancouver, when the murders occurred, if she had access to your purse without you knowing it?"

"Good god." Michele shook her head and held her hands out like the answer was obvious, "We see each other all the time. Of course she would have been able to get into my purse. But why would she?"

"I'm not certain that she did, Mrs. Reddig. I'm just asking."

She glared at Richie for a solid minute, then asked, "What else do you need?"

"I'd like to take a look in your closets."

"My closets?" She peered at the detective with her eyebrows pressed together.

After Richie's nod, Reddig turned and led him to the bedroom and clothes closets. He slid the garments along the rails, then asked if she had any garments currently at the cleaners. When she said she didn't, he said, "I think I'm done. Thank you for your time."

Richie walked back out into the hallway, out to the living room to the front door, and let himself out. He pulled out his cell and called his partner.

"Did you find the clothes?" he asked Sweetland.

"Nobody's home. The place is dark and no cars in the garage."

"Well shit. I've got a passport but it's expired. No stamps. Couldn't have been used by Leyna Henberlin. She must have applied for a passport in her sister's name."

"How about the dress?"

"Nothing."

"We need to find her. You going back downtown?"

"Yeah. See you there."

―――――

Leyna Henberlin sat in her office staring down at her hands. She didn't know she'd been picking at the polish on her nails. She didn't actually see what her eyes focused on. For that matter, her eyes weren't focused. Her thoughts weren't either. They came at her from all directions at once. Her job, her father, the old Chinese man under the bridge, the yard behind the house, her marriage, her husband— but mostly her sister's phone call telling her of the detective's visit to her house, looking for her passport.

They'll be looking for me now, she thought, then picked up the telephone and called her husband.

"I hope you weren't planning on leaving soon and expecting dinner to be ready," she said when he answered the phone with his usual greeting.

"Umm, well, what time is it?"

"Not late yet, but getting there. I phoned to let you know I still have a few things to deal with, so you're allowed to work late yourself. In fact, you may be on your own for dinner." She tried to portray a joking forgiveness for his being late.

"Okay, I could use the time. I'll see you when we're together again."

"Yes, when we're together again. And soon I hope." Her voice dropped, lost in thought.

"I won't be too late. Do you think you will be?"

"Huh? Oh, no. I shouldn't be long." She paused then said, "Thanks, Neil. I love you."

"Love you too. See you later."

They hung up.

———

Two hours later, when Henberlin turned the corner to his home, he reached up and clicked the garage door opener. He stopped in the garage, got out, and was opening the door to the house as the garage door touched the concrete floor. He didn't bother calling for his wife since he found Leyna's car's spot in the garage empty. He flicked on a hall light, a living room light, and stepped over to pull the cords that closed the curtains. It had been so long since the police had watched his house that he didn't think to look for a strange car.

Loosening his tie, he began unbuttoning his shirt as he walked to his bedroom. There, he stripped and took a shower. The shower supplied the sought after stress relief after a day riding a desk chair. He noticed a few persistent bruises, but otherwise his ribs were close to normal. Wearing workout shorts and a T-shirt, he returned to the living room to make something to sip on while he searched the refrigerator for something to eat.

———

Leyna leaned against her car, waiting. Without looking at her watch she couldn't tell if the time passed slowly or if it raced and she chose not to look at her watch. She didn't care if she stood beside the car the whole night yet she wanted to get done what she knew she had to do. There were no other cars in the parking garage, which set her at ease. Whatever she did next wouldn't be witnessed. In the parking garage the security cameras were located at the entrance and the exit, not on the individual parking levels. From time to time she looked at her fingers, noticing the chipped polish, not remembering that she had been picking at them since the phone call from her sister.

She lifted her head and turned to the door that led to that floor's lobby. The door opened and Detective Richie stepped through, stopping when he spotted Leyna leaning against her car.

"Mrs. Henberlin, I've been looking for you," he said.

"Well, now you've found me. Where's the other detective?" She continued to lean against the far side of her car, away from the detective who now stood at the back of the vehicle.

"I'm here to take you in. I want you to go with me down to the station."

"Am I under arrest?"

"No."

"Then I'm not going."

"I can put you under arrest for not cooperating and take you in without charging you with a major offense. Either way, you're going to be coming with me."

"I don't think I will. So now what?"

"Mrs. Henberlin, if you don't cooperate I'm going to have to put the cuffs on you and escort you to my car. Do you want to go out like that?"

"You want to rough me up?"

"That's not how we do this. You need to accept that you're going to have to answer for what you did and come along peacefully."

"Well, I told you, I'm not going to."

Detective Richie watched her for a few seconds then as if he'd made up his mind that talking wasn't going to accomplish anything he stepped closer to Leyna. As he did he reached behind his back to grab a pair of handcuffs snapped to his belt on a leather. As he did, Leyna reached down and grabbed the tire iron she'd taken from the trunk of her car in her right hand. While Detective Richie's hand grappled with the cuffs Leyna cocked her wrist with the tire iron in it and whipped it at Richie. He saw it coming and leaned back but it still caught him at the base of his neck and slid up the side of his head. He remained standing, reaching to the side of his head where the tire iron had scraped, folded, and crushed his ear. Leyna step forward. With the tire iron in both hands she stabbed the beveled end into his abdomen. Richie folded over and toppled down to the cement floor. He lay on his side for a few seconds then rolled onto his back. Leyna stood with the tire iron lifted above her head.

"First that woman thought she could take him away from me, now you think you can take me away from him. I guess both attempts end up the same way." Leyna brought the tire iron down with all her strength and a cracking thud sounded from the middle of Detective Richie's forehead. He laid motionless behind her vehicle.

Leyna stood with the tire iron brought back for another blow if needed. Her shoulders heaved with the intake of deep breaths. She spit out a skein of hair that had made its way into the side of her mouth. Seeing that Detective Richie wasn't going to move again she straightened upright out of her athletic stance and took a few more deep breaths. Once she calmed herself she opened the door of her car, threw the tire iron onto the passenger side floor, and lowered herself into the driver's seat. She started the car and reversed it, not even noticing the bumps lifting the car as she backed over the detective. She knew she'd been lucky that just one of the detectives had come to arrest her but her anger also rose now that she had to go find the other one and take care of him too. If her luck held, the other detective was on his way to arrest her husband.

––––––

Outside the Henberlin home, Detective Sweetland pulled up after receiving the message from dispatch of Henberlin's return. He parked behind the unmarked police car then climbed into the back seat with the two officers.

"Did the other car arrive?" he asked.

"No, sir."

"Drop the 'sir' stuff. It was only him in the car that arrived?"

"We only saw one head."

"Okay, thanks guys. We'll give it an hour." Sweetland went to climb out, but couldn't open the back door of the car from inside. The driver heard Sweetland swear, and he flipped a switch that allowed him to open the door. The officers watched in their rearview mirrors as the detective returned to his car.

––––––

With his mind numb from work, the only thing Henberlin could come up with for dinner was an uninspired stir-fry. He sliced up a few vegetables while defrosting a chicken breast. He cut that into cubes and tossed it into a wok. When the meat turned nice and brown, he added the vegetables and cooked them until they developed some browning of their own. Then he poured some soy sauce over it and plopped it out into a bowl. Rice would have been nice, but he didn't want to take the time. As he carried the hot bowl of stir-fry and his drink to their television room, the doorbell rang.

He scrunched his face, wondering who could be dropping in. His food and drink landed on the coffee table in the living room and he went to open the door.

When he saw Detective Sweetland, backed up by two uniforms, he sighed and tilted his head while his shoulders slumped.

"What can I do for you, Detective?" he asked.

"I have a search warrant," Sweetland said, handing him the document. "Please step aside."

Henberlin pivoted out of their way. "Haven't you already gone over this place enough? What are you looking for? Maybe I can just get it for you and you can be on your way."

"I need to look in your wife's closet, and in all desks and drawers for passports," Sweetland answered.

"She uses most of the closet in our room, and has some things in the closet in the guest room. But you guys have our passports. Did you forget that?"

"No, I didn't." Sweetland's tone had a strong dose of don't-call-me-stupid to it.

"Okay. Carry on."

Sweetland asked, "Where's your wife?"

"She called me at my office and said she had work to do."

"So she's there?"

Henberlin shrugged. "Or at a client's office, or her meeting turned into dinner. She must have known that might happen, because she told me I was on my own as far as eating was concerned."

Detective Sweetland looked down at the bowl of fried vegetables then up at Henberlin giving him a chin-lift. He left without saying anything to Henberlin and went to the bedroom where he took Leyna's clothing from the closet and laid each piece on the bed. He arrived at one particular dress and stopped. He held it out to the full length of his arms, pinching the garment by its shoulders.

"This looks like the one," he said to Henberlin, who stood in the doorway.

Sweetland bagged the dress then went through the nightstands followed by a thorough search of every drawer in the den, kitchen, and living room. When he finished, he hadn't found any passports.

"Do you know who your wife was meeting tonight?" he asked Henberlin, who had followed in silence as the detective searched.

"No, sorry."

"Can I have a look at your phone?"

Henberlin thought about this for a second. He had some questions he wanted answered, and knew he wouldn't get them if he didn't cooperate. He pulled out his phone, keyed in the security code, and handed it to Sweetland.

"Okay," Sweetland said after he'd scrolled through the messages app. "Please contact us if she gets in contact with you. It'll go easier for her if you do, and if she turns herself in."

"What's going on? Why are you after her again after all this time has gone by?" Henberlin asked evenly, even though dread filled his heart anticipating the answer that might come out.

"We have enough evidence to charge your wife with murder, Mr. Henberlin," Sweetland said. "Video evidence."

Henberlin's head shot up to stare at Detective Sweetland. "Video?"

"From the Calgary airport, around noon the day of the murders. Your wife returned to Calgary that day," Sweetland provided.

Henberlin shook his head. "That's not possible, she was in Vancouver with me. We went over that. She couldn't have returned." He hoped he sounded convincing, but it sounded phony inside his head.

"When did you know she was the killer?"

"No. She isn't the killer. You've had it in for her for so long, you're starting to make this stuff up. She couldn't have returned to Calgary that day. She had a conference and people saw her there."

The detective watched him and held his gaze when he made eye contact. Then Henberlin looked away, his eyes jumping around the room, down at his feet, out the window, and finally at the Sweetland again.

"Call me if she gets in touch with you," Sweetland said. "It's important for both of you that you do."

———

Once Sweetland returned to the police car he sat for a moment and thought, He texted her, asked her where she was and told her I was looking for her. She knows, and if she has that passport, she could try to leave the country. Her sister told her we were looking for a passport. She may not use it again if she thinks we called the border crossings but we'd look pretty stupid if she did and we hadn't called it in.

He sat a minute longer then asked himself, "Should I take him in now?"

He stretched the tired muscles in his back then opened the car door to go and arrest Henberlin. Inside he allowed Henberlin to change his clothes and then they walked out to the car. After making sure Henberlin sat safely in the back seat, they drove away.

———

Standing behind the fence at the side of the garage, Leyna stood with the tire iron in her hand. She watched the police car pull away, following it with her eyes until it turned the corner. She stared after it for a short while after it had gone, the image vivid, as if it were still in view. Gradually she slipped down into a squatting position. With no chance to clean up everything that needed to be cleaned up, especially with the presence of the two uniformed police officers, she stayed beside the garage of the house. In her squatting position she cried for a long time. When she finished she found herself in a place at which she couldn't remember how she'd arrived. She stared at the bottom rung of the fence. The tire iron had left her hand and she picked at her fingernail polish. Then she remembered her sister's phone call and she knew she had to run. She had a passport she could use, so she headed south to the nearest border crossing.

32

—

As Henberlin picked at the grey, sound-absorbing material, he wondered if he was sitting in the same interrogation room where Leyna had been interviewed. She'd told him the room had been extremely cold. This room lived up to that description. It had been about two hours since they asked him to have a seat and wait. He tried to keep his mind busy by going back to certain days with Leyna, rebuilding each day from the morning up. He never finished a day or found what he was looking for in the rebuilt timeline. Instead, his mind drifted to Leyna on the run. Where was she? Was she struggling, trying to stay ahead of the police with no one's help? She couldn't do it alone.

The door opened and Detective Sweetland entered the room. Henberlin noticed that he had never seen Sweetland without his jacket. His white shirt sleeves were rolled up to mid-forearm, and he carried a mug from which Henberlin picked up the smell of coffee.

"You doing okay?" Sweetland asked, his voice full of concern.

Henberlin gave a brief chuckle. "Did you check my phone? Did she call?"

"No calls. Where do you think she went?"

He scratched his head, accepting that he had no choice but to cooperate. "My first guess would be Coutts, but then that seems obvious because it's the closest. South of Creston, maybe."

"So you think she's going to try to cross into the States? We do too, but what if she were to stay in Canada?"

Henberlin took a deep breath. He had to ask his next question because he didn't know where he stood with the law. "Do I need a lawyer? Am I under arrest?"

He watched as Sweetland took a long time choosing his words.

"You're not under arrest, yet. We need you to clear up a few items before we can decide."

"So I can get up and leave if I want?"

Sweetland squirmed in his seat then said, "It wouldn't look too good if you left."

"As long as I'm free to go, I can find my way to cooperate. A lawyer's going to try and place a guard on what I say. I'd just as soon be completely honest."

The detective appeared to weigh Henberlin's words.

"When did you know your wife killed the Albins?"

"I'm still not certain."

Sweetland slumped a little as he leaned forward. "I told you earlier that we have proof. Your wife came to Calgary that Saturday. Video proof in the airport, coming and going, Calgary and Vancouver."

"You could be mistaken. Even if you aren't, that puts her in Calgary. It doesn't prove she murdered the Albins."

"There's the video of the woman shooting Mrs. Albin. We had people analyze the video. They concluded a woman shot and killed Mrs. Albin. They're going over it again, trying to identify the woman—with your wife in mind. You know they're going to prove it, because you've known all along that your wife did it."

"I admit it's easy to conclude she did it. You do have some circumstantial evidence. But mostly because she's decided to run after you found out about her using her sister's identification to travel. Once we've found her and she tells us what happened, I'll believe it if it's true." His chin tightened and quivered, but he didn't intend to let the accusations go unchallenged.

Sweetland asked, "Why did you set up a meeting with us when you had no intention of keeping it? The captain wanted to send an arrest warrant to the FBI when he heard you'd taken off with her."

"I've explained that to you. It was because of your behavior toward her. I'd asked you to back off a bit with your harsh approach to my wife. As strong as she is, she's had her issues. The first time you two met her, you put her in the hospital. I thought I had that to look forward to every time you came near her. I owed it to her to prevent that from happening again. You guys don't care that she'd been hospitalized in the past, when her father ended his political career. She enjoyed that part of her life, people admired the way she thought about important topics. Her opinion mattered. Then her father ended it, and she no longer had a platform. No one cared what she thought. Her work life didn't provide the same opportunity, and she slipped into a depression that took her way down. You were putting her back in that place. I had to keep her away from you because you didn't care how much damage you did to her. I only wanted to save my wife."

"We have to do our job. People try to drop sad stories on us all the time," Sweetland said, sitting back in his chair, arms crossed over his chest.

"Yeah, well, when you choose not to believe those stories, someone has to look out for the people you could destroy." Henberlin looked at the detective, his lips pursed, trying to hide the numbing sorrow that his wife's current condition generated.

Sweetland shook his head then said to Henberlin, "I have a few things to follow up on. We'll take a break. Can I get you anything, a coffee?"

"Sure. Coffee would be fine."

The helpless desire to get out of the room and go home to sleep in his own bed wore on his patience. He knew he had to keep his cool until they let him go. Get these questions over with then go find Leyna. That's all he wanted right now. His head dropped onto his chest and he tried to steal a nap.

———

Sweetland turned in at another room down the hall outfitted with a desk and three chairs where the captain of detectives watched Henberlin on closed-circuit television. The interview room wasn't built for comfort. Henberlin shifted and shifted again as he tried to get comfortable. They knew how difficult it would be because they'd made it so.

"How's it going with Mrs. Henberlin?" Sweetland asked the captain.

"Not here yet. Richie hasn't come back. Must have had to go looking for her somewhere other than her office."

"Did he call in where he was going?"

"I'll have to check," the captain said. "Henberlin's known for a while that his wife is the killer. Why else take her away?"

"He's not asking for a lawyer. Is he trying to make it look like he doesn't need one because he's done nothing wrong?"

"And that bullshit about wanting to help us now."

"No, that I think is genuine. He's worried for her," Sweetland said, still staring at the monitor. "He thinks he can make it easier for her if he's with her when we catch her."

"Well he won't. We better try and find Richie, we got to get the wife in the room."

Sweetland twisted his head and screwed up his lips. "Maybe send a patrol car to Mrs. Henberlin's office. That's the last place we knew he intended to go."

———

The door clicked and Henberlin opened his eyes. He hadn't slept or rested. Sweetland again held a mug of coffee as he entered. Henberlin took in the aroma and stared at the mug.

"Did you ever get your coffee?" Sweetland asked.

"No," Henberlin replied.

"Ah hell. I'll get someone to bring you one." Sweetland turned to leave, but stopped at Henberlin's voice.

"It's okay, I don't need one." He waited as Sweetland took his seat across the table. "Can we get this over with? Did you look at my phone? Has she tried to contact me?"

"Nothing on the phone," Sweetland said.

"You need to let me try to contact her. Keeping me tied up in here isn't helping you or Leyna. I promise I'm going to help you find her."

"Do you think your wife tried to set you up for the murder?" the detective asked.

Henberlin blew out his lips in shock and opened his eyes wide, pulling his head back. "What? No."

"Just saying. She got you to fly to Vancouver in a manner that made it so you couldn't prove you'd gone. She keeps you tied up in the spa with a person that doesn't work at the spa, so no one at the hotel could say you were there. You were our first suspect. We did arrest you based on those facts."

"My wife isn't devious enough to put a plan like that together."

"She put a plan together to slip back to Calgary, do a couple murders, and get back in time to have people see her at the final reception of her conference. We've proven she's devious enough to do that."

"Yes, but… she wasn't in her best state of mind." Henberlin sat for a minute. Could Leyna's jealousy and quest for vengeance against Yanmei have made her vengeful against him as well? She would never harm him. But if her mind had been taken over by thoughts of revenge, could she have meant to punish him too?

"Impossible. She couldn't have done any of this," Henberlin stated.

"You just said she'd previously been in a very low place. It's your affair that seems to have put her back there."

Henberlin sat up in his chair then took his time placing both of his hands on the table. He leaned in and rested his weight on them. "There was no—" he raised his voice, giving a violent shake of his head on the last word—"affair."

"She believed there was an affair. That's all we need."

"She believes me now. There was no affair. You have to stop saying there was." Red faced and hands in a tight clench, he wished he was at home or on the road somewhere looking for Leyna. Instead, he had to stay here at the detectives' disposal, to save himself before he could save Leyna.

Sweetland stared at him. "Okay. Mr. Henberlin, we want to monitor your phone for a few hours. We'd like you to stay here in case your wife tries to contact you. So you can respond under our direction."

Henberlin hesitated. "Give me the phone, let me go home and try to get in touch with Leyna. I promise I will contact you if I talk to her."

Sweetland held still in thought, giving Henberlin slight hope, then he shook his head.

"Then, yes, of course I'll stay. The best way for me to help my wife is to help you." Henberlin knew he had no choice. They could make it more difficult for him if they chose.

"Unfortunately, the only place we can accommodate you is in one of the holding cells. You'll at least be able to lie down there."

"Are you arresting me? If you are, then I'll have to call a lawyer." He tried to sound as if they'd let him down.

"No, Mr. Henberlin, you're not under arrest. We can all react faster if you're nearby. The cell is going to be more comfortable than this room," Sweetland said.

————

When Sweetland left the room the captain was standing outside. He twitched when Sweetland looked him in the eye then dropped his gaze. His shoulders drooped as he said, "We found Richie."

"Good," Sweetland said. "He can take over for a while. I need a rest."

"Sorry, Detective, that can't happen. Richie was in the parking garage of Mrs. Henberlin's building. He's dead. He was laying on the ground behind Mrs. Henberlin's parking spot. He'd been run over but it also looks like he'd been attacked."

"Attacked. By who?"

The captain looked away when he saw the realization in Sweetland's face. The color drained, his lips pursed and his jaw muscles ground his teeth. He lifted his head and looked off in the distance beyond the room's walls. Lifting his hands up with splayed fingers, palms inward, he said under his breath, "Maybe she is crazy."

"She's a cop killer," the captain said.

Sweetland took a seat, looking down and shaking his head. He allowed himself a moment of misery, guilt and second guessing then fired up out of his chair saying, "We gotta get her... soon. This is going to make them want to get away even more. We can't let that happen."

––––––

Henberlin, hoping to sleep for a few hours, had no idea why all of a sudden his body jerked up into a sitting position. "What the hell's going on?" he demanded.

Sweetland stood over him taking deep breaths. He turned and looked at the cell wall, seeming to be gathering his thoughts. When he turned back his breathing had steadied though his face remained tight, appearing ready to crack.

"What's going on?" Henberlin asked in a quiet voice, staring at Sweetland's scar.

Sweetland waited, watching Henberlin. When Henberlin saw he was being watched, he made eye contact with the detective, then looked down at the table.

"Have you still not gotten use to the mark on my face?" Sweetland said, his voice a little loud.

"Sorry, I was staring again. It's mystifying."

It was Sweetland's turn to look down at the table. "Mystifying… that's a new one. I think most people find it horrifying. That they can't find the words to ask for an explanation makes them wonder about its origin even more."

"Is it worse when they ask or when they don't?"

Sweetland tilted his head to one side, thinking. "I don't know," he said.

"You said your ex-wife gave it to you?"

Sweetland stared at Henberlin for a full minute then said, "Maybe it's worse when they ask."

"Why did you yank me out of bed? Did Leyna call my phone?"

Sweetland's posture straightened and the air in the room changed. For the first time Henberlin felt anger radiate from the detective. Sweetland had always been the calm one, the one of reason, now he seemed an intimidating menace.

"No. But we found Detective Richie."

"I didn't know he was lost."

Sweetland gave Henberlin an evasive smile. "He's dead."

Henberlin's brow raised as his mouth dropped open. He didn't speak.

"Dead, laying on the ground in front of your wife's parking spot at work. He'd gone there to arrest her."

"I'm sorry, I… I'm sorry."

"It looks like he was attacked and beaten, then he was run over by a car."

Henberlin's healed ribs began to ache. His breathing accelerated and he felt his stomach begin to clench. "I have to get out of here. I need fresh air."

"Me too. Come on," Sweetland said then led the way out of the station. They walked across the street and around a corner to a small coffee shop, the walk doing much to settle both men's moods. They chose a booth that looked out on the street.

Henberlin picked up the laminated menu and asked, "You going to have something?"

"Nothing. I don't eat breakfast."

Henberlin looked up, concentrating on not looking at the other man's scar. "So am I still free to go?"

"Yes, but we need to know a few things and I want to tell you that you're making the right decision. Helping us is going to make it a lot easier on both of you. Right now, you have a real chance to help your wife. If you're playing us, then you're going to make it worse than you can imagine."

"I'm not playing you."

"The captain thinks you are. He's hoping you are because he wants to arrest you. He wants to keep you locked up until your trial. Especially now that Richie's been murdered. If your wife is in the mental state you say she's in, do you think she could have attacked Richie?"

"I'm not an expert in that sort of thing. I don't think she could. Not the Leyna I've lived with all these years. She just isn't capable of killing someone." When he emptied his lungs through his nose he knew he had exhaled his moral worth. He knew he couldn't and shouldn't protect his wife, now he could only help her get better. And to do that he had to be free. He had to lie and deceive his way to keeping his freedom.

"Your wife is in trouble regardless of who killed Detective Richie. She needs to be in custody and it has to happen soon. Cops are going to interpret what happened as a cop killing whether she did it or not, whether she's mentally unstable or not."

Henberlin continued to look hard into Sweetland's eyes but said nothing.

"You need to help find her and you need to stay out of jail. She's going to need your help. I think for you to be free is the best way you can help her. If you go to jail and can't act on her behalf when she's in custody, she's going to be a ward of the province. That is, if she goes into a mental health institute. Do you have power of attorney if your wife becomes incapacitated?"

"I don't know. How do I find out?"

"It's something you would have done with a lawyer or a notary public."

"Then no, I don't think I do."

"Look into it. It's important in a situation of mental incompetence. But if she's found fit for trial and she goes to jail, then she'll be treated like a regular prisoner. And if she did kill Detective Richie she'll have a pretty rough time of it in jail. Cop killers don't last long."

All this worry because he wanted to help his country. If Delaney had picked someone else to help, he and Leyna wouldn't be in this position. He sat up and stared out the window.

How could Delaney help get us out of this mess? he wondered.

A few hours later, while still waiting in the police station for Leyna to call, Henberlin accepted the sandwich offered. Time had passed at a slow pace.

During the afternoon, a sergeant offered him a book. He filled a few hours reading but without retaining what he'd read. He asked about his phone every hour. Always told there'd been no calls, no texts. He waited. He asked to leave, but Richie wanted him to stay. Leyna might be getting to a hotel to rest after a long day of running. She would likely try to make contact after she'd settled for the evening and given her situation some thought. Again, Henberlin stayed to show his willingness to help find her.

The evening brought no contact either, but the police again asked him to spend the night in the cell. He wondered if that was a good idea. Some of the looks he'd received from a few of the officers made him a little uncomfortable.

If she didn't contact him by noon the next day, he could go, they told him. At noon, there had still been no word from Leyna. They gave him the phone and arranged for a patrol car to take him home.

"Remember, you said you intend to help us. Make sure you call us right away if she makes contact," Sweetland said as the two men stood beside the open door of the police car.

"I will."

"You better," Sweetland said. After a short pause, he said, "Neil, we all think you knew your wife murdered Yanmei shortly after she'd done it."

"Then you're all thinking wrong." Henberlin found himself looking at Sweetland's scar, and Sweetland left him to it for a good long time.

"It's amazing what a man will do to protect his wife," Sweetland said. "Even if it means committing a crime, holding back evidence, lying about intentions, maybe helping a guilty person hide from the law."

Henberlin continued to stare at the scar even though he knew that's what Sweetland wanted. When he finally shifted his gaze to meet Sweetland's, he remained silent. But he saw the light of understanding in Sweetland's eyes.

"Now you know," Sweetland said, as they continued their stare down.

"You've been through this?"

"Nobody got killed." He lied.

Henberlin broke away and climbed into the back of the police car.

33

———

Leyna awoke a few times over the two days since she received the call from her sister telling her about the visit from the detectives. After calling her husband that night to say good-bye, she knew she needed to take care of the things that were getting in her way again. The detectives were surely going to come for her. Maybe if she could convince them once and for all that she hadn't left Vancouver they would leave her alone. But inside, she knew they weren't going to believe her, she knew she would have to take matters into her own hands. When she saw only the one detective coming to get her she relaxed enough to form a new plan. She knew that she could surprise one of the detectives but not both. Her first plan to immobilize both had odds stacked against success. The odds changed when she only had to deal with them one at a time. It meant she had to drive across the city to find the other one but she knew her chances for success were much better now.

But when she saw the other detective drive away with her husband she knew she'd lost her chance to take him out. She didn't want her husband to see what she was capable of, and she felt a little easier when they drove away.

When she arrived at the border a few minutes after eleven o'clock, she parked within sight of the crossing. One last moment to think about whether she should cross, making it a point of no return moment.

As she put the car in gear and started for the crossing, it hit her. The passport is the thing that started her on the run. Now it was useless. The police would have alerted all border crossings. The crossing agents would be looking for the passport and her car. She couldn't take the chance of leaving the country. Best to lay low for a day or two.

Turning the car around, she returned to Lethbridge and checked into a small hotel to sleep and gather her thoughts. And sleep she did. The times she did wake up, she only drank a glass of water to wash down the pills that allowed her to sleep some more. The third morning, she sat up at the end of the bed and took a first look at the place she had picked for her hideout. Faded green striped wallpaper, old-style radiators, simulated wood laminate on the desk/television stand. The rest of the room was only less impressive.

The first pang of hunger struck and now she could think of nothing but food. Pulling back the curtains, which she could reach from where she sat on the bed, she looked out hoping to see a restaurant nearby. Across the street stood a low, two-story stone building covered with weeping brown and grey stains. On the main floor a blinking neon sign indicated the place was open. When she looked closer, it looked like a place to eat.

She scrambled her hair into a ponytail, then looked at the clothes she had with her. She wasn't going to wear the dress she'd been wearing her last day in the office, so she congratulated herself for stopping at the discount store on the way out of town. She had bought a sweatshirt, a pair of jeans, running shoes, and a light green jacket. She put them on and stepped out of her room, then over to the restaurant.

The smell of greasy food made her hunger more acute and her cravings became urgent. Still, she knew the first bite she ingested would be painful when it hit her stomach.

Her cell phone vibrated in her purse. When she'd looked at it this morning after she first woke up, she'd been shocked that her husband or the police hadn't tried to contact her. No voice mail, no texts.

Has Neil been in custody? she thought. Should I look at this now?

She didn't know how long she'd sat in a funk staring at the small screen until the interruption by the young man behind the counter bringing her food—his name tag read Dennis—drew her back from her returning despair. She paid for the meal, thanked Dennis, and realized she'd already forgotten what she'd ordered. She also found she no longer had the hunger pains.

Back in the room, she wondered why she had ordered French fries with the salad. It made no sense since she never ate fries. She forced herself to eat a few for the carbs they would provide, carbs she knew she needed.

She returned to her phone and began to read the text message.

➜ I'm out now. They let me go this morning. Please let me know you're okay. Please call me. I love you.

"I love you too," she said to the phone.

She'd purchased a throw-away cell phone like the one her husband had used to contact Jian Liu and soon found it in the bottom of her purse. She sent a text of a sad emoticon to her husband from the new phone, hoping he'd realize it came from her. Seconds later, she received a return text on the throw-away.

➜ Leyna?

Leyna sent another emoticon message—this time, a smiley face. Then she turned off the phone.

She looked up at the curtains covering the window. "It's not fair to you," she whispered to the dead phone, "but I have to do this without your involvement if we're ever going to be together again."

It was wonderful of Neil not to turn me in the minute he knew I killed his mistress, she thought. It could have gone either way. He may have wanted revenge against me if he'd loved that woman. It turns out he loved me. I need to distance him from me so he can remain free. They've already arrested him again, and somehow he's free. I can't let them arrest him again.

This she thought over and over while she fought the urge to dial his number. To resist the urge, she turned to planning how to get away. First, she showered so she could be fresh and think fresh. It came to her as she dried her hair. She knew she'd be leaving a clue as to her whereabouts. Her car, when they found it, would tell them that anyway.

———

Henberlin searched deep into his memory, trying to come up with an idea of where his wife might have gone. He thought of places from their past, places where they'd enjoyed good times. The previous day and night at the police station, providing information to the police about his wife's activities and state of mind had opened his eyes to her mental plight. The pressure of what she'd done must have finally put her out of her right mind if she thought she could run from the police, especially if she really had killed Detective Richie. It took a while for him to convince the police officers that he wanted what they wanted, the safe capture of his wife. And if the police believe Leyna was a cop killer he wondered how committed to her safe capture they really were.

What he still didn't know: Had he completely convinced the detectives that he didn't know his wife had committed the murders? Did they trust him enough to allow him to assist them? With that doubt in mind and with the increased level of danger coming from the police themselves, he knew he would have to inject himself into the search. If they saw his willingness to cooperate, they may concede that his involvement would be helpful.

The RCMP and their large web of observation was now involved. The detectives had sent them the all-points bulletin with pictures and a description of her car. He knew that her car would be spotted and her capture would occur soon. They were pretty sure she hadn't crossed the border at this point, but still thought it was her ultimate goal. To that end, they concentrated their search on towns nearest the border. An outside chance existed that she'd already crossed, but only if she had gone south immediately after she called her husband. Since they hadn't been able to notify the border crossing until not long before midnight, she had a window when she could have passed through unnoticed. If she'd used the passport there would have been a record of the crossing. Then again, late at night, in the middle of a good book or a crossword puzzle, the border agent might not always record the passports they see along the safest border in North America.

Henberlin had come to realize his quest to retain Leyna's freedom by aiding in her concocted cover-up didn't serve her well. She needed medical help. Being placed in a hospital would be better than being sent to prison. His goal now was to keep his own freedom, in order to be available for her when she did get caught and afterward while she was incarcerated. He had to maintain that he didn't know Leyna had killed Yanmei, even though the detectives believed otherwise. His cooperation now would be viewed as the right thing to do, in light of emerging evidence indicating her guilt. Wanting to do his best for his wife is what he'd always been after.

Still believing he may need help from elsewhere, he turned to the only other source he had: Delaney.

After a minute or two of idol talk, Henberlin began on the topic he'd called Delaney to discuss. "The police are about to arrest my wife for murder."

The line remained silent. Henberlin could hear the other man's breathing.

"You're kidding, right?" Delaney said.

"No. They have pretty convincing evidence, and they're trying to pin some of it on me."

"I have to ask: Is she guilty? Are you?"

"I'm shocked. I had no idea it happened." The shock he expressed in his words existed, but he didn't know if it was because he had just acknowledged his wife had murdered Delaney's agent or because he lied to the man who's help he was going to need soon.

"Why? Why did she kill Yanmei?"

"Jealousy." He wanted Delaney to think about that.

"Neil, I'm sorry."

"Yeah. I wanted to help you. I shouldn't have kept it a secret from Leyna. If she'd known the affair wasn't real, none of this would have happened."

"Well... maybe."

"I'm trying to find her now. I'm hoping they'll see I want to take care of her. That's all I want." He waited to let his concern set in. "I wanted to let you know, in case you tried to contact me for something related to the Chinese. I don't think I can help right now."

"Yes, that's understandable. There's not much I can do, but let me know if you need anything."

"Right."

He hung up then checked his cell phone again to see if she'd sent another text. Nothing. Time to check in with the police again. Again, he had nothing to tell them.

When he made his call to Sweetland, there was news. The police in Lethbridge reported finding Leyna's car at a parking meter in the downtown area.

"I'm going to drive down there," Henberlin stated.

"I don't think that's a good idea. I'm about to head there myself. You leave this to the police," Sweetland responded.

"I don't care if you think it's a bad idea. If she's there, she's going to need me to help settle her down. You guys have a terrible effect on her. Don't worry, if I find her I'll let you know. It's best for her to face what she's done."

"You'll forgive me, Mr. Henberlin, if I disagree. We'll be able to take care of your wife."

"I'm going down there. If you don't want my help while I'm there, that's fine, but I'm willing to help. I'm leaving now. I'll have my phone." He disconnected, packed a bag, and went to his car.

Henberlin hit a hundred and forty kilometers an hour as he reached the valley leading into Lethbridge. He slowed, trying to remember what he knew about the city and its layout.

As he entered, he looked for hotels and motels, stopping at each one and showing them a picture of his wife. No one on duty had seen her, so he knew he would be doing the rounds again later in the evening. He called Detective Sweetland to update him on what he'd done since his arrival. Sweetland would be arriving in the city soon and indicated he would be going straight to the main police station where Leyna's car was now parked. Henberlin invited himself to the police station to help look over the car. But before going to the station, Henberlin checked with the rental car companies in downtown. He found nothing.

At the police station, Henberlin waited in an interview room while the police took a look at her vehicle. The keys were on the driver's floor mat. She'd thought enough not to inconvenience them, and therefore provided her keys. When asked what type of objects they would find in Leyna's car, Henberlin told them things that she always kept in her car: gum, change, a hairbrush, and side pockets stuffed to overflow with scraps of papers and receipts.

Detective Sweetland went through the paper debris and found a Clothes Barn receipt dated three days earlier, time-stamped after six PM. The fact she had on different clothes, and that they could place her in the south of Calgary at that time, didn't amount to the slightest fraction of a clue.

He joined Henberlin in the interrogation room.

"Well, at least she's more comfortable than she would be wearing the dress suit she would have had on in her office," Henberlin said.

"We found blood in a number of places on the undercarriage of the car. Don't know if it belongs to Richie but it doesn't take a genius to connect those dots." Sweetland shot a deadpan look in Henberlin's direction as he spoke.

Henberlin nodded while deep in thought as more of the worst possible situation came true.

After a minute Sweetland continued, "The border crossings report no record of her crossing. We're still going to have to go down there and show them a picture."

"Did you check the bus station?" Henberlin queried, still not over what he had concluded about the blood marks.

"Do they run buses to the US from here?" Sweetland asked.

"That's something I can ask when I show her picture to the ticket agent," Henberlin responded. "Would you like me to do that? I need to do something, I can't just sit here."

"No, we'll send someone. I guess we better check the train station while we're at it."

"There's no passenger service by train in Lethbridge. It's all freight," Henberlin informed him with a blank stare.

"Good, that'll save us some time," Sweetland said.

"I'll check the hotels again and let you know if I discover anything."

Sweetland nodded even though Henberlin kept his eyes away from the detective.

Thinking that Leyna would have wanted to stay at the edge of the city closest to the border, Henberlin started at the south end of town. Two hours later, back in the downtown area and able to walk to the few hotels located on the main street, one desk clerk recognized Leyna's picture. Feeling like he was getting somewhere Henberlin called Detective Sweetland.

"When did she leave?" Sweetland asked the clerk, who had to go back to the records of the night she checked in. He searched for the time she arrived and got the name she used and the room number.

Then he could see when she checked out: Eleven AM, the posted check-out time.

"How did she appear when she left?" Henberlin asked.

"Sorry, I didn't see her then."

"Then how did she seem when she checked in?" Henberlin's voice showed signs of exasperation.

"Quiet. I'd say she was pretty tired. I had to repeat things to her a few times before she understood what I was saying."

"Did you see what she did during her stay, when she went out? Did she say where she'd been?" Sweetland asked.

The clerk shook his head. "I never saw her again after she checked in. Sorry."

"Okay, how did she pay?"

The clerk looked at the screen again. After a few keystrokes, most of them backspaces, he said, "Cash."

"Could we see the room?"

"Sure, but it's been cleaned."

"Then did housekeeping take anything out of the room that she might have left behind?"

The clerk went into a back room to look in the lost-and-found. Customer possessions were bagged and stored in case the customer called back looking for something. When he returned he had two large white paper bags. Inside one were the clothes Leyna had worn to work that day, and in the other were her shoes. Henberlin identified them as hers immediately.

"We'll take these," Sweetland told the clerk. They walked out the door, crossed the street, and stepped into the restaurant to wait for a report from the border.

As expected, they found out nothing at the crossing. The bus station revealed that a passenger could get to Great Falls from Lethbridge, and from there to everywhere else. She could have also caught a bus west to the Kootenays, east to Saskatchewan, and back north to Calgary. The ticket agent couldn't make an identification, saying only that there had been some women that looked like her.

He couldn't be sure, and wouldn't know which bus she got on if he did recognize her.

"Okay," said Sweetland. "I guess we head back. Her picture's already been sent to all the police departments. We'll ask them to check out the bus depots to see if anyone saw her."

"Okay, when can I have her car?" Henberlin asked.

"We'll keep it for a while. I'll have it shipped to impound in Calgary," Sweetland said.

———

The next day, Sweetland called Henberlin. Henberlin answered the phone and asked, "How can I help you?"

"We found out your wife withdrew some money from a bank while she was in Lethbridge—five grand. You sound like you're on a speaker phone. Where are you?"

Henberlin hesitated a few seconds, then said, "I'm in my car, on the highway."

"Headed where? Did your wife get in touch with you?"

Henberlin continued to drive in silence. He couldn't think of how he should answer the question. He knew he had to cooperate with the detectives but he also knew he had to protect Leyna.

"Five thousand dollars?" Henberlin asked, hoping to change the subject.

"Leyna withdrew her daily limit of one thousand dollars from a bank ATM," Sweetland explained. "She then went into the bank and withdrew another four thousand dollars. A nice paper trail, but we already knew she'd been in the area at the time. But now we know she has more cash, anyway."

Henberlin figured they could ask for the security camera recordings, but that would only confirm she'd been there and let them see the clothing she wore. That didn't amount to much. She could have bought another change of clothes shortly after being seen on camera.

After a few long seconds, Sweetland said, "So, what about your wife? Did she get in touch?"

He had to cooperate. "She did, actually. From a new phone number. She sent a text saying she was all right. I'm on my way to get her."

"Get her from where?" The tone of angry command couldn't be missed.

"She went east. She's in Weyburn. I'll call you when I get there."

"Where in Weyburn? How did she get there?"

"I don't know where exactly, she wouldn't tell me. She will when I let her know I'm there to be with her and that I'm alone. She said she'd run again if I didn't promise to go get her alone. I'll call you later."

Henberlin disconnected and turned his phone off. He knew he'd bought himself a few hours. The next time he talked to Sweetland, the detective was going to be hopping mad.

Earlier, his phone had rung and he didn't recognized the number. Leyna had purchased another new phone. His hands fumbled with the answer button, "Hello, Leyna? Is that you, are you all right?"

The phone remained silent. He decided he'd better start telling her things or she would hang-up.

"Leyna, it's going to be all right. You've done a good job staying away on your own, but it won't work. The police are looking for you everywhere. The RCMP have all your information, and they're concentrating on places close to the border. You have to give yourself up. If you do that, they'll try to make it easier on you than if you continue to try and get away. Leyna, do you hear me?"

Henberlin heard air escape from Leyna's nose.

"Leyna, you have to let me know where you are."

"I will," she said.

"Leyna, thank God. Are you okay?" His heart battered his rib cage when he heard her voice. Relief blanketed his entire body.

"Maybe… I don't know."

"Tell me where you are, please."

"I'm done with this, Neil. It's too hard."

"Do you want me to come and get you?"

"Yes, can you?"

"Yes, of course. Where are you?" His hands shook during the silence that seemed to go on and on. He could tell she held some reservations about revealing her location.

"Just you though, Neil. I only want you to come."

"Yes, but first tell me where you are."

Again she forced him to wait before saying, "Weyburn."

"That's a long way. The police can be there to help you faster than I can get there."

"No!" she shouted. "Only you. As soon as I hang up, I'll leave here and keep going on my own if you don't come by yourself."

"Leyna, it's over. You have to go to the police."

"I will, but with you. Please."

He didn't want her to feel he was hesitant and said, "Okay, I'm going to leave now. Where are you in Weyburn?"

"Text me when you get here."

"Okay."

He had a couple more hours to go on the Trans-Canada Highway before arriving in Weyburn, Saskatchewan—happy to be on his way to get his wife.

34

—

Eight hours to think about what to do once he had his wife back hadn't been enough. Henberlin's elation at hearing from Leyna allowed him to breathe again. Air lightened his head with oxygen for the first time since she'd gone missing. From days of not eating, sleeplessness, and expecting bad news, he now verged on elation. The first two hours, he distracted himself by searching the radio for a suitable station, changing every time the static overtook the sound of the music. Then the elation fluttered as the trip neared its end.

The thought of Leyna attempting a solo escape entered his mind. Could she take her own life? The longer he went without hearing from her, the heavier an expectation of a phone call informing him that his wife's body had been found weighed on his mind.

This morning's phone call from a number he didn't recognize caused a rise in his pulse. He hoped it was her. He heard her voice when he answered. Contacting him meant she still wanted to survive. When she said she wanted him to come and get her, it meant she either needed his help to continue running, or she'd had enough and intended to pay the price for the murders she'd committed. He hoped she meant it when she said she'd had enough. Either way, a resolution to their life of limbo dangled a few hours down the highway.

The music began to get on his nerves when he realized he had a decision to make and he had to make it on his own. At the time Leyna came into his life, he began to make his decisions based on what most benefitted the two of them and their relationship. He disassociated with his previous acquaintances in order to resist the temptations he thought were bound to cause tension in his relationship with his wife. He avoided his family and their stubborn belief in their right to meddle in anyone else's life. He knew they would clash with Leyna's stubborn desire for independence, now that she no longer acted on her father's will. They became their own self-sufficient unit once they were together. They chose goals for their lives, goals for all the important matters they would deal with as a couple, goals seeking to strengthen their quality of life. That was what caused his confusion over the last two months: She'd made bad decisions on her own. Decisions that forced him into a position where now he had to make a self-serving decision.

She's taken herself away from me, even though she wants me with her, he thought. She's changed, she's become a killer. How can I live with a killer? If she goes on like this, she could run up against another person she deems a threat and she could cross the line again. She could kill again. Like it appears she did with the detective. It would be best if she saw this eventuality, best if she turned herself in.

She could get help, serve her punishment, and then return to a life with him. Not a normal life, but maybe they could cobble together a pleasant, loving world where they isolated themselves from society. If she asked him to run with her, there would be no hope for her to repair mentally, no hope of having a life that simulated a time before she thought an affair with Yanmei existed.

Could he run with her? Could he turn her in? Those two thoughts ping-ponged inside his brain, rebounding in different directions, colliding with each other on every bounce.

As he closed in on Weyburn, his speed increased without his realizing it. He pulled into the hotel entry going the wrong way, and angle-parked blocking the entire drive. It was luck that he managed to put the car's transmission in park. He heard the engine still running as he pried open the auto-open doors. Words flew from his mouth the instant he saw someone behind the desk.

"My wife's checked into your hotel under a phony name. I need to get to her right away," he said, almost gasping.

He described Leyna to the clerk, who immediately told him which room she occupied. He thanked the clerk then asked if he could have a key.

"If you get over there now, I'm sure the police will let you in."

Henberlin froze. What the clerk said sunk in. It was okay. "Which way?" he asked.

The clerk pointed, but said, "You can't leave your car like that."

Once outside, he ignored his car and ran in the direction the clerk had pointed. He saw two RCMP cruisers parked in front of one of the rooms. The room open, two officers standing outside the door. As he approached, one of the officers stepped toward him with his arms raised, palms outward.

"Officer, I'm her husband," Henberlin said, leaning to look around the officer and into the hotel room. "Is she okay?"

The officer didn't answer but asked him a series of questions. Once Henberlin had satisfied the officer that he was the husband, the officer led him into the room and introduced him to the officers inside. Henberlin paid them no attention as they sat at the bottom of the bed trying to talk to Leyna. Henberlin's eyes went to her, sitting up at the top of the bed, blankets pulled up above her waist.

She had on a jacket and blouse, appearing to be fully dressed under the blanket. Her hair lay flat against her head, signs of lipstick still on her lips, her skin pale. Still, in her eyes he saw the gleam of life, impossible to hide. The few faded freckles scattered on her nose and cheeks visible. She'd always powdered them, and he wondered why she would hide what he thought made her so attractive. Exhaustion and confusion didn't diffuse her beauty. She stared straight ahead, not noticing he'd entered the room. He watched her for a minute, then crouched at her side.

"Leyna?" he said. She recognized his voice, turned, and smiled. "Leyna, are you okay?" His voice soft and solicitous.

"I just woke up," she said.

The police officers yielded to him.

"How long have you been here?" he asked.

"Let's see. When did I call you?"

"This morning at about seven."

"Maybe another day or two. I've been sleeping."

"Excuse me," said one of the officers who had been in the room. "We found these." He held out a prescription bottle. "Do you know how many of these she had?"

Henberlin took the bottle and read the label.

"Sorry, I didn't know she was taking these. Don't know what it's for," he said, shaking his head.

"It's for anxiety."

Henberlin nodded. "She's probably got some sleep aids around here, too."

He grabbed Leyna's purse and reached in to find two more bottles of pills. He showed them to the officer.

"Mr. Henberlin, we're here to arrest your wife for murder. You're aware that there's a warrant out for her?"

"Yes, I've been working with the detectives in Calgary to find her."

The officer stared at him for a moment. "You have?"

Henberlin nodded.

"The detectives from Calgary said to expect no assistance from you."

"Now that we've all found out they were right about the murders, they want to make it look like they solved the crime on their own," Henberlin said. "I helped look for her. I only asked to be present when they caught up with her so I could make things a little easier for her. Her mental state is what's important to me—and they couldn't give two shits about her. How can I help you?"

The officer nodded a little longer than required to understand Henberlin's meaning. "Because of the pills, it's procedure for your wife to be examined by a doctor. She'll be under arrest and considered to be in police custody."

Henberlin smiled and nodded.

———

Leyna slept through the rest of the day handcuffed to her hospital bed, with Henberlin nodding off in the chair beside her from time to time. As soon as the hospital staff had settled Leyna into captivity, Henberlin left the room to place a call to Detective Sweetland. His cell phone had been taken from him and there were two guards assigned to the room, one for Leyna, one for him. His guard accompanied him to the pay phone. He knew Sweetland would be in a mood, but he could accept Sweetland's chastisement without losing his cool.

"So you decided to check in, did you?" Detective Sweetland said.

"Yes, things have settled down here."

"I know. They're going to keep her overnight for observation. We'll be coming to get her when they say she's okay to be transported. Until then we'll have guards outside her room."

"I don't think a guard is necessary, and two is overkill. But, suit yourself. She's had enough. I decided on the way here she was going to turn herself in."

"It's easy to sound like you're helping when she's already under arrest."

"I've been helping all along."

"You hung up on me and turned your phone off without telling me where your wife was hiding. How is that helping?"

"I had to be with her when you caught her. I couldn't trust you to allow me to be with her."

"Why should we?"

"Because I'm the only one who cares about her. Your only concern is getting an arrest. You don't care what harm you do to her. I've been trying to protect her from your badgering the whole time. If I'd hired a lawyer to protect her, you would have called it an indication of guilt. Okay, you're right, you've proven she did it. I tried to pull the reins in on you because I didn't believe the direction your investigation was taking. To me, she'd been innocent all along. That is until now, since you've proven she's guilty."

"Okay. One of the guards is for you."

"I figured as much, he's standing right here, really close, doing his job. I ask again: Am I under arrest?"

"We're working on it."

"You're all stuck on your belief that I knew. I know she's guilty now, but didn't until you proved it to me. I'm sorry for what she did."

After a long pause Sweetland asked, "Where are you staying?"

"Here, with Leyna."

Silence came from the phone receiver. It seemed forever before Sweetland spoke.

"I don't like it."

"Come on," Henberlin said, "You have two guards, we're on the third floor, and my wife doesn't have her wits about her. The nurses and doctors are sworn to take care of her but I'm the only one who's looking out for her. You have to let me stay with her. Handcuff me to my chair if you have to."

"Still…"

"Look, Detective, you led me to believe you have some experience in the position that I'm in. She's about to break and nobody's trying to prevent that from happening."

"Let me think about it," Sweetland hung up.

"Will do," Henberlin said to the dial tone.

Leyna slept the entire next day. The hospital staff gave Henberlin encouraging updates about her vital signs, and indicated she'd be waking up soon. Then she'd be able to travel. He knew these updates were also being supplied to the Calgary Police, so he wasn't surprised when the following day Sweetland called and confirmed they were on their way.

Around midday Leyna sat dressed in jeans and a shirt, handcuffed to the chair. The guard had remained inside the room after the nurse and Henberlin helped her dress. She needed the help. She stood like a doll and allowed them to grab and move her limbs so they could be placed in the articles of clothing. She didn't help in anyway, didn't comment on anything they were doing. She didn't answer to any questions they asked her, including requests to lift an arm or bend a knee to make dressing her easier. Her eyes followed her husband's every move and remained on him the whole time. Her expression blank.

Sitting in the chair, she continued to watch her husband. No one else existed for her.

When Sweetland and another detective showed up, Leyna took her eyes off her husband. She stood up in front of the chair with one hand drawn back due to the handcuff attached to the chair's arm.

"Please sit down, Mrs. Henberlin. We won't be leaving for a while. I'd like to ask you a few questions before we go," Sweetland stated.

Leyna sat. Her eyes returned to her husband.

"Mr. Henberlin, we want to talk to your wife alone."

"No, I'm going to stay."

"Mr. Henberlin because of our concern regarding your level of involvement in your wife's crimes, we can't have you in the room."

"No, I can't leave you alone with her. I still don't have medical power of attorney for my wife but as her husband I feel I have a right to be in the room."

"Sorry, but you have no such right."

"Then I'm going to advise her—"

"That's why you can't be in the room, you aren't allowed to advise her. Now please leave."

"No, I have to be here."

Sweetland shook his head as if admonishing himself. "Mr. Henberlin, I think I've been more than kind with you. I could have been a real bastard and kept you away from your wife this whole time. You say you intend to cooperate with us but you really are getting in the way. I've asked you politely to leave the room and now I'm going to have to insist." Sweetland gave a slight nod to one of the officers who then walked toward Henberlin.

Henberlin balanced on a thin edge. What's best for Leyna? I piss them off and I can't help her from jail. I leave her alone and she could withdraw from me.

"Neil, just go. I'm not going to say anything."

All eyes turned to Leyna and everyone froze looking at her sitting in the chair, legs crossed, the elbow of her free arm resting on the armrest with her hand in the air. Relaxed in posture, tight and explosive in attitude. Henberlin saw hatred beam from her eyes toward Sweetland daring him to be alone with her.

Sweetland turned to Leyna as the door shut on Henberlin and said, "Other than your prescriptions, we had your belongings shipped to us in Calgary. We were looking for a passport in your sister's name—one you used when you came back from your trip with your husband to Los Angeles back in July. The passport was in your purse and it showed that you did travel using your sister's identification."

Leyna's eyes stayed fixed on the detective but she remained silent and still.

Sweetland continued. "Because of that, we thought you may have travelled as your sister on previous occasions, and we did, in fact, discover that you had. Do you want the details, or will you concede that you did travel to Calgary on the Saturday that Mr. and Mrs. Albin were murdered?"

Leyna continued to glare. Her eyes still and still, she said nothing.

"Okay, then I will tell you," Sweetland said. "Your sister's name appeared on the passenger list for a flight leaving Vancouver for Kelowna at ten forty-five AM on the day in question. You had a layover of—"

"Spare me," Leyna interrupted.

Sweetland stopped. He waited while watching Leyna before he said, "Very well. Let me just state that we have considerable evidence that will be presented to your lawyer before and during trial. Enough evidence to justify the charge of murder for which you are under arrest. You do understand why you are in custody?"

"What?" Leyna said. "Since when?"

"You were arrested three days ago when we found you at the hotel. You'd been there for two days before calling your husband to come and get you. We got to you first, and arrested you for murder."

Leyna held a twisted smile. "Yeah, that's right. My husband thinks I killed his mistress. I didn't deserve to be treated like that."

With Leyna talking, Sweetland's energy level increased as he suggested some thoughts. "No, not at all. You deserved to be treated better. He did a bad thing to you, and for that his mistress must be killed,"

"It wasn't his fault. They made him do it."

"Who made him do it?

"The other men he works with."

"What other men?"

Leyna shook her head. "I don't know. He doesn't tell me things anymore and I find him going to an apartment with another woman."

"Mrs. Albin?"

"I guess that's her name."

"Mrs. Henberlin, you killed Mrs. Albin because she was taking your husband away from you," Sweetland said.

"No," Leyna said, shaking her head.

"And you couldn't stand the way it made you look. The embarrassment from seeing the story of your husband's mistress's murder in your husband's secret apartment in all the papers and on television. You thought your friends and coworkers laughed at you. You thought all the people who admired you for your poise and control during your father's political career were now seeing you as not good enough for your husband and you couldn't stand that. Reporters who'd lived to hear your opinions, politicians who wanted to know where you stood on issues, and citizens losing their respect for you because your husband had to go find another woman to fill some of his needs. It didn't matter who made the problem, you knew how to solve it. You had to keep what belonged to you, so you killed the Albins. Now you need to get it off your conscience. We have all we need, but don't you think you'll feel better if you fill in some of the details?" Sweetland crowded her as he drilled in his insinuations.

Leyna continued her eye contact, ready to challenge Sweetland. Then she gave up. Her eyes softened and sought the floor. She focused on some deep, low point while emitting a soft, single-tone hum. Sweetland watched her for a few minutes then turned and asked for the nurse to come and check on her. Niether could extract any further response from her.

Detective Sweetland stood and towered over Leyna.

"Okay, Mrs. Henberlin, if that's how you're going to cooperate I'm going to unlock the cuff connecting you to the chair and add a waist lock to secure you while we move you to the squad car. It's about time you started to feel like the criminal you are."

The detective pulled a key from his pocket then bent over to the side where Leyna's right hand was cuffed to the chair. He unlocked the cuff and separated it from the chair's arm so that it dangled loosely from Leyna's hand. Leyna looked up at Sweetland then placed both of her hands on the arms of the chair and began to push herself up. As she rose, she burst a scream at Sweetland and swung her arm, whipping the dangling cuff to catch Sweetland under his left eye. She whipped it again and again catching Sweetland on the head and shoulders.

Henberlin, waiting outside heard the first screams and shot up out of his chair, brushing the guard aside and flew through the door. He saw Leyna flailing at Sweetland and charged into his wife, tackling her, taking her to the ground and holding her body as tight as he could so he could shield her. As he landed he could feel the grip of the other police officers in the room ripping at his shoulder, their hands trying to peel him away from his wife. His head pounded with blows from the officers trying to separate them. He hung on even tighter, willing to take the blows that he knew were meant to land on his wife. One of the officers locked his hands under Henberlin's chin and pulled back on his head, stretching his neck, crushing his throat. Henberlin's hold on his wife slipped and the officer swung him to the floor, pinning him so he couldn't interfere. He watched the other officers toss his wife like a rag doll to establish control over her. They dragged her along the floor, flung her face down and yanked her arms behind her, almost lifting her from the ground so they could attach the handcuffs behind her back.

The nurses had turned their attention to Sweetland as soon as he went down. They had pads of gauze pressed to his face. The other officers yelled instructions at Leyna and Henberlin, hyped on the adrenalin speeding through their veins.

Henberlin yelled at Sweetland, "She didn't know what she was doing. She snapped, you saw that, Sweetland. She snapped."

35

—

Henberlin exited the psychiatric hospital through the main entrance, where he met a small clutch of reporters—the ones who were willing to wait for his side of the story. It looked like four years of the weekly three-hour journeys were coming to an end. It wouldn't be long until his wife transferred to a regular penitentiary for women.

Two hours earlier, the Crown attorney assigned to prosecute Leyna's case had left by the same door. Her entrance fifteen minutes prior to that caused a great commotion among the reporters who this day showed up in numbers. They'd heard the prosecutor had requested a special meeting with Leyna Henberlin. The reporters barely finished shutting down their equipment after the prosecutor's entrance when the circus started up again as she left. They hadn't had much time to speculate further on the subject of the meeting, so they fired the same questions at her as she pushed past them on her way to the parking lot.

The attorney fielded the reporter's questions by referring them to her upcoming press release regarding the current status of Mrs. Henberlin's case—the same response she provided on her way into the hospital. Before the reporters were able to ready their equipment to tape again, hoping for a better response, the attorney entered her vehicle and pulled away. This left them with only Henberlin's exit as an opportunity to capture a sound bite for the five-thirty news. Their hope drained as they remembered he liked to wait until after the news broadcast had started before leaving his wife.

Henberlin hoped they thought he waited until broadcast time before leaving so that he caused them to miss their deadlines. But, in fact, Leyna liked to watch the news while she ate her dinner, which she took in her room. Once she seated herself at her small desk, her meal in front of her and the television tuned to her favorite news channel, she fixated on the happenings of the outside world. Henberlin, seeing her settled into her nightly routine, left to start the long drive home.

"Mr. Henberlin, is it true your wife has now pleaded guilty to the murders of Stephen and Yanmei Albin and Detective Richie?" one reporter asked louder than the others.

"Apparently, there will be a press release coming from the prosecutor's office," Henberlin responded.

"We're just wondering if she's getting the same treatment you received when your charges were dropped. Is her case being dismissed?"

"In my case, the Crown did the right thing."

"You've never responded to the question of how one of the most expensive lawyers in Calgary came to work on your case pro bono. Will you comment now?"

"Somewhere in your archives, you'll find the answer I've always supplied to that question. I know you love hearing it so here it is again: I've been advised not to answer."

"How is it that he managed to get all of the charges dismissed?"

Henberlin smiled, relishing the enjoyment of this response. "The Crown saw that my belief in my wife's innocence was genuine. They used their ability to perceive things rationally and made the correct decision. All of these same facts have been reported to great extent in all forms of the news media, including yours. Yet you and your editors have not shown the ability to make the same rational decision. The charges were dismissed because the system works."

After Henberlin had been charged with aiding a wanted person to avoid capture and obstruction of justice, he immediately contacted Hec Taylor, Jian Liu's former lawyer. Hec seemed less than cooperative, which Henberlin had expected. He waited for Hec Taylor to come out of his office one noon hour and walked with him on his way to the courthouse.

"Hec, you provided me with the video that identified my wife as Yanmei's murderer," Henberlin said.

Without breaking stride the lawyer said, "I did no such thing."

"I stored a copy of the video out somewhere in the cloud. What do you think detectives Sweetland and the Calgary Police will think if they see it? They'd think you've been a little selective in what you shared with them. I'm sure they asked you when you showed them the short version if more video was available. If they saw the extended, more revealing video, they'd know you had it all the time. Undoubtedly, a lawyer withholding evidence that would solve a murder is frowned upon." Henberlin loved the irony of blackmailing the man who had been blackmailing him. Using the lawyer to retain his freedom, the very thing Taylor had threatened to take away.

And so, Mr. Taylor prepared a strong case demonstrating Henberlin's belief in his wife's innocence up until the detectives provided proof of guilt. But the strong case didn't dissuade the Crown prosecutor's intent to go to trial, even with the odds stacked against the likelihood of conviction. The public wanted a show and the visibility wouldn't hurt the prosecutor's career. Still, even with a strong case, Hec Taylor continued to emphasize to Henberlin that he couldn't guarantee a favorable outcome. The case had been so publicized the public had strong opinions on both sides of the situation. His freedom would only be maintained if the prosecution couldn't prove he knew his wife had committed the murders. Many a jury had considered circumstantial evidence proof.

Throughout the preliminary procedures, Hec noticed a reluctance in Henberlin, as if he was holding something back, and he pressured him to come clean. Henberlin resisted providing the whole truth because he didn't know how strong Hec Taylor's ties were to the Chinese government. Did they end when Jian Liu died or did another contact for the Chinese come into play? Henberlin worried that if he played his CSIS card he would be revealing Delaney's surveillance of Jian Liu. The Chinese may or may not know of the surveillance. If they didn't, he would be blowing CSIS's operation.

Not wanting to take a chance on a trial, he determined it necessary to contact Delaney without informing Hec Taylor. He dropped in at the rent-an-office site only to discover that Contract Geo had moved out, leaving behind a post office box address. Not panicking, Henberlin pulled out the phone Delaney had supplied him and pressed the speed dial. The phone rang but no one answered. Now, a little panic and a great deal of disappointment set in.

The next day, while Henberlin debated the benefit of dropping in at the CSIS office, his Delaney phone rang. He answered and was happy to hear Delaney's voice.

"I tried to call you. There was no answer," Henberlin said.

"Right. That phone has been archived. There's a group that monitors previously-used phones. If a call comes in they don't answer, they just pass along the information to the relevant agent."

"So, the project we were working on has been shut down?"

"Essentially, yes. All of Jian Liu's contacts have disappeared. We're still watching Roy Warren, Gordon Venzi and Hec Taylor to see if someone on the Chinese side approaches them."

Henberlin thought about complaining about not receiving an official thank you and the acknowledgement that his services were no longer required. But he didn't want to create an obstacle that would prevent Delaney from helping him in his current situation.

"Well, that's a relief, I guess. I hope you and your people get what you want."

"Yeah, maybe." Delaney said with a dismissive tone. "So, what can I do for you?"

"I need your help," Henberlin started. "It has to do with the charges the Crown brought against me. Do you remember me telling you I may need you to put in a good word for me?"

"Vaguely, but go ahead."

"The prosecutor is trying to get a conviction against me by presenting the case that I lied to the investigators that the affair with Yanmei didn't exist. They're saying that I insisted on that so strongly that I finally convinced my wife there was no affair. If I lied about that for as long as they say I did, then I could be just as likely to lie in regard to not knowing about my wife's guilt. I need to convince them that I hadn't lied about the affair being non-existent."

Delaney remained silent for a long time then said, "And?"

"I need you to set that record straight."

"Our policy is to stay out of the legal system as much as possible."

It was Henberlin's turn to remain silent. As he did, his thoughts went back to his desire to help his country. Then his thoughts jumped forward to now, to Delaney's cold words telling him his country didn't want to help him.

"You know I'm using Jian Liu's lawyer to represent me. He let it slip that he knew early on that my wife had killed Yanmei. He's dead set on getting me off because he saves himself in the process. One thing he keeps telling me is that he thinks I'm holding something back from him. That I have a card to play."

Silence again. Then Delaney said, "Go on."

"I don't know how strong Hec Taylor's ties are to the Chinese, so I don't want to tell him about my involvement with you. Even if he does know, I don't think he can use the information with the prosecutor to the same effect it would have coming from you. I'd rather not tell Mr. Taylor about our activities, but if it's the only way I can save myself from jail time, so I can be on the outside to help Leyna, I will testify that I was asked to rent the apartment and stage an affair with Yanmei. The prosecutor would then come looking for you to confirm my testimony and the details would be on the public record."

"Do you think this prosecutor will drop the charges once he knows this information?"

Henberlin knew he had Delany's attention. Now he had to plant the words he wanted Delaney to use in his conversation with the prosecutor. "You'll have to make sure he knows I got involved with your project with the best intentions and that I whole-heartedly cooperated at every turn. My willingness to go along with the fake affair is a good example of my willingness to help. I didn't have to do any of this stuff. I wanted to help my country and look what it got me. I've lost everything. If they see you trying to make right a situation that my involvement with you made wrong, I think they'll drop the charges."

"Leave it with me," Delaney said and they ended the conversation.

Out of courtesy to their sister law enforcement division, and to protect an operation designed to protect national security interests, a few days after the conversation with CSIS the Crown dropped the charges to no outward fanfare. It took three weeks before a curious reporter for the *Herald* checked the court schedule to see when the Henberlin trial was scheduled to begin. When the reporter didn't see the trial listed on the docket, or even listed as pending, he asked the question. The prosecutor's office, in a brief response, stated that during their pre-trial review, they concluded they would not be making good use of the public funds required to prosecute the case. The press reacted as if they'd been cheated out of their big windfall story and took it upon their collective selves to find out how Hec Taylor made the case disappear. The press went after Hec Taylor knowing there would be nothing more from the prosecutor.

Henberlin enjoyed the scrum that developed between Hec Taylor and the press. Taylor took credit for the smooth legal maneuvering, yet had to maintain secrecy because he didn't know exactly what secret he was keeping.

293

Outside the hospital, Henberlin again provided the press with his official response as to why the case was dropped. "Mr. Taylor used his considerable powers of persuasion to help save the public the expense of a senseless trial." Using the Crown's own limp words of justification to jab at the press, while giving Hec Taylor kudos for nothing, provided him with a small level of satisfaction, something that eluded him these days.

Another reporter tried a new tact. "Will this be the last time you'll be making this drive? Will your wife be moved to a closer jail or is she coming home?"

"Why? Has coming here to Ponoka to badger us been an inconvenience for you? I didn't see you here that often."

"So it's all over?"

Henberlin stopped. It never entered his mind that it could be over. "This is only a new phase in my wife's incarceration. I'm worried for her. It's dangerous enough for someone who is mentally unstable to be in a psychiatric prison. Even though that is where they belong. When that person, a person who killed a police officer, gets moved into a general prison population, they're often taken advantage of, abused by other inmates and by the staff."

"So you're saying there will be no trial?"

"You'll have to wait for the press release to get your answer."

"Did she enter a plea bargain to avoid going to trial where the details of the murder and its potential cover-up would have been made public?"

"Our lawyers advised that the amount of coverage provided by the press and the amount of misinformation included in that coverage made it impossible for Leyna to get a fair trial. Leyna and I agree. She doesn't need the attention that the media would turn in her direction during a trial. It's best for her to remain out of the public eye. The media isn't capable of understanding the mental illness aspect of the crime committed. You've tried and convicted her as a jealous, cold-blooded killer. Her mental state at the time of the killings is difficult for anyone to understand. Getting any jury to understand the fragility of such a state would be a daunting task. Add to that the fact that she is guilty of multiple murders, and she doesn't stand a chance in any court. All parties involved on both sides of the case agree this is the best outcome. You guys are the only ones who wanted a trial. You're going to disappoint your public again, just like you did when my charges were dropped."

The reporter pool remained silent. Henberlin moved past the group on his way to his car. Once he had passed them, one reporter shouted out, "Will you finally provide all the details of the murder and the nature of your relationship with Yanmei Albin?"

"No."

"Where will your wife be confined?"

Henberlin turned to answer. "To begin with, they are moving her to the Fraser Valley facility. I'm going to be working to get her moved to Edmonton, so she'll be closer to me and in her home province."

"Is that what we're going to be told in the Crown's press release?"

Henberlin smiled again. He knew the media read his smile as a sign that they weren't going to get a satisfying answer. "You'll have to read it and see."

————

From the Deerfoot Trail, Henberlin turned east on Memorial Drive. He thought it likely that another herd of reporters would be waiting for him at his home, so he decided to spend some time at work. The reporters had enough new information for one day.

At an office building halfway up the hill he turned in and parked in the large uncovered parking lot. The lights in his second floor office were on, so he knew Kyle was working late again. They moved into the building because of the not-in-downtown rental rates, and it proved to be a wise decision.

When he decided he needed a respectable lawyer to handle his wife's legal issues—Hec Taylor's reputation being more of a detriment than a benefit— he knew he would need all the money he could save. They hadn't had to sell their home yet, but all of his reduced income from the new venture went to legal expenses. He didn't care that he no longer had a social life. Not having the expense of one helped with the legal fees, and being out in public without Leyna made socializing pointless anyway.

With the cases finally concluded, the legal fees would be significantly reduced. However, the new expenses—travel out of province to visit Leyna, lawyers to file applications with the correctional facilities to have her moved—would no doubt continue to eat into his cash flow. He didn't know if he cared where the funds went, as long as he spent them on necessities to make Leyna's life better.

He remained free. That is, free to live a life among the general public and free to see Leyna. At one time, he thought they were both going to get away with the crimes his wife committed. Then there was a time when he thought they would both end up behind bars. This outcome, one of them jailed while one remained free, amounted to the same thing as both of them in a lockup.

He didn't know how long he could have lived with the guilt of Yanmei and her husband's murders going unpunished. Now that wasn't a concern. Guilt, he realized, was a force of nature. You don't get rid of guilt. When one instance of guilt disappears, another equal level of guilt replaces it. Now, his wife sat in an isolated room and soon the room would become a cell. No matter how he looked at it, she would live in jail because of something he did. Indeed, she had pulled a trigger twice and in the end taken the lives of four people who didn't deserve to die, but the guilt was all his. Because of him, his wife was a murderer.

OTHER NOVELS BY MITCH DAVIES

The Inn of Fallen Leaves

Finalist 2015 Best Indie Book Awards – Contemporary Fiction

Journey to feudal Japan and the banishment of the samurai class. In a quiet inn on the Nakasendo highway, disillusioned samurai, Itashima Chobei is confronted by Akiyama, a samurai on a mysterious errand. Akiyama's actions turned the serene mountain Inn of Fallen Leaves into a state of chaos.

Also at the inn is a beautiful woman, Miyo. While she is attached to one, she is coveted by the other. Both men are driven by the respect for her love. When Miyo abruptly disappears, Chobei must pursue Akiyama across the beautiful yet brutal Japan of the 1860s. Both samurai face an ultimate question: is there still a place for loyalty to a clan, or are the lives of individuals more important?

Information regarding books by Mitch Davies is available at:
www.pensmithbooks.com

Stolen Breeze

Finalist 2015 Best Indie Book Awards – Action and Adventure

All Ben Beck wants is to start over with a new opportunity so he decides to throw himself in the middle of the Pacific Ocean with a confusing group of strangers.

No level of smooth sailing could prepare him for being attacked or being at the wrong end of a pointed gun. From the idyllic life of charter sailing and Polynesian island hopping, to a life and death struggle on a tilting yacht deck at night, Ben can't help but wonder if the other members of his crew are friends or enemies.

He doesn't find out until he wakes up with a throbbing headache after sneaking into a mooring at night and has a meeting with the law.
Will the crew, the sea, or a stretch in jail shred Ben's canvas? Find out. Catch a Stolen Breeze!

A Wind In Montana

Bronze Medal Winner – 2011 eLit Awards Young Adult/Juvenile

Enjoy the ride through High School with Rory and Victoria. They see changes coming so they begin to make decisions for themselves. First Rory drops out of the school band and basketball programs, alienating his teachers, in order to pursue a prestigious chemistry scholarship. Then they start a relationship and Victoria begins to consider alternatives to the music career she is being groomed for.

Keep reading to find out how to get more information about books from Mitch Davies.

On Twitter at @mddaviesagain

On Facebook at
https://www.facebook.com/Mitch-Davies-204759449534161/

Join the mailing list at:
www.pensmithbooks.com